A Rose O'Brien Series - Book 1

Saving
Lily

S. S. DUSKEY

ALSO BY S.S. DUSKEY

THE ROSE O'BRIEN TRILOGY:

SECRETS IN THE KEYS
DECEPTION IN THE BITTERROOT
REDEMPTION IN THE TAHOE BASIN

Printed in the United States of America
First printing, 2024
Cover images by Debbie Driggers
Cover design and author photo by Debbie Driggers
Editor - Carrie Padgett
Publishing Coordinator - Sharon Kizziah-Holmes

SakiRose Publishing
Hamilton, MT

www.ssduskeyauthor.com
www.instagram.com/ssduskey
ssduskey@yahoo.com

ISBN - 13: 979-8-9893427-0-9

ACKNOWLEDGMENTS

I would like to thank Steve Weinstock, Charisse Rose, Teri Albrecht, and Stacy Cortes for their expertise in their respective fields and for being tolerant of my crazy questions. I would also like to express my gratitude to my editor, Carrie Padgett. Your guidance has played a significant role in my development as a writer. Last but not least, my dearest friend and superb book cover designer/photographer, Debbie Driggers. Undoubtedly, we had a great time designing the covers.

PROLOGUE

◆

"ROSE … ROSE O'BRIEN, get up," a man shouted as my bedroom door slammed against the wall.

I rolled over, thinking I was having yet another one of my nightmares with bullets zinging overhead. That was until someone flung the covers off me.

"Move, move, move. We gotta go," a female ordered as she yanked me off the bed.

"What the hell?" I yelled and swung a right hook. A night light provided enough illumination behind the gal that I saw her jerk backward to avoid the impact of my fist.

"Motel's been breached," the female FBI agent named Jess roared in her earpiece headphone. "Need immediate extraction."

I reached for my gun that I kept on the nightstand. And then remembered I didn't have one. I shook my head and realized I was not dreaming.

The attack was real. The bullets were real.

A third agent pushed me from behind.

"Not without my dog!" I hollered, diving into my muck arctic boots. "Sue, come on girl." My sweet rescue Red Kelpie was already sitting at attention on my bed, growling at our intruders before I finished calling her name.

As I peered over my shoulder, the time on the clock read three. Heavy eye roll. Not again. Here I was somewhere at the top of the world, tucked away in Utqiagvik, Alaska, and they found us. Whoever *they* were. The moment we exited my bedroom, more incoming bullets shattered the windows.

Jess yanked me to the floor and tossed me a ballistic vest.

I tugged it over my head and attached the Velcro straps. The bullets kept coming and glass exploded everywhere. I pulled Sue closer to me. If only her K-9 bullet-proof vest was in reach, but it was in the living room. I tried to shield my ears, but protecting Sue took precedence.

Two federal agents returned fire with their M4s, covering the large front bay windows, as Jess was on me like flies on crap. If only I had my AR15, or even my 40mm, as I was itching to get into the gunfight. But I'd had no time to pack anything, let alone firearms, when they snatched me from my yacht in Florida.

"Cavalry's here." Jess jutted her chin to the back door as she continued to return fire.

Sue and I edged out of the bedroom on all fours as the zinging bullets flew past us. This was most definitely not a dream. Unfortunately, this was not the first time Sue and I had our haven shot to hell. Her little body trembled and all she could do was stay under me in a low crawl. It was a fun technique we'd been practicing. Little did I know we'd have to use it in real life.

The glass from the exploding windows peppered me, but my adrenaline was on octane, so I didn't feel it. I reached up to turn the handle, but it was locked. I wasn't about to call my security detail for something I could manage, so I kicked at the door until it burst open. Just as it flung wide, two more armed federal agents yanked me off my feet, throwing Sue and me into the rear of an armored Chevy Suburban.

The snow was so intense, the taillights from the second Suburban were barely visible. While continuing to return fire, the three agents jumped into the vehicle with us. The driver, whom I did not see, was a female agent with dark hair. I was not sure what agency she was with, but it was irrelevant at the moment. We were in her hands as the vehicle sped away on the snow packed road. The Suburban ahead guided our way, as we had zero visibility.

No sooner had we left than the gunfire ceased. As if someone ordered them to stand down. The reason did not matter; but it stopped. I released a gasp I'd been holding since they ripped me from my slumber. All I could do was hold Sue. She was a pro and knew the drill. Sue was on my lap the second my butt hit the seat.

Two agents sat across from me, a third up front with the driver.

Because they often rotated, I barely remembered their names. But one thing was constant: there were at least two CIA, the other two FBI, one always being female.

Jess turned on the light and handed me my jacket that was on the seat next to her.

I nodded a thank you. I couldn't stop shaking. I wasn't sure if it was the early-March thirty-below temps or the fact that we were almost eliminated again.

"Will one of you tell me who is after me?" I shouted. I didn't mean to yell, but my ears were ringing wildly from being exposed to at least 140 decibels. The last assigned agents had been tight-lipped. Maybe I'd get lucky this time.

"A cartel member by the name of Stanley James, or SJ, as you know him," Jess said.

The male FBI agent, Charles, gave her an elbow to the ribs.

"What?" Jess said with a shrug. "Rose has a right to know."

"Thank you," I said, tugging the parka over Sue and me. "Finally, someone is honest with me. But it makes little sense. I was not scheduled to testify against him, nor was I ever a witness. Hence, no US Marshals babysitting me." I snuggled Sue. "The cartel's washed their hands of SJ. He's of no consequence to them. From what my intel has told me, they've moved on and found someone new to take over. Max Ryan was the one who would've testified, and my father. And since Max is dead, that leaves my father."

"How do you know this?" Charles asked.

"Have *you* forgotten who I am related to?" I replied.

"Yeah, yeah," Charles said, flicking his wrist. "From what we hear, SJ is negotiating a plea deal. So, there may be no trial."

"Then why am I under federal protection? And my family?"

The two agents exchanged glances.

"The intel we received is that you have a hefty bounty on your head," Jess said. "Preferably served dead, not alive."

"As for your family," Charles said, "there's been no talk of them. Agents Powers and O'Malley have them covered in Florida as a precaution." He looked out the window. "O'Malley will have our heads on a platter if we don't keep you safe," Charles added.

"Leave O'Malley to me. And he's out of the country right now. Neither my dear brother-in-law, Powers, nor Kevin O'Malley can have that much pull in either of your agencies," I said.

"O'Malley has more than you realize," Charles said. "Your boyfriend would jump through fire for you."

I shook my head. "But is my *boyfriend* aware this is the third safe house in a month that's been crashed? Haven't you asked yourselves why? There's an obvious rat in one of your three-letter agencies," I said. "I'm safer on my yacht out to sea with *my* security detail."

I was not used to hearing those two words, "my yacht." It had only been nine months since I became Richie-Rich-loaded, and it felt so pretentious. I looked out into the black abyss. "I'm not a freakin' damsel in distress," I said, furrowing my brows. I was tired of running away like a frightened buck at the prime of hunting season. I was not my father. I was done running. It was time to be the hunter.

"Here's the deal. You drop us off at the airport in Utqiagvik. End of story."

Both agents shook their heads in protest.

"It's not up for negotiation." I held up my phone—the third disposable this month. I turned on the light above my head and dialed. "Good morning," I said, "it's me, yep, another burner. Good thing I have your number memorized. I know it's early but are you available—ugh." I rolled my eyes. "Not like that. I'm still with Kevin. I'm talking about your schedule—Yep, the full-blown training. Yes, I'm finished with my PT." I nodded to every other word as if he could see me. "It only hurts when it's cold—Monday morning? Thanks, Simon Rae. Oh, sorry Simon. I'll have a chopper get you."

Jess and Charles sat with their mouths opened, staring at me.

"What?" I said, touching my hair. It dawned on me it was in a half-assed ponytail. The light above must've illuminated me. I took down my hair, running my fingers through my tangled waves only to twist it in my signature high pony. "Is that better?" I snorted.

"It's not that, Rose," Jess said. "You just don't look or act like the typical trust fund, spoiled billionaire we have to deal with."

I peered at my clothing. I wore my comfy alma mater navy-blue UC San Diego Tritons' hooded sweatshirt, now with holes, and matching sweatpants. "Hey, you try being yanked out of bed, multiple times, I might add. And see what you sleep in." I leaned back and threw my hood over my head.

"Not your *wardrobe*, or your hair. But your attitude," Jess said.

"Agent O'Malley is a lucky man," Charles said.

"What, because of my money?" I scowled. "It's newly inherited."

"Don't be so defensive," Charles said with his palm to me. "I meant your attitude. You don't treat us like servants."

"Thanks," I said. "I didn't mean to snap. I treat others how I want to be treated. Unless you're a dirt bag, then it's game on."

"Agreed," Jess said, turning to the driver. "Change of plans. We are going to the airport."

"Are you sure that's a good idea?" the female driver said.

If it wasn't thirty below outside, I would've had them drop us off here. I pondered. But we would certainly freeze to death.

I nodded to Jess.

"Affirmative," Jess replied.

I considered the four agents in the vehicle. My Spidey-senses told me one of them was the traitor.

CHAPTER 1

◆

WHEN YOU'RE AN inch away from death, your world flashes before you. I've been there before and faced God, sort of. I'd never actually seen Him, only a brilliant light. That thought entered my mind as Sue and I paced on the private airstrip, the Montana May morning chill slicing through me.

"Where is she?!" Simon snapped. He peeked at his iPhone as if Lily would magically appear because he demanded her presence.

I fished my cell from my jumpsuit pocket and dialed. "Hmm, her phone is off, straight to voicemail," I said. "Lily's late … again. It's the second time this week. We were supposed to meet for lunch yesterday, and … well, she never flakes."

"Rose, we gotta go … now." Simon tapped my shoulder and inclined his head to the plane. "Storm clouds coming in, not to mention Sam is moving cattle today. So, unless ya want to train in the rain and land on a few cows, we have to roll." He twirled his finger in the air.

Sam and his family owned the three-hundred-acre ranch just outside of Whitefish and was the perfect place for us to sky dive.

"All right … all right, let's do this," I said, removing my parachute from the back of Simon's GMC Denali, shouldering into it. I handed Rayo my cell phone for safe keeping as did Simon. As I made my way to the awaiting Beechcraft King Air, Sue leaped into my arms.

"Oof. What's up, girl?" She drenched my face with her tongue and tugged on my harness. "Honey, we'll be down soon. Mama promises," I cooed in baby talk.

Sue was a sweet pup I rescued. Hell, I stole from an abusive tweaker on this very day one year ago. She was well-behaved most days. But today, she was ill-mannered. I put her down and motioned for Rayo to take her.

Rayo McQueen was my grandma's latest ranch hand and was filming our jump from a boat on Flathead Lake.

Just as I bent to tie my 5.11 boots, Sue snatched the throw-out ball, dragged the bridle line, and popped the pin of the main chute. Causing the parachute to fall out.

"What's wrong with you, doggo? It's not playtime," I said, and removed the chute. I stared at her handy work. "This isn't going to work." I chuckled.

Rayo ran up and grabbed hold of her.

Simon returned moments later from his GMC with another chute in hand. "Here is Lily's. She's obviously not making it." His scowl implied the delay miffed him. On a normal day, Simon was happy-go-lucky. But, for work, he was serious. Today he wore his Army Special Forces game face.

"Hey, I didn't plan this." I furrowed my brows back at him and hurried toward the plane. As I peeked over my shoulder, Sue barked feverishly with her hackles raised. I considered her reaction but dismissed it.

"So how long do we have your friend's field?"

"Until the cows come home," he said with a crooked smile, his humor returning.

Simon was a handsome gent and if I were not happily involved in a relationship, I would consider him an option. He was six feet, four inches and pure muscle. He had crewcut brownish-auburn hair mixed with a touch of black. And lashes to die for. When he smiled, his brown eyes crinkled in the corners. And don't get me started on his dimpled chin.

Our pilot, Kate, taxied down the private air strip as the Beechcraft King Air, known as the "rocket ship," quickly lifted off the ground. The King Air was the choice of aircraft for skydiving as it gets divers to altitude in ten minutes.

As we made our way to the heavens, I tightened my chute's straps and Simon briefed me on today's jump. I was not a skydiving novice and had close to two-hundred jumps under my belt. But today was different.

"Why are we doing this?" I yelled over the roar of the King

Air's engine.

"You're paying me a boat load to do *this*. Besides, it's great for your training." He showed me the M4 was clear and handed it to me.

"Ha!" I snorted again. "I'm *paying* you to train me to protect myself. Not jump with an M4 strapped to me." I shook my head.

"Yesterday's jump was pure fun. Today, you asked for the military experience. And I figured you missed the adrenaline rush of your job." He adjusted his helmet and goggles.

I tightened mine as well. "Yeah. This isn't what I had in mind." I rolled my eyes.

"Hey, we could do a HALO jump … at night."

The High Altitude, Low Opening training was specific to special forces, but I was not looking for that level of intensity, at least not yet. I turned my attention to the window. The sky was a heavenly painting of white, mixed with swirls of gray clouds. I closed my eyes and felt the warm embrace of the ambient light. I opened them just in time to see the sun peeking over the horizon.

Sunrise had always been my favorite time of the day. To me, it's God's promise of a new beginning with endless possibilities. As I contemplated what today had in store, I noticed one cloud took the shape of a dog. My mind drifted to Sue and then to Lily.

What was going on with Lily?

"Hm-mm," Simon cleared his throat. "Earth to O'Brien. You ready?"

I returned my gaze to his.

"I need your head in the game." He switched on the Go Pro that was attached to his helmet.

"I'm here and in it," I said.

"Good. Now remember, like we trained on the ground, engage your target when you land."

Kate announced our altitude of 10,000 feet.

Simon slid up the door. "See you at the DZ, O'Brien." He motioned for me to jump.

I drew a deep breath and looked at my pilot, Kate Orr. "I'd rather be flying the plane than playing *Army* at the Drop Zone," I yelled.

Kate laughed and threw me a thumbs up.

How hard could it be? I jump and engage my target. Simple,

right? I rolled my neck. A millisecond later, I flung myself out of the plane. At first, the familiar gust of the air hit my face, and my heart pounded like a racehorse on the final lap. And then the freefall. The ultimate in freedom. I was a bird soaring through the atmosphere as the wind rushed through my body.

After freefalling for a few seconds, I checked my wrist altimeter. Okay, 3,000 feet. I pulled my main chute.

Nothing!

CHAPTER 2

◆

DON'T PANIC, ROSE, you got this. I tried to convince myself. But my visceral response was in fight *and* flight. I was falling at least 120 mph, but my blood pressure was much higher. I immediately spread my legs and arms to reduce my rate of descent. I'd practiced this in indoor skydiving centers.

I cut away from my main parachute, peered to my left, and found my red clothed reserve handle. With my left hand, I yanked it and deployed my reserve chute. Phew! It opened. But when I looked up, I saw a shit show of epic proportion. The lines whipped around, slapping my face, as my parachute was not fully inflated. I started in a slow spin and sped up as I was approaching earth faster than I'd liked. I was beginning to spin out of control.

Remember, breathe through your nose and out through your mouth. Or was it the reverse? Suddenly, I was swallowing air and gasping. I couldn't breathe. My body tingled, and I was getting dizzy and lightheaded. All symptoms of hypocapnia. Now can I panic? Was I going to meet God and reunite with my mother and beloved husband, Bradley?

Snap out of it, Rose! I had to keep my wits. My family needed me. *Breathe deep through your nose and exhale slowly out of your mouth. Remember your training*, I chanted. As soon as my breathing regulated, I grasped a steering line, only to discover one was severed. Crap again.

I was too far away from any marsh or wooded areas to land, and the snow was ice-packed. My only saving grace was the lake. Although the temps in the water were hovering somewhere in the upper thirties, I had no other options. While trying my best to control my malfunctioning parachute, I steadied myself for impact into Flathead Lake. And if I didn't slow down, the surface tension in the water would be equivalent to landing on concrete. More panic.

Okay, so I may be shattered … again. I'd just about recovered from a broken pelvis and arm, dislocated shoulder, fractured ribs, and multiple gunshot wounds from a year ago. But at least I'd be alive, right? As I braced for water impact, I was swiftly yanked upward. It was Simon. I'd forgotten he jumped after me. He hooked into my partially collapsed parachute with his feet, and, with both our weights, steered us to a frigid, but safe water landing.

Note to self, he needed a raise.

CHAPTER 3

◆

CK SAT AT the boat launch in her rented black Jeep Grand Cherokee, peering through binoculars. "I can't believe she survived it," she mumbled, lowering the Bushnell. She picked up her phone, rolled her neck and inhaled a meditative breath as she dialed.

"This must be important for you to break protocol by calling," a lady with a Spanish accent snapped on the other end.

A brief pause fell on the line. "This is beyond the protocol, Cora. The target is still alive."

"Unacceptable ... CK. She shouldn't have survived the jump," said the woman. "And how many times must I tell you? It's Agent Alvarez or just *Alvarez*."

"The target didn't show, and Rose obviously took her parachute by mistake," CK said.

"How do you mean ... is Rose dead?"

"No. I'm watching them fish her out of the lake."

"How can you be certain?" Alvarez asked.

"Considering the target has long black hair and Rose has long *red* hair. Yeah, I am."

"Things are getting sloppy. Do I need to send in someone else?"

"No, you do not!"

"Fix this. And what happened to the tight tail you had on her?"

CK pulled the phone away from her ear and sucked her teeth. "Listen ... *Agent Alvarez*. I can't be on her too tight or I'd blow my cover. Lily Cazier is not a stupid woman."

"Never use that tone with me." Alvarez's accent was extra thick.

"Yes, ma'am." CK rubbed her face. "Something is up. Lily must be meeting with her contact. It wasn't supposed to go down until tomorrow."

"If Lily finds the truth, well ..." Alvarez said. "But now that she's still alive, find out what she knows."

"Interrogate her?" CK said.

"Did I stutter?"

"I can't play that role," CK said.

"Not my problem. Handle it," Alvarez said. "I want a daily *emailed* report. Oh, and for now, keep the target alive until I give the green light." Click. The call ended.

CK rued the day Cora Alvarez, without warning, became her new handler. And she found it peculiar that the agency gave her a covert domestic assignment. Since becoming a field operative, CK has had international jobs. All that CK was told was she would go dark as usual, and her only CIA contact would be her handler, Cora Alvarez.

CK tossed her phone on the Jeep's passenger seat, picked up the Bushnell, and watched Simon climb on the boat. She opened her encoded computer that sat on the seat, accessed the app, and located Lily's phone, but it was off. So CK pulled up Gil's phone. Good, his was on.

She reclined and wiped the sweat from her forehead and relaxed her shoulders. CK rifled through her duffel bag, looking for her black book. She was old school and didn't store numbers on her phone. Not to mention, she often used burners. CK thumbed through the pages and found Mac V. She dialed.

A man with a gruff voice answered. "Yo."

"You still have eyes on G?"

"Yep," Mac said.

"I've got another job for you," CK said. "I'll text you the details."

CHAPTER 4

———◆———

"**WHAAT THE HELL** kinda traiining wass that?" I chattered through my freezing bones.

Rayo tossed me and Simon large, thick towels.

I nodded a thank you because I couldn't form a complete sentence at the moment.

"Oh my God, Rose." Simon patted his body with the towel and removed his parachute harness. He unstrapped the M4 and helped me out of my harness. "I jumped after you and waited for you to pull your chute, but saw you were in trouble. You scared the shit out of me."

My teeth stopped chattering. "You and me both." I wrapped myself in the towel. The instant I sat, Sue immediately jumped on my lap, whimpering. She trembled as fast and furious as me, but she also helped warm me. "And why are you turning something I love to do into work?"

"It's called training," Simon said as he tilted his head, drying his ear.

"What happened to the parachute?" Rayo asked as he steered us to shore.

"I had to cut away the main, and the reserve malfunctioned," I replied and turned to Simon. "I owe you big time."

"Call it even, since I forced you to jump," Simon said in a sardonic tone.

"I'm sorry. I didn't mean it like that. I appreciate you," I said and clutched my left side.

"Thank God for CRW," Simon said.

Rayo and I tilted our heads.

"Canopy Relative Work. It's advanced parachute training. We'll work on that for next time, Rose."

I squinted and pursed my lips.

"But seriously, you would've survived it with your experience. At the least, you'd have some broken bones," Simon said. "Wish I could've seen how the main was packed, but it's in the lake. And we may not know how it happened since it's a mangled me—wait a minute. Somebody cut this." He pointed to the severed lines on the reserve. "Who the hell packed your parachute?"

"You mean Lily's." I continued to squeeze out my long, braided, soaked hair, contemplating. "Do you think it was on purpose?" I met Simon's gaze.

He sat across from me and sighed, staring back. "It's suspicious. We need to talk to Lily and find out who packed it. Unless … it *was* meant for you," Simon said. "Chatter is there's still a hefty bounty on you. Or someone from your old job that would want you pushing up daises … you know, with your sunny disposition?"

I shook my head. "No one I supervised could afford a hit on me. And I've only been in Montana a few days. I've stayed under the radar, using only cash, and double backed on my driving. Nobody knows I'm here, except for Grandma and you all. I didn't tell my sisters."

"More secrets, Rose?" Simon asked.

"No." My voice rose an octave. "Omission is not being secretive. Besides, Kaylee is completing her residency in Jacksonville. And Saki is busy with baby Violet and managing her fitness center in Miami."

"Not even Kevin or James?" Simon raised his brows.

"Kev is out of the country. He's on another secret squirrel assignment. Gotta love the FBI/CIA Joint Terrorism Task Force. And James, well, between family and the FBI's SWAT team, he has no time to breathe." I cleared my throat. "After all that happened the last couple of years, my family encouraged me, as did my employer, to take a leave of absence, sail around on Max's Super Yacht to exotic islands, collecting seashells," I said. "Heck, even Sue gets bored with it." I snorted.

"You mean *your* yacht," Simon said. "Back to the target on you."

"That's why you're training me," I replied. "To *face* my

enemy." I raised my arm with a tight fist.

"Don't be snarky. I'm serious, Rose. You could've been the mark." He wrung out the saturated towel. "And you only hired me a couple of months ago," Simon said. "You don't want to be kidnapped a second time, do you? You need to keep your security detail closer." He scowled.

"Seriously! You going to lecture me now?" I frowned back. "I'm tired of babysitters."

"Hey you two, chill," Rayo said. "You two fight worse than me and my kid sister."

"Whatever," I said. "He started it." I flicked my thumb at Simon.

"If you were my sister, I would've drowned you when they brought you home from the hospital."

"Wow!" I said with raised eyebrows.

"You know I'm kidding," Simon said and tore off a couple sheets of paper towels.

"What's this for?" I asked.

"You got a little something," he said, pointing to his nose to show me.

It was then that I felt the warm iron taste in my mouth. Drats. Bloody nose. Just as I reached for another wad, I clutched my ribs. Damn, not again! That familiar pain. I'd wondered how many I injured this time. I did a mental eye roll.

"You're lucky that's all you got." Simon sat beside me. "You need to get checked out at the hospital."

"Remember, under the radar," I said. "Disregard, I took a first aid trauma course. I can do it."

"Stubborn ass woman." Simon smirked. "I was a medic. *I* can do it."

CHAPTER 5

◆

"OUCH!" I WINCED as Simon leaned over and palpated my ribs. I'd just about punched him in the nards when he jerked away.

"Easy. I may wanna have kids someday. You bruised a couple. At least. Maybe a fracture. Not to mention, you are going to have a good shiner. Now, unzip your jumpsuit and lift your shirt."

"No way purv," I said. "You are not looking at my girls."

"Girls?" Simon scoffed. "You really are a sister. And an annoying one at that."

"You were so sweet when I met you," I said, gingerly unfastening the top part of my sodden suit. "What happened?"

Simon gave me a cheeky grin. "Lift your damned shirt so I can look."

I rolled up my top, but only up to my bra line.

"Not too bad. I don't think they are more than just bruised. You'll live," he said with a chuckle. "But I'm serious, Rose. You need better security. I'm not convinced you weren't the target today."

"That's why you're here," I said. "And him." I inclined my head to Rayo.

"Him?" Simon said. "He's fresh out of college and a computer geek at that."

"Hey, I graduated with a criminal justice degree, played college football *and* I'm learning to be a ranch hand," Rayo yelled back. "I also just received my CSI certificate. I could be bad ass!"

"Rayo, Grandma vetted you, so I know you have serious potential," I said.

"Or did your gran hire him because he looks like a young Sam

17

Elliot?"

I considered Rayo. "I knew there was something familiar to you," I said.

Rayo was in his early twenties. He stood 6'2" with thick wavy, brown hair and a mustache with a scruffy beard. His hazel eyes twinkled when he smiled. Rayo also had the actor's trademark gravely deep voice.

I shook it off. "I'm serious. I've got all I need," I said as I pinched my nose, my voice nasally. "The whole point of this training is to help me, help myself. I need no more people around me twenty-four-seven."

Simon and Rayo chuckled.

"What?" I asked again.

"It's hard to have a serious conversation when you sound like a cartoon character." Simon pulled my hand away from my nose. "And I promise you, Rose. This—" He waved his hand at the mangled chute— "is not how I train."

"After today, I'd rather stick to the ground for a while. Perhaps learn how to hot wire a car, or even pick locks," I said with another pained grimace. I didn't know what hurt worse, my nose or my ribs. "Are you sure my grandma didn't put you up to this?" I twirled my fingers in the air. "If Gran thinks I'm going to take over her secret squirrel business and turn me into Jani Bond … she's got another think coming."

"I assure you, Rose," Simon said. "Your gran would not want to see how you react to falling to your death with a malfunctioning parachute."

"I know." Just then, my phone rang. I looked around then remembered I'd asked Rayo to hold it for me. He handed it to me. I peered at the caller ID. "Speak of the devil." I answered it on speaker.

"How did the jump go?" Grandma asked.

"Uh … okay," I said. I didn't want to give her a coronary. But I was sure she would find out sooner rather than later. "A slight mishap with a chute. We're in one piece."

"Huh?"

"Nothing," I said, "we're good."

"We have a problem," Grandma said, thankfully ignoring my comment. "Something's going on with Lily. I thought she was jumping with you today. But she woke late and was in a tizzy. She mumbled something about forgetting to meet you and tore out of here on her bike. I'm worried. She's been flaking on her duties, too." Grandma sighed. "Are you headed my way?"

"We hadn't planned it. We were going to hang out at Simon's friend's ranch for the day and grill burgers and ribs," I said. "And we need to get dry clothes." I wrung my shirt. "Wait a minute. Her phone is in Simon's car. Does she have a burner?"

"First, why are you wet, Granddaughter? And yes, she has a burner."

"Long story. We'll change and head your way. I will call you in a bit and give you the details. The Beechcraft also must be returned, it's a loaner and Max—uh, my Stream is at the Kalispell Airport. See you soon," I said. I was still not used to the fancy toys being mine.

"Rich people problems," Simon muttered.

I squinted and gave him a half-raspberry.

"Okay, it will give me a chance to see where she's going," Grandma said.

"Wait! Graan ... what did you do?"

"Nothing I would *not* do for you. I asked Griz to place a tracker on her bike," Grandma said.

"Lily is smart and knows your tricks. Remember, she's put trackers on for you," I said with raised brows.

"This is new," Grandma said. "I've been working on it. She won't know it's there."

"I don't feel right about spying on her," I said.

"For the greater good," Grandma said. "Oh, before I forget, your attorney, Keith Fenner, has been calling here. He said it's urgent he speak to you."

"I forgot to call him back. Perhaps I have yet *another* form to sign." I caressed my aching face. "Who knew inheriting billions would be so much work? It may also have to do with Max's mother's wounded vet foundation," I said. "We're doing another fund raiser."

"You mean *your* foundation," Grandma said. "Doesn't Keith have your number?"

"Yes and no," I said. "Few people have my main number. Please let me know if you hear from Lily." I disconnected.

Something was amiss. First Lily flaked on me twice, then someone sabotaged her parachute. Were they connected? And why did she need a burner? What had Lily gotten herself into?

The hair on my arms stood on end.

CHAPTER 6

---◆---

LILY'S MOTORCYCLE PIPES roared as she pulled her 'sixty-six Genny Shovelhead into the only gas station in Darby. As she fueled, a chill sliced through her. It was eight-thirty, and the temperatures were in the low forties, but the day promised to warm to the seventies. Montana weather was so unpredictable that Lily almost regretted taking her bike. But since the Genny had belonged to her father, riding it livened her spirit.

She rummaged through her saddlebags, looking for her balaclava. She located her tool kit, but no face covering. Instead, Lily found a small, yellow padded envelope with no return address. Only that it was postmarked Missoula. Lily had forgotten about it when she checked her post office box the other day. As she opened it, a locket dropped out and fell into her hand. It was an antique with lilies etched on the front. She smiled as it was her mother's favorite flower, hence Lily's name.

Lily shook the envelope, looking for a note or letter revealing the sender's identity, but there wasn't any. She assumed it was yet another birthday present from Lillian. Lily grinned again as she slipped it over her head and tucked it under her black turtleneck. But why would Lillian mail it? Who else would have sent this mysterious gift?

Thinking of being secretive, why did Gil, her private investigator, want to meet Lily at a park in Hamilton? For a PI, Gil was paranoid and downright cryptic in his correspondence.

Soon after she returned from her rescue mission of Rose in Lake Tahoe a year ago, Lily received a box in the mail. The package contained letters between Lily and her parents, pictures, and other family memorabilia. The box was tucked away in her parents' villa in Italy. Lily's parents, both in the CIA, were on assignment there. The new renters of the villa found the box hidden in their cellar, so they called a number found on a Post It note taped to old papers.

One letter written by her mother, Maisy, was alarming. Lily couldn't understand why she'd never mailed it, but it was dated a month before her parents perished in a private plane crash four years ago. Maisy wrote that Lily's father, Gerald, was undergoing "standard pilot testing." And since he flew for the CIA, the reported stress tests were mandatory. Maisy had stated Gerald was experiencing sudden mood changes, trance-like states, and at one point got up in the middle of the night and disappeared for several hours.

Upon his return, Gerald had no memory of where he went. Maisy confronted her husband, and they decided he was going to back out of the testing. Shortly after, Gerald and Maisy flew to the Alps on a mini holiday, but their plane crashed. Gerald and Maisy reportedly perished; their bodies were never found. The investigators informed Lily that pilot error caused the crash, but she always had doubts. Gerald was the best pilot in the Air Force, which was one reason the CIA recruited him.

In the letter, Maisy urged Lily not to tell a soul, especially anyone associated with the CIA. Lily interpreted this to include the woman who took her in, her mentor and second grandmother, Lillian. So, Lily searched underground chatrooms and conducted her own investigation. She ran across bizarre theories from a deadly virus to mind control to bubonic plague. A few months ago, Lily received a message. One thing led to another, and she hired a private investigator by the name of Gil Fox.

As soon as she fueled her bike, Lily hopped on and took off to get answers to long-awaited questions. At least she hoped.

CHAPTER 7

TWENTY MINUTES LATER, Lily pulled up to Hero Park at the north edge of town. Near the park's entrance was a veteran's memorial to pay tribute to local fallen heroes who served and protected our country. The park also sat next to the Valley Inn. A restaurant and bar with the same name were a stone's throw away. A little over a year ago, Lily and Rose drugged and abducted Rose's stalker from this very hotel. Lily sighed. She missed her friend and felt awful for flaking on her bestie twice this week. But she knew involving more people than necessary in her quest for answers could be dangerous.

And Rose had plenty of that in her life.

Just as Lily hopped off her bike and removed her helmet, a young female wearing a hotel uniform exited the rear entrance.

"Excuse me, are you Ms. Lily Cazier?" she called out.

Lily looked around and nodded.

"Oh, thank God, you wouldn't believe how many long-haired brunettes came by this morning." The gal darted to Lily.

"How can I help you?" Lily asked with furrowed brows as she kept her hand on her bike, in case she needed a quick getaway.

"A tall, bald man asked me to give this to you." The gal handed Lily a cell. "He said you would know the phone's password."

"Okay … thank you," Lily said hesitantly as she watched the woman return to the Valley Inn. The passcode was the same as the last burner she received from Gil.

Since they met, Gil had given her two throwaways, which she was told to destroy after one use. This one would be no exception. She'd asked Lillian for a separate disposable and stopped using her iPhone. It was too easily tracked, so she purposely left it in

Simon's truck.

Lily entered the code and a text message appeared. Gil informed Lily there was a change in plans and for her to proceed to the south side of the park, cross the footbridge over the canal, and continue to the farthest picnic table. An envelope would be taped to the underside. Once she read the text, Lily deleted the message, dropped the phone, smashed it beneath her boot, and tossed it in the trash.

Afterward, she followed Gil's instructions and made her way through the sixty acres of mature cottonwoods and meadows.

Lily was always fond of this park and often caught sight of osprey, bald eagles, and even moose. But today, she was on a mission and power walked to her destination. The second she crossed the footbridge, she continued to her right and went around the fishing pond.

It was 9:00 a.m. and people milled about, enjoying their walks, some with dogs. Paranoia crept in as she felt the eyes of total strangers fixed on her. Everyone was suspect. Lily didn't enjoy the cloak and dagger routine like Rose would have.

Lily spotted the picnic table, and as luck would have it, it was unoccupied. With her head still on a swivel, she sat and ran her hands under the table but found nothing. Dang. Sliding to the other side, she found the envelope. She snatched it and stuffed it in her pocket and sped back through the park.

When she reached her bike, she looked around to make sure no one followed before she pulled out the envelope. Again, with her mind's eye vigilant, Lily opened it and a USB flash drive popped out with a handwritten note that read:

Sorry for the secrecy, but I'm being followed. Meet me where we first met. Watch your back. Keep the drive close and don't let anyone get hold of this. If something happens to me, there's no turning back. Stay safe. Trust no one. Regards, G.

"Lake Simi? Is he serious?" Lily mumbled as she stuffed the note back in the envelope, jamming it deep in her right inside jacket pocket. She put the USB in the opposite side. She took a moment to think. She didn't have an overnight bag but wasn't going back to Lil's secret squirrel ranch outside of Darby. So, she put on her helmet and braced herself for the approximate two-hour drive on a bike with a small gas tank and not-so-comfortable seat.

CHAPTER 8

◆

ALTHOUGH I INHERITED Max's Gulfstream G450, it was too big for Grandma's private airstrip behind her house, so Kate landed it at the newly expanded Ravalli County Airport. Since I was intent on staying under the radar, we filed the flight plan under Kate's name.

Kate Orr was my pilot and flight instructor. She was in her early thirties, divorced, and loved traveling with me. Her smile would light up any room. Her fair complexion was smooth, with a sprinkling of freckles. In a girlish way. Yet, her jet-black, wavy hair, with heavy white highlights, gave her a remarkably alluring appearance. She was stunning.

Per Grandma's text, there was an Escalade waiting for us at the airport. The keys were at the front desk inside the Fixed-base Operator. After loading our gear, we set off to Darby. We arrived at Grandma's at a quarter to twelve and rolled up to her unmanned security gate. Kate, who was driving, punched in the code I gave her, and we made our way through.

Grandma's two guard dogs, Brian and Stevo, greeted us. The dogs circled our vehicle, barking, baring their teeth. Had I not met them, I would have thought twice before exiting. When I opened my door, they wagged their tails and welcomed me like a long-lost friend.

"Hi boys. Miss me? I was only gone a few months," I said.

Simon and Rayo, who were familiar with the dogs, exited the vehicle, too. While Kate clutched the steering wheel. Her honey brown eyes widened.

"Uh … is it okay?" Kate's voice quavered.

"Yes. They're guard dogs, but you're with us. They will take you as a friendly. The pit is Stevo, and the Cain Corso is Brian."

"Cain Corso?" Kate inquired, with a head tilt.

"Corso's are an Italian breed of mastiff. Used for protection, tracking or companion. In Brian's case, he's all three. And a big cuddle bug, too." I scratched behind each dogs' ears as they sat on either side of me like giant book ends. "They both are."

Sue jumped out and was in total dog mode. The three of them scampered off, wildly running towards the pasture.

Kate slid out of the Escalade and joined me. We bolted up the steps onto Grandma Lil's wrap-around deck that overlooked her private two-hundred-acre horse ranch. She had two ponds, one loaded with trout and the rear backed to thousands of National Forest acres. Her views of Trapper Peak were breathtaking.

"In here," Grandma Lil called from the kitchen, where I could smell her famous elk stew. She turned, beaming. Her smile lines were distinct. I ran up and gave her a bear hug.

"You look wonderful, Granddaughter. Minus the damage to your beautiful face." She held my cheeks between her fingers and thumb and turned my head side to side, examining my injuries. "You'll probably have a nice black eye later. I guess it builds character." She laughed, smoothing my hair. "Something else is different." She stepped back and glanced side to side. "Did you change the shade of red? It's lighter."

"No. That's what sea air and sun do." I chuckled.

"It makes your sapphire blues pop," Grandma said.

I put my hand on her shoulders and kissed each cheek. "You look amazing too." Grandma Lil stood my height at five feet eight inches, but appeared she'd shrunk. Grandma had her silver hair cut into a bob. She looked ten years younger and did not look in her late seventies.

"You've had quite the morning," Grandma said. "Are you shaken?"

"A bit." I formed a crooked smile. "But not stirred. Unless you throw in a couple of olives," I said.

"Don't make me crave a martini this early," Grandma said with a laugh.

"Let's get down to business." My smile faded. "Where is Lily?"

"Let's eat first." Grandma motioned for us to sit at the kitchen table.

Simon, Kate, Rayo, and I joined Grandma, and we wolfed her amazing stew. The chunks of vegetables, lean meat, simmered in broth and herbs created perfection. Or darn close. My eyes rolled so far back in their sockets and I craved a nap. I hesitated to rehash my morning.

But I did. After, I pushed away from the table and pondered Lily's circumstances.

"Granddaughter, you are doing that lip-biting thing," Grandma said. "What's going on upstairs?"

Simon chuckled. "That's a frightening place."

I shook my head at him and returned my attention to Grandma. "As much as I don't want to invade her privacy, can we peek at Lily's room?" I scrunched my nose.

She nodded. "But just the two of us, for now."

Sue had rejoined us and cocked her head like a curious puppy.

"Three," I chuckled.

CHAPTER 9

———◆———

AFTER A QUICK stop in Missoula to fuel again, Lily arrived at the Lake Simi Cemetery at 11:15 a.m. The Genny's pipes were so loud they could raise the dead.

It was Lily's idea to first meet Gil at her parents' gravestones. Since their bodies were never found, the graves were empty. And being this meeting was about them, she felt it appropriate he chose it today.

Lily made her way through the wrought iron gates and since she was on her bike, she could not bring fresh flowers as she'd done every time before that. So, she removed the dried lilies from her previous visit and crushed them over their plots.

"Hi Mom, hi Dad. I'm back," Lily whispered, with tears streaming down her cheeks. She knelt between the two headstones. "I miss you both so much. Life has not been the same without you. Ms. Lil takes great care of me. She is just as spunky as ever." Lily sighed.

"And, yes, I am still single, but happy. I have not found the right guy." Lily picked up the dried flowers and rolled them between her fingers. "I would have brought you fresh ones, but I rode the Genny, Dad." Lily looked up and tears welled in her eyes again. She used the sleeve of her jacket and wiped her face. "Sorry, I don't mean to be such a ba—"

Suddenly, she heard branches rustling and spotted a woman's shadow. At least, what appeared to be a shadow of a woman. She bolted to her feet and ran to catch up to the mystery figure. But whoever was there vanished into the tree line as quickly as they emerged. Lily's heart pummeled as she scanned left and an even quicker right.

Shivers traveled down her spine. Ghosts were not an uncommon sighting in graveyards, she told herself. Just as Lily took a few steps backward, she bumped into a giant of a man with dirty overalls. His steely gray eyes locked onto hers as he raised his left hand with a claw-shaped tool.

Lily created more distance and looked around for an escape while she reached for the Sig Sauer 9mm she kept in her hip holster.

"Easy," the fellow said, scratching his thick salt and pepper beard with the tool.

"You scared the heck out of me," Lily said, panting as she released the death grip on the butt of her pistol.

"I didn't mean to frighten you," he said and lowered his hand that held the clawed instrument. He looked at it. "My apologies. I was doing some gardenin'. And my beard gets so dang itchy. The wife keeps threatenin' to shave it off in my sleep."

"Oh. I am sorry. I … I was just, you know, talking to my parents. You probably think I am a bit off."

"Not at all. Plenty of folks do it," he responded with a toothless smile. "I don't listen to no conversations. It ain't polite."

Lily peered beyond him into the trees. "Did you come from over there?" She pointed to the line of pines.

"No. I was just comin' from the other side of the shed. If ya can't tell, I'm the groundskeeper."

Lily nodded. "Um … have you seen a lanky, bald gentleman?" She scanned the cemetery. "We were supposed to meet here."

"You're the only one that's been here all mornin'. Well, gotta get back to work." The man turned on the heels of his muddy boots and walked away.

"Oh … okay. Thank you," Lily said and fished her phone out of her jacket and texted Gil: *Where r u?*

No response. So, she did what Gil instructed her *not* to do and called him. But it went straight to voicemail. Could Lily have gotten the meeting place wrong? Or even the time? Perhaps Gil meant the café where they stopped for lunch the last time they were here. That must be it. As Lily made her way back to her bike, the sun was fading behind dark gray, ominous clouds. The forecast projected light rain.

The darkness that filled the sky was anything but a mist.

CHAPTER 10

GRANDMA LIVED IN a thirty-nine hundred square foot log home, with four bedrooms, three and a half baths, granite kitchen counters, massive master suite, office, laundry, wine room, and double attached three-car garage. I was especially fond of her dual sided fireplace. Since she was alone, she hired ranch hands to help with her mustang rescues.

Lily was her main ranch hand, along with Griz. He was our third stooge when Lily and I abducted a man who was haunting me. Another story for another time, as Grandma would say.

Lily and Griz had shared the guest log cabin that was three-thousand square feet, with two master suites on opposite sides of the house, a laundry room, and fireplace. The guest log cabin matched the main house on the outside, same inside with the vaulted ceilings and enormous windows.

After Grandma unofficially adopted Rayo McQueen into the family, Lily moved into the main house with Grandma. Lily fought it at first, but since Grandma took her in after her parents died, she became another granddaughter. So, Lily obliged.

Grandma and I entered Lily's room and the second we opened the door, a woman whose back was to us quickly spun.

"Whoa, who the hell are you?" I reared my head.

Sue had been on my heels, as usual, and even let out a low growl.

"Stand down, Rosie." Grandma put her palm to me. "This is Charly. She and Griz are dating."

"Ookay. So, what are you doing in Lily's room?" I crossed my arms. Charly stood an inch shorter than me but met my weight. I could take her, I considered.

"I … I was looking for my sweatshirt," Charly said as she picked up a black hoodie.

"Why are you holding this?" I asked, snatching an envelope addressed to Lily from Charly's grasp.

"Easy, Granddaughter," she scolded. "Charly and Lily have become good friends."

"We have." Charly stood tall, shoulders back. "Griz and I were watching a movie with Lily the other night and I must've left my sweatshirt." She turned to Grandma. "We didn't want to wake you, so we watched it in here."

"What movie?" I asked with furrowed brows.

"Rosie! That's enough."

I breathed in a deep, meditative breath. But forgot about my throbbing ribs. I crossed my arms again, discreetly pushing against my ribcage while holding in a pained moan. And cleared my throat instead. I was a pro at masking pain.

"Sorry," I said, but not meaning it. "You caught us off guard." I shook the envelope. "But it still does not give you permission to snoop," I snapped. Although that is why Grandma, and I were in Lily's room. But Charly didn't need to know that.

Charly stepped closer to me. Her deep, dark brown eyes glared through me. She was stunning, but there was an emptiness and coldness in her gaze. Even the veins in her neck bulged. "It was sitting on my sweatshirt," she said through gritted teeth.

"Let's take five." Grandma shuffled between us. "It was a simple misunderstanding."

Charly stepped back as calm returned to her face. "Yeah. A misunderstanding." She shot me a tight, closed smile as she rolled her long raven, wavy hair into a bun. "Let's start fresh, shall we? My name is Charly Kane. And you must be the infamous Rose I hear *so* much about." She gave me a strong, confident handshake, looking me straight in the eyes again.

I lowered my shoulders that I had been wearing as earrings. "Sorry, I can be overprotective of my family," I said.

"Anyway," Charly said and glanced to Grandma. "Have you heard from Lily? I texted and called her, but she hasn't responded."

"That's what we won—"

"Gran, she took her Genny out ... *remember.*" I shot Grandma a wide-eyed look.

Grandma must've caught on. "Oh, that's right. A long ride if I recall," she said.

"Okay. Good to know." Charly ambled to the door. "Later," she said. "It was a *pleasure* meeting you, Rose." She flashed me an obviously fake smile.

After Charly exited, I shook my head and turned back to Grandma. "What were you thinking, allowing that woman in your home?" I said, fists on hips.

"Rose O'Brien!" Grandma mirrored my stance.

Uh oh. When Grandma used my full name in that tone, I knew the poop was gonna hit the fan.

"Sorry, Gran. But I don't trust her, nor do I care for her." I threw my hands out. "Even Sue's hackles are still raised. And you said dogs know who to trust. And boy, don't get me started on the age difference between Griz and her. Was he looking for a MILF?" I snorted.

"Granddaughter," she laughed as levity returned. "She's not *that* much older."

"You know I'm right," I said.

"Eh, so she has a few years on him," Grandma said. "And to answer your question before you ask, yes, I cleared her."

"Okay, if you say so," I said and continued to peruse Lily's room, the envelope still in my hands.

"Charly served in the Army. She was in the intel unit. She's a pilot too. No criminal history, not even a speeding ticket," Grandma said.

"Okay ... okay. I get it. But what about now? What does she do for work?"

"She received a full medical discharge," Grandma said.

"I kinda feel like crap, treating a wounded vet that way." Sort of. "Lily never mentioned her," I said.

"You haven't been available and have been off the radar lately," Grandma Lil said.

I plopped on Lily's bed with my shoulders slumped. Sue joined me.

"Rosie, it's okay. You still have a target over your head. You're in survival mode," she said, stroking my hair.

My mother used to call me Rosie. How I missed Mom. I let out a heavy sigh again and picked up a framed picture of Lily and her parents at one of her mounted shooting competitions. Lily was always proud of this photo, as she'd won several buckles and saddles. No doubt Lily missed her parents, too. At least I had my father back in my life.

"I know, Gran. But Lily was there for me when we almost lost Saki and her baby. Heck, she helped us rescue Saki and Kaylee when they were kidnapped and left to die in these mountains."

"Yeah, no thanks to Max."

"It feels like a lifetime ago." Sue plunked her head on my lap. "I mean, for goodness' sake, Lily also flew all the way to Tahoe when Dad and I were abducted." The memory of waking up in the van with my father and Max tied up, the shootings, and the explosion made me shudder. It was too much.

"Stop, Rose. You would do the same for her," Grandma said as she checked the other side of the bedroom. "That's why it's critical we find out what's going on with Lily."

"You're right." I rose to my feet and scanned the bedroom one more time. "Nothing out of the ordinary. Unless we *really* want to toss her room or peek at this," I said, waving the envelope in the air.

"Toss her room? Boy, you still have that parole agent mentality. And what kind of spies would we be if all we relied on was reading a personal letter from a mother to her daughter? Besides, I've got something better." Grandma snatched the letter out of my hand and stuffed it in her pants' pocket, inclining her head to the other room.

Spies? I pondered.

What *did* Grandma have in mind for me?

CHAPTER 11

◆

MAC VIG SAT in his white panel van across the street from the Lake Simi Café, watching his target named Lily through binoculars. Although he did not know her exact whereabouts, locating Lily's bike was not difficult. It was a classic and the only one of its kind in town. Heck, anywhere. It was twelve-thirty, and his mark did not appear to be leaving anytime soon, not to mention he hadn't eaten all day, so Mac entered the small café-casino and slithered into a booth opposite her.

Lily must've looked at her cell at least fifteen times; she seemed oblivious to Mac's presence. Each glance at her phone resulted in her big, round hazel eyes down turned. The gal was a stunning, athletic-framed woman in her mid-twenties. Her silky black hair was tied into a braid that fell to her waist. Yep, stunning. If only she wasn't the target. Oh well, that's how his business went sometimes.

The gal kept looking out the window and back at her phone. It was obvious she was waiting for her PI. But he would not be showing. The dark-haired beauty picked at her hamburger and moved the fries around the plate with a fork. The check had been sitting at her table since Mac ordered the fish and chips special.

Another half hour passed, and Mac finished his meal, paid his tab, and quietly slithered out back through the casino door. He looked over his shoulder to make sure no one spotted him as he returned to his van. After pulling away, Mac backed into a parking spot next to Lily's motorcycle.

As luck would have it, few cars remained as the lunch crowd dispersed. He jumped out and loosened a spark plug wire. With his head on a swivel, he reached into her saddlebag and took out her tool kit and tossed it in the rear of the van. He was a rider too and knew she'd come prepared.

Mac was on to the next step when his phone vibrated. He yanked it out of his black jacket side pocket. It was a text message from CK: *Change of plans. I rented a room at the Lake Simi Motel. 2 blocks from you. Corner room, #5. The clerk left the door unlocked. Take them both there. Wait for further instructions.*

Mac growled as he felt his neck redden. He was proficient at his job and did not like last-minute changes. Sloppy work was how people got caught. Now he had to move two bodies undetected. She'd first told him to interrogate both targets and then kill them. Dumping their corpses into the lake. Simple job he'd done a few times.

Mac: *WTF. I have 2.*

CK: *I paid the clerk to help.*

Mac: *Gonna be extra.*

CK: *Not my money.*

Mac frothed as he jammed the phone back in his pocket. He reached into his bag of tricks and removed a loaded syringe, set it on the seat, and waited.

A couple minutes passed, and his target finally paid her tab.

"Perfect," Mac said as he opened the passenger side sliding door. The still body that lay on black plastic rolled, almost falling out of the van. Mac caught the man—Gil—before he kissed the pavement.

"Oof." Mac groaned and grunted as he strained to catch Gil. "Talk about dead weight." He moved the sedated guy back over the tarp, but he did not appear to be breathing. "Shit, you can't die yet," Mac said, checking for a pulse over Gil's radial artery. It was faint, but still there. He exhaled and swiftly moved him to the opposite side of the van, making room for another body. Mac closed the door and returned to the driver's seat.

A few minutes later, Lily exited the front door of the café. He sized her up. Five feet four inches, not a pound over one-hundred and twenty-five. Mac stood a few inches taller but had at least seventy pounds on her. This should be easy.

The target approached her bike and frowned at her loose wire. She opened her saddle bag, most likely looking for the kit that wasn't there. She tossed the contents of the bag onto the ground with more force than necessary and peered around her motorcycle. She stood there, hand on hip, scratching her head.

That was Mac's cue. He rolled down his window. "Ya need help?"

"Not unless you have tools. I could've sworn mine were in here," she said, returning the items to her saddle bag.

Mac grabbed the needle from the front seat and removed the cap. He crawled into the back and said, "I have tools," while opening the sliding door.

"That would be great," she said, with her gaze on him.

Mac jumped out, hiding the needle behind him. He put his left hand over her mouth while he jabbed her neck with his right. She battled him, but he was stronger, and the drug worked quick. In a matter of a few seconds, her eyes fluttered, and she weaved and collapsed into his arms.

Mac peered to his left and then a quicker right, before swooping her into the van next to the other body. The timing was perfect as a patron was leaving the café. He returned to the driver's seat and kicked up rocks on his way out of the parking lot.

CHAPTER 12

SUE AND I followed Grandma and rejoined Kate, Simon, and Rayo in the living room. Gran slid behind her mahogany desk that sat in her breakfast nook overlooking the backyard, then eased onto her oversized leather chair, opening her laptop. She put her right index finger on a USB fingerprint scanner and the computer unlocked.

Kate's eyes widened.

"This is where I get all my James Bond stuff," I said with raised eyebrows.

"So, is this how you 'cleared me'?" Kate laughed and air quoted.

Although she sniggered, Kate was not off the mark. Since Kate worked for me, Grandma vetted her and ran a complete background. Grandma, being former CIA, still had connections and passwords to programs I'd never heard of. As the apple doesn't fall too far from the tree, my employees were also required to sign non-disclosure agreements.

Grandma's fingers danced over the keyboard at lightning speed, and there was a sparkle in her eyes. She missed getting into the mix.

"Lily's first stop was Hero Park at the north end of Hamilton," Grandma said. "You know, by the restaurant and hotel."

"Yeah, I'm familiar with that part of town." I chuckled.

Grandma gave me a quick sideways glance and wore a Cheshire Cat grin. I assumed she remembered that day as well when Lily, Griz, and I took a scoundrel named Titos from his motel room and brought him here for "questioning." That seemed ages ago, when I first learned what my grandparents and father did for the CIA. I shook my head and returned to the computer screen.

"Lily then went to the Lake Simi Cemetery. Most likely visiting her parents' gravesite." Grandma scrolled. "And then to the Lake Simi Café right off the main highway. She's been there since eleven-forty-five." She turned her chair. "So, you wasted a trip here for nothing. You were closer when you were in Kalispell. I apologize."

I laid my hands on her shoulder. "It's never a waste seeing you." I bent over and whispered in her ear. "Plus, you have all the necessary equipment downstairs." I stood. "I left mine on my boat. I was not expecting it this trip."

"Boat? Ha. What I have on my lake is a 'boat.' You have a floating village with an arsenal, and as much security as I do," Grandma said with a laugh.

"Maybe." I grinned. Just then, my phone rang. I fished it out of my jeans back pocket and looked at the caller ID. "Speaking of boat, it's one of my staff."

"My staff," Simon said, shaking his head mockingly.

I squinted at him. "Hello, Mr. Khan," I answered in my most polite voice.

"Pardon the intrusion, Madam," Khan said.

"That's fine. Is everything okay?" I asked.

Khan Fullerton was Max's employee and knew the yacht like the back of his hand. So, I kept him on. Besides, it was in the trust. Khan was in his late forties and easy on the eyes. He looked and spoke like the late Cary Grant with his sexy Mid-Atlantic accent. And like Cary Grant, Khan was born in England.

"Madam, first your attorney, Mr. Fenner, phoned and said it was most urgent you return his call," Khan said.

"I am aware," I said. "We've been missing one another's calls."

"Very well. Second, there's been a slight—" Khan cleared his throat— "mishap."

"What did TJ do this time?" I asked with an eye roll.

"Mr. Hooker tripped on the upper deck with the grace of a rhinoceros."

I snorted. Mr. Khan was always good at making me laugh. "Was anyone hurt?"

"Not at all. It was quite amusing. But he broke one of the newly acquired chaises and ripped a hole in the rear of his trousers," Khan said. "Wouldn't he be better suited out there with you? After all, he is your Security Officer."

"He means well and has two left feet." I snorted again. "But he is also the best at his job. Except his weakness for the ladies."

"That's why I called," Khan said with a chuckle. "A young lady snuck past Mr. Hooker last night. Or he may have invited her. I'm not certain."

"Let me guess. Another of Max's twinkies." I rubbed my face.

Grandma spun in her chair and slowly looked at me while Simon and Kate laughed. They mouthed *Twinkie* at once.

"Khan, please assist the gal to the bereavement room and offer her a nice bottle of wine from Max's selection. And thank you." I disconnected.

All three threw their hands out, obviously urging for juicy details.

"Since I inherited Max's money and yacht, I've been getting, um … visitors sneaking on board looking for him," I said. "I even had one crawl into bed with me. That was until Sue growled."

Simon raised his brows and grinned.

"Easy purv," I said. "I threw her onto the floor after I pulled my gun on her. I had to console her after I broke the news of Max's untimely death. I think his women were more upset about losing the wining and dining and less about Max. He wasn't the most romantic guy. And that's when I began giving away his reserved wine that I don't want. You know, as parting gifts. I need to change the name of the yacht. I guess having *The Max 1* on the exterior hull is a dead giveaway. It keeps slipping my mind."

"Rich people prob—"

"That's getting old, Simon," I said.

"Wait. You said TJ was your Security Officer. You might have to can him if he lets unauthorized individuals sneak on board." Simon was back to being serious as he towered over me.

"TJ is the best. But a softy with the ladies. He's a great D-Bag detector. Max's women are harmless floosies. The gal last night was probably working at the fundraiser dinner put on by Max— um, my foundation. I guess she stayed behind."

"You don't strike me as one of those socialites," Kate said.

"I assure you, I'm not. Last night's event was too uppity for my taste. I was conveniently absent for it. And Khan was gracious to cover for me. But I must comply with having them. It's a condition of the trust. Sheesh, that document was longer than a hardback dictionary. Good thing I had Mr. Fenner to help me muddle through the BS."

I returned my attention to the computer screen. "Speaking of long," I said. "Gran, you said Lily's been at the café since eleven-forty-five? It's now one. Over an hour?"

Something was wrong.

CHAPTER 13

LILY AND I both ate at lightning speed as if it were our last meal. My reason was because of my occupation. I never knew when I had to arrest or run after someone. I paced behind Grandma.

"What if she met up with a guy?" Simon asked. I could tell he didn't want that to be the case. I'd noticed a twinkle in his eye whenever she was around or her name was uttered.

"No. Lily totally would've told me," I said.

"Are you sure? Perhaps she didn't fancy you all giving him a colonoscopy," Kate said.

"Pfft, no," Grandma Lil and I responded at once.

I watched Simon raise his eyebrows.

"Okay. Maybe we'd scope … a little," I said. "But after this morning's incident, I'm convinced something's going on. I can feel it." I picked at my dry cuticles.

Grandma rose. "I agree. Lily's been there too long. Take my new Sprinter Van Conversion. It's loaded for all your needs." She winked.

Kate gave a head tilt.

"I'll tell you later," I said.

"Can I go too?" Rayo asked. His voice was so deep and booming it startled me as he stepped up behind us.

I studied Grandma.

"He is a computer whiz," Grandma said. "Just keep him safe for me. He's on loan from his folks in Idaho."

"Of course," I said. "But let's get on the road. Grandma, please let me know if she calls."

She nodded.

"I'll take Rayo with me and follow in my truck," Simon interjected. "A second set of wheels can't hurt. Besides, the van will be a tight fit for all of us. Especially when we pick up Lily." His tone was hopeful.

"And I'd love to drive the Sprinter," Kate chimed.

"It's all set. Let's find Lily." I looked at my crew. "Worst-case scenario, it's a fun road trip." Sue stood on her hind legs and put her front paws on me. "Don't worry. I'm not leaving you out of this, baby." I kissed the top of her head.

"Granddaughter, when you return, we need to have a discussion. You know about your future ... oh, remember to call Mr. Fenner. He left *another* message."

Calling my attorney was not on my to-do list. I was avoiding him. He most likely wanted me to host yet another fund-raising event. Inheriting billions was way too peoply for my liking.

As I was loading my and Sue's overnight gear into Grandma's Mercedes-Benz Sprinter Van, I saw a black bag tucked away in the corner. I opened it and shook my head. Grandma was always prepared. There were the makings of a kidnapper's kit. She equipped the bag with rope, zip ties, duct tape, a black hood ... I'd need to talk to her. But what caught my attention were a couple of vials of SP-117. I chuckled as I remembered using it on Titos. But we also used a cattle prod. Thank God *that* wasn't in there.

Note to self: ask Grandma about the last time she used the van.

On second thought, maybe it wasn't such a great idea. I didn't want to know.

CHAPTER 14

◆

LILY'S HEAD THROBBED as if a vice-grip constricted her, and the odor of chlorine tingled her nostrils. As she pried her heavy eyes open, she saw double everything. She lay on her side, her face smashed on a pillow, hence the bleach smell.

What happened?

The Genny. A man offered tools. She did a quick body scan and breathed a sigh of relief. She was still fully clothed and unscathed.

Lily rolled over. Great. Her abductor had secured her wrists with zip ties in front and a rope bound her arms to her side. She kicked, only to find her ankles restrained in the same manner. Suddenly, her vision was in full focus and there he was. She screamed a muffled shriek, but the cloth binding her mouth prevented any noise from escaping.

Gil lay motionless on the opposite bed, bound with zip ties, but not gagged. "Lily," he murmured as his eyelids fluttered. He was only in his boxers and socks. But why?

Lily furiously wiggled to a sitting position. She sat up on the edge of her bed, watching as Gil thrashed around. He was perspiring and shivering at once. As Lily leaned over, she heard him mumble.

"Things ... not ... what they seem. She's a—" his words were breathy. Gil's head lolled to the side, and he appeared to lose consciousness.

"What? Who's she?" Lily said with a muted cry. "Gil ... Gil. No!" With tears in her eyes, she bolted to her feet. Whoever took her was gone.

Lily hopped like a rabbit toward the front door but just as she turned the knob, the bathroom door flung wide, slamming against the wall.

"Hey ... where the fuck do you think you're going?" a gruff voice yelled as a stocky man with a black ski mask lunged at her.

Now that Lily was facing her attacker, she wasn't going down without a fight. Hell, she'd handled stallions bigger than his ass. She jumped up and donkey kicked the man's shin. But he had quick reflexes and he hopped to the side to avoid the other leg getting hit, too. When he leapt, he stumbled and knocked over the end table. The lamp crashed to the floor and shattered.

"A feisty one, are ya?" he snarled as he swooped her up, flinging her like a rag doll back on the bed. For his small stature, he made up for it in strength.

Lily screamed another subdued yelp. She glared at him. Who was he? His voice sounded familiar. But from where?

As he approached her, Lily drew her legs to her chest and was ready for a fight. She was not going to be raped and mutilated. She'd seen too many headlines and refused to be another statistic. But this was Montana, and things like that were not a common occurrence.

The man pulled a Glock 40mm from the low of his back. "Kick me again and see what happens."

Lily saw the gun and then looked for her holster. It was gone.

The fellow picked up her Sig 9mm from the table with a motel towel and asked, "Looking for this?"

Lily's heart dropped. "What do you want from me?" she strained to ask.

"If I take the gag off and you yell, I will shoot ya. Get it?" he said, leveling the gun to her head.

Lily's eyes widened, and she nodded.

He removed the cloth muzzle and jumped back. She assumed he was preparing for another kick.

"Who are you and what do you want?" Lily spouted.

"You don't ask the questions. I do." He waved the pistol.

"I ... I don't know what you want from me," Lily cried. "And is Gil okay?" She looked over at his unresponsive body.

The dude's phone rang and he turned away to answer. "Yeah—she's awake. Her friend, on the other hand, didn't do well with the serum." He scratched his head with the hand holding the Glock.

The man's ski mask shifted to the left, exposing a two-inch scar on the right side of his jaw. Lily could make out a thick, black mustache. He wore non-descript blue jeans, a black leather bomber jacket. But his boots were wide square toed, gray Caiman Hornback alligator boots. Not a scuff on them and the soles were not worn.

A guy Lily went on a date with was a boot snob and had a pair. He'd bragged to Lily they cost at least a thousand dollars, hence her one date and done policy. But this man's jacket was designer as well. So, if he was not there to rob or rape her, then why? She thought as she peered at Gil's bobbling head. And then it hit her harder than the drug he gave her. It must have something to do with what Gil was going to tell Lily about her parents and what really happened to them. Hence Gil's paranoia.

And then she remembered the flash drive. Did he have that too? Since he tied her up, she could not check her pockets. All she could hope was that this man, whoever he was, did not thoroughly search her.

The bloke took the drive out of his pocket and examined it. "Yep, I've got it," he said. "Chip? I didn't find a chi—fine."

If he has the drive, why keep her alive? Lily leaned her body toward him to eavesdrop. She heard a woman's voice on the other end.

He disconnected and stared at Lily. "So. Do you want to tell me where the chip is?"

"Huh? Wha?"

"There's more than this USB," he said as he waved it in the air. "This guy here," he wielded the gun at Gil's bed. "Gave it to you."

"I swear on my parents' grave. I … I know nothing," she said. "I was meeting with Gil." Lily jutted her chin at him. "I picked up the drive, but I did not look at it. And he did not give me a chip. Did you find a chip on me or my bike when you took out my tool kit?" she snapped. "My bike. Is it all right?" Lily moved towards the edge of the bed and sat tall.

"It's still at the café. But I can change that." He pulled the only chair in the room closer to her and sat. He leveled the gun at her head again. "Start talking. The truth for once."

"I'm telling you the truth. I don't have a chip," Lily said slowly and deliberately.

"Okay. We'll see." He stood and walked over to a black duffel bag and dropped it on the bed. Her kidnapper yanked Lily by her jacket's collar and tossed her onto the chair. He reached into the bag again and retrieved a pre-filled syringe. The needle was unlike any other she'd ever seen.

Lily's eyes widened when he held one side of her head. "Please, no!" she begged, with tears streaming down her cheeks. "I'm telling you the truth." Lily tried to jerk away, but her attempt was futile. She felt a prick behind her ear.

She instantly grew drowsy, and her world went dark.

CHAPTER 15

WE ARRIVED IN Lake Simi a little after four-thirty and the rain started coming down in buckets. Lightning lit up the dark skies. Gotta love the spring in Montana. It can be sunny one minute, the next rain and even snow. But the temperature was close to seventy, so zero chance of the white stuff. But one thing was certain: I was not prepared for the foul weather and only had my hooded zipped sweatshirt.

Based on Grandma's last known location of Lily, we found her bike still parked in front of the Lake Simi Café. My heart was pounding in my throat as I quickly unbuckled my seat belt and leaped out of the van.

"Rose, can you let me stop the vehicle before you fly out?" Kate yelled.

I was used to jumping out of partially moving vehicles in my job. But this was personal. As I inspected the ground around Lily's bike, I noticed her spark plug wire was loose and her Genny was cold to the touch.

The skies unleashed a torrential downpour as I continued to scan the area one more time. And then my attention was drawn to the café's neon Open sign flashing. Kate, Rayo, Simon, and Sue were now standing next to me. Simon, Rayo, and Kate were the only ones smart enough to have raincoats and umbrellas.

"Let's go in the café and ask around," I said and peered at Sue, who'd been doing a little dance. "Rayo, can you please walk Sue while we check out the café?" Typically, I would put her service vest on her since she was certified and take her in with me, but no time now.

Rayo obliged my request and handed me his coat, as did Simon. I shook my head.

"I'll hang back with Rayo," Kate said, opening her umbrella. "The two of you can handle questions. We'll walk around the block and do some checking."

Before Simon and I entered the café, I unzipped my sweatshirt and shimmied out of it, shaking off the excess water. When we stepped inside, I saw one other patron sitting at a table.

"We're closed," a gal shouted from the back. "The oven just died on me!"

I walked around the counter and peeked my head into the kitchen. "I'm sorry, but we're not here to eat." I pulled out my cell. "Do you mind if I ask you a few questions?" I scrolled through, looking for a photo of Lily I took the other day.

The young gal, whose name tag read *Paisley*, stood with one hand on her hip, the other with a dish towel thrown over her shoulder. "Excuse me, I've got to clean." She sighed. "And I'm alone … again." By Paisley's tone, she was in no mood for a conversation.

"I apologize. But my friend is missing," I said, following her to a dirty table.

Paisley was cleaning and didn't look at me.

I shoved my cell under her face. "Do you recognize her?"

She inspected the picture. "Yeah, someone who looked like that was here a few hours ago."

"We know. But can you tell me if she was alone? Did she leave with anyone?"

"Not that I'm aware," Paisley said as she continued wiping off the salt and pepper shakers.

"You see that bike out there?" I pointed. "That's hers. It's her pride and joy. Lily would never leave it. Especially in this weather," I said without coming up for air.

Paisley shrugged again and threw her hands out. "I don't know what to tell ya."

I rolled my neck, cracking it from side to side and curled my lip. "Look! Paisley," I said with a tight jaw.

Simon must've read my body language. He shuffled between us, elbowing me away. He leaned in and whispered. "Easy, Rose. Remember your breathing techniques."

48

He turned back to Paisley. And since he towered over the five foot and change waitress, he bent his neck like Big Bird and grinned.

"Ms. Paisley, we are really concerned about our friend." He flashed his toothy smile. "Can you think of anything … at all, that would help us locate her?"

Paisley smiled and giggled like a schoolgirl. Simon could charm the pants off an ant.

"She ordered a burger and fries. Didn't eat much, just played with her food." She looked up and to the left. "Oh … and kept looking out the window, as if she was waiting for someone, but no one showed." Paisley resumed her cleaning.

I stepped up to her, heaved a deep sigh, and put my hand on hers. "Paisley. Can you please think … real hard, at *anything* that may appear out of the ordinary?"

She crossed her arms and shook her head.

I stood with my right leg back and squeezed my fingers into my soaked jeans and pulled out a twenty-dollar bill and handed it to her. "I urge you, this is important," I said.

Her eyes widened and her demeanor changed. Whether it was the money or my desperate plea, but she finally said, "There was a man sitting across from your friend." She pointed to a booth. "I wouldn't normally pay attention to a customer's clothing or jewelry, but this guy had on a real expensive watch, ya know, with diamonds on the face.

"Oh, and a real nice leather black jacket. And his alligator boots cost more than my car." She stuffed the money into her bra. "Another thing, it's probably nothing, but he kept staring at your friend. I mean, she's beautiful and I'm sure men check her out all the time."

"That she is," Simon said with flushed cheeks.

I cleared my throat. I'd have to have a chat later with Simon about his obvious crush. I turned back to Paisley.

"What did he look like? Any scars, marks, or tattoos?" I asked.

"Um … no tats that I could see. But he had a two-inch scar on the right side of his protruded jaw. It made his snaggletooth stand out." Paisley touched her jaw as if forming the blemish. "He was stocky. He had a thick black mustache and goatee. Black hair, but—" she laughed— "it looked like a wig. I could tell because my uncle wears a toupee. Most definitely not a local."

"Did you see his vehicle? Make, model, dents?" I peppered her with questions as if I were on the job.

She tilted her head and looked up again. "He was driving a white van with no windows. Nothing on it. And he parked across the street." Paisley jutted her chin to the window.

"Did he use a credit card?" I asked.

"No, paid in cash and left out the back door before your friend."

"Did you see her leave?" Simon asked.

"No. I was waiting on another customer."

I looked up, and that's when I saw the CCTV. "Um … Paisley. Are those functional or just a deterrent?" I pointed.

She scratched the nape of her neck and shrugged. "I'm only part time and have no clue. The owner will be back tomorrow morning."

I puffed my cheeks. "Is there *any way* I can have his or her number?"

Paisley bit the side of her lip.

I reached into my pocket and pulled out a fifty. I had more money than I ever desired and believed in sharing it with those who worked hard and were in need. By the look of her holey, dirty tennis shoes, all tips were needed.

Paisley snatched it, stuffing it with the other twenty. She drew her order pad, jotted a number, and handed it to me.

"Thank you very much. I'm sorry I came at you hard earlier." I looked at my feet. "We're really worried about her."

Paisley reached into her shirt and returned the fifty. "I don't feel right about taking all this."

"Please keep it. You were very helpful." I gave her a genuine smile, and we walked out.

CHAPTER 16

WHEN LILY OPENED her eyes again, she was staring at the spinning floor. The man's alligator boots slowly came into focus.

"She knows nothing," Lily's kidnapper said as he spoke to someone on the phone. "And her friend is not doing so well. Couldn't get him to talk much. The drug had an adverse effect. Not like you said it would."

Lily swayed her heavy head to the side.

"Mac, are you sure you gave them the *full* dose?" A woman's voice sounded. "And am I on speaker?!"

So that was the worm's name, *Mac*. Lily was positive she'd heard the woman's voice before. Maybe? Lily was too drugged to be certain of anything. And what did he give her? Lily was not a recreational drug user—unless you count whiskey—so she had nothing to compare this haze to.

Mac fumbled with the cell phone as he took the caller off speaker mode. "Yeah, you were. She just woke … and, of course, I gave them both the full dose. I don't need you telling me how to do my fuckin' job, CK," he groused.

Lily watched as Mac grabbed the Glock from the table that now had a suppressor attached and leveled it at Lily's head.

"We're done here. I'm going to finish up and leave," Mac said. "Send in someone else for a body dump."

"Please, please. Don't kill me," Lily cried. "I won't tell anyone. I … I don't even know what you look like." Tears poured down her face.

"What do you mean, stand down?" Mac said. "Change of orders?" He lowered the weapon. "What do you want me to do with—yeah, I have that in my bag. And *that* is gonna cost you extra!" He cursed as he disconnected the call. "Well, beautiful, you've been given a reprieve," Mac said.

"Thank you, thank you. I promise I know nothing. Turn your head and I will run out the door. I won't tell a soul. I swear." Lily's voice perked. She was going to be free.

Mac cut her ankle restraints and motioned for Lily to move back to the bed.

"Please, please. Don't hurt me." She dropped to her knees, wailing. Her hands in a praying motion.

He yanked Lily by her elbow with his free hand. "I don't do that to women. Now get on the bed."

She stood on wobbly legs and fell backward. "Wha … what. You said—"

"It's not what you think." He snarled, keeping the gun trained on her. Mac opened the mini frig and pulled out a can of cola. He popped the top, took a sip, and let out a heavy sigh. "Before we do this, do ya need to use the toilet or something?"

She didn't but nodded and bolted into the bathroom. Just then Gil moaned, and she spun. "Aren't you going to help him? He doesn't look so well."

"Are ya gonna go or not?" Mac snapped.

"How can I with these restraints?" she barked back as she stared at her PI's motionless body. Lily regretted getting Gil involved in this. Whatever *this* was. If he wasn't going to kill her, what was Mac planning to do? Lily's thoughts were interrupted when Mac cut her wrist ties.

"It's hot in here," Lily said, removing her jacket and tossing it on the bed. She continued scanning the room for a way out. But there wasn't one.

"Don't get any bright ideas. Now move before I change my mind." He shoved her. "And leave the door open."

Lily rubbed her wrists and gazed at her reflection in the mirror. She sucked back a strangled sob. She peered around the bathroom. No window. Dang. She heard the refrigerator open for the second time.

"I got a cola for you."

"Th … thank you?" Lily furrowed her brows in confusion as she stood over the sink and splashed water on her face. He said he wouldn't kill her, now he offered her a soda. Nothing made sense. She wet her cheeks and neck again, ran a hand through her hair. And that is when she felt the searing pain behind her ear. Lily traced her fingers around where the louse had jabbed her. She twisted her head to the right, straining for a glimpse of the site in the mirror. It was a red, raised mark. What was the crap in that vial? She dried herself and returned to the room.

"What are you going to do to me? And what did you give me?" she asked with her hands on her hips.

"I'm not at liberty to say." Mac shoved her back on the bed and handed her a soda.

Without asking, Lily took the soda. Who knew why she obeyed him. She could've kicked him again, but she'd risk getting shot. Gil too.

Lily gulped half the can, watching Mac as he looked at his watch and back at her. Suddenly Lily started getting drowsy, and the room spun once more.

"Wh … what did you put in soda?" she slurred.

"No sense in fighting it," Mac said.

"What am fighting?" she garbled.

"You seem like a nice gal. I'm glad I didn't have to kill ya." Mac removed black latex gloves out of his bag and slipped them on. He then retrieved a loaded syringe with a brownish-looking substance. Mac pulled out a silicone strap that Lily had seen in the doctor's office.

Lily's body was heavy, and she couldn't speak. She fell back on the pillow and stared; her body frozen. She watched Mac roll up her sleeve, tie off the strap, and jab her. The room became blurry, and she had a sudden rush without a care in the world. Lily just gazed as Mac placed her Sig in her left hand.

Her eyes became too heavy to stay open. Lily felt Mac's hand over hers, followed by the squeezing motion.

Pop … pop … pop!

CHAPTER 17

AFTER WE EXITED the café, Simon left his truck parked, and we piled into the Sprinter in search of any signs of Lily or this white van Paisley told us about. Rayo tossed Simon and me towels. While we dried ourselves, Kate continued her services as the driver. We cut down side streets and passed the Welcome to Lake Simi sign twice. The sun was setting as we drove by the sign a third time.

Apparently, the town of Lake Simi had a population of around 1,500 people. Lake Simi had a marshal's office, community hospital, post office, an old cemetery, elementary, middle, and high schools, three gas stations, and five restaurants. All "fun facts" I wasn't the least bit interested in knowing. But Rayo was. He kept giving us nuggets of info as he continued his internet search.

"The lake is two hundred feet deep. It's fifteen square miles and sits between two rivers. It's surrounded by national forest along the Lewis and Clark historic trail," Rayo read from his iPhone. "Grizzly bears and gray wolves exist in the area and tourists can enjoy fishing, camping, canoeing, boating, hiking an—"

"That's enough, Rayo," I barked. Since I was riding shotgun, Rayo did not see my eye roll too.

The van suddenly went quiet. I turned around and saw judgy eyes gazing at me. Even the dog cocked her head. Okay, so maybe Sue wasn't being critical, but if she were a person, she would be.

"Sorry, Rayo. I don't mean to be so snippy," I said, giving him an apologetic, faint smile.

"It's all right, Rose," Rayo stated. "I understand. We will find her." He put his hand on my shoulder.

I fought back tears and cleared my throat. I was more comfortable with the stony silence.

"Let's take a break," Simon said.

"Sounds good to me." Kate yawned as she pulled over to a lake-front park.

We all got out and stretched our legs, while Sue attended to her business. I was relieved when a light mist replaced the downpour from earlier, but my jeans were still drenched and sticking to my thighs. I needed to change. It might lighten my mood.

When Sue and I returned to the van, Rayo was pulling out food from a large cooler. Once again, Grandma to the rescue. She'd packed roast beef sandwiches, chips, fruit, vegetables, and whatever leftovers Rayo could squeeze into our vehicle. She even packed Sue a few chicken, rice, and vegetable meals.

My mind was spinning like a squirrel on cocaine, so I did not enjoy the sunset, nor did I taste the sandwich. I just wolfed it and changed my pants. I plopped in the driver's seat so Kate could chill in the back with Rayo and Sue. While Simon sat in the passenger seat.

As we sat lakeside, Rayo was toying with the state-of-the-art computer system Grandma installed in the Sprinter when he suddenly started laughing. I turned and found Sue belly up on her dog bed. Her paws were moving as she woofed in her dreams. She was probably playing with her doggie friends. I smiled ever briefly. Then she snored so loud it got a giggle out of us. Sue brought joviality to the somber van.

"Rose," Rayo said. "I've been meaning to ask you. Why the name, Sue?"

I released a weighty sigh. "Long story. I named her after my murdered friend Sue Sullivan. Hitmen gunned Sue down in a hotel a year ago today. I will spare you the bloody details." I sighed again. "But I was the target. Anyway, the same day I rescued Sue from a tweaker. I had no plans to keep her." I looked back at my sweet girl and smiled. "Sue had other plans. Anyhow, I was doing recon on Stanley James's mansion. You know, the cartel dude who wants me dead. When I got too close to his house, one of his guards asked me what I was doing. I told him I was looking for my lost dog.

"The mansion, ironically, was in the same neighborhood as my friend Sue's parents. The ogre must not have believed me and demanded the name of my dog. I blurted out Sue. Little did I know she'd jumped out of my vehicle and was on my heels. So, she kind of named herself." I stared straight ahead as I relived it. "I'd lost two friends that day. Both murdered in a case of mistaken identity." I wiped a tear that trickled down my cheek. I shook my head. "So that's how she got her name. Sue saved me."

The Sprinter went silent once more, and I felt eyes on me. But this time, they were sympathetic.

"She also helps me not murder dumb asses."

"You mean mentally, right?" Rayo said with a shaky laugh.

"Oh, naturally," I replied.

"It's called anxiety, Rose," Simon interjected.

"Pfft, no. How can you say that?"

"Let me see … how many people have you shot on and off duty?"

"Really?! You want to go there, special ops man?"

"Point well taken. I've just learned how to channel my stress and anger. Which is now part of your training."

I furrowed my brows. "I don't have anger problems. I have dumb ass people problems." I paused. "Sue calms me so I won't throat punch them." I snorted.

"She really is your therapy dog," Kate said.

"Yeah, she's trained in personal protection, but the bonus is she picks up on my moods. Hence, her vest."

Just then, Sue woke up and snorted.

"Ha, she snorts like you, Rose," Rayo said.

"That she does." I checked my phone for the millionth time. No calls, but the time read nine. As I set it on my lap, it rang in my hands. I flinched as I answered it on speaker. I'd hoped it was Lily or even Grandma telling me Lily was okay.

But the caller was Lake Simi Café's owner, Isabel. She'd informed us there wasn't anything suspicious on the CCTV. Isabel mentioned the man in question's facial features were blurry and Lily's bike must've been out of view. I hung up and slumped my shoulders.

"I feel like we're missing something," I finally said.

Kate leaned forward. "A good night's sleep might clear our

minds." She yawned again. "We should find a place to crash for the night."

"We can bunk in here, but it might be tight. Or we can find a motel?" Simon said.

"All five motels had no-vacancy signs," Rayo said. "If we had more notice, we could get one of those vacation rentals. There's a lot here."

"I'm not a fan of hotels or motels." I chewed on my lip. Not to mention I could not rest until I found Lily unharmed.

"You're doing that lip-biting thing, Rose," Simon said. "I've been around you long enough to know you're planning something."

"Can we hold off for the moment on bedding down?" I asked. "There must be another camera somewhere near that café." I sat up straighter in my seat. "Wait, there was a bank across the stree—"

Just then, sirens wailed past us with flashing red and blue lights. One right after the other. Two marshals' vehicles, followed by an ambulance, and then the Marshal himself.

We looked at one another in silence for a spell. Even Sue's Red Kelpie ears were at attention.

"I got a bad feeling," I said.

"Me too," Simon and Kate uttered simultaneously.

CHAPTER 18

◆

I TORE OFF out of our lakeside parking spot as the last emergency responder passed and followed them. We didn't have to go far because you can practically throw a stone down Main Street. Red and blue lights converged on the Lake Simi Motel like flies on a carcass.

The moment I screeched to a halt and angled the van behind a patrol vehicle, two deputy marshals made entry into the motel, room number five, with guns drawn. My gut told me it had something to do with Lily. I jumped out and ran toward the scene. I was not thinking, and I was on automatic.

As I had taken a few steps, a chunky man wearing a uniform who stood close to six feet yelled at me.

"Stand back. This is an active crime scene," the deputy, who looked to be in his late fifties, bellowed. His name tag read *Pane*.

I pushed through. "I'm Agent O—" No, I wasn't. I stood motionless with a gaping mouth as the rain returned, pounding on my bruised face. And for the first time since I took a leave of absence, I did not know who I was.

"I said, back off, ma'am," he ordered again and held his hand to me.

Simon was behind me in seconds and yanked me off my feet. "Rose, he's right," he whispered in my ear.

My heart sank as the two deputies exited. The female uttered "body bag" and waved a paramedic into the room.

I stood on my tiptoes, stretching my neck to see into number five. "No!" I shouted and broke through their barrier, bolting again as fast as my long legs would carry me. And that's when I spotted Lily's jacket draped over the edge of the bed.

"Grab her," Deputy Pane yelled.

The second my feet hit the threshold, they yanked me from behind and whisked me away. A female deputy clutched my left elbow. And a male, who looked as if he was barely out of puberty, was on my right.

"Ma'am. We gave you one warning, so unless you want to sit in the backseat of my patrol car, you need to back off *now*!" the female pressed.

Just then, Sue bolted from the van and ran into the room, whimpering. She jumped on the bed where Lily's jacket had been. I breathed a sigh of relief when I heard Lily mumbling something inaudible. Sue on the job.

"Whose dog is this? Get her out of here!" the paramedic ordered.

I called Sue back, and she was immediately by my side, her tail tucked. "Good girl. It'll be okay," I uttered in a weak attempt to convince myself too.

The female deputy marshal positioned herself in front of me with her arms out.

I shook out of it and looked at her name tag. It read *Moxmar*. Moxmar stood an inch taller than me and had at least five pounds on me. Moxmar had curly chocolate-brown hair and was in her mid-to late-twenties. Another young one. But she wore the confidence of a seasoned professional.

"My friend is in there. Is she all right?" I asked.

"I am not at liberty to discuss it with you," Moxmar replied calmly.

"Please. Someone abducted her today," I bellowed.

Deputy Moxmar looked at me with furrowed brows. "Abducted? Are you certain?"

"Uh … not really. But I'm almost positive."

"Almost doesn't cut it. Now, back down," Moxmar demanded.

I stood, biting my nails, and nodded. "Please tell me, is my friend, all right?"

"They are checking her out," Moxmar replied.

"Are you taking her to the hospital? Can I see her the—"

Deputy Marshal Pane stepped out of the room and stared

through me. "She doesn't want to go to the hospital. They will medically clear her here."

"Okay … o—wait, cleared?" I squinted. "She's going to jail! For what?!"

CHAPTER 19

"**THAT'S ALL I** can say," Pane said. He rested one hand on his weapon and the other on the iron railing outside the room.

Just then, the Marshal himself exited the room. He bore a striking resemblance to Sir Winston Churchill. The Marshal was in his late sixties, stood 5′6″, and was roughly 185 pounds with gray hair and blue eyes. He even had an unlit cigar hanging out of his jowly cheeks. It was fitting his name tag read, *Church*.

"This is going to be a long night," Church said to Pane. "The coroner's office can't get here for the body. They're on a triple in Missoula, so the inn will be full. We will process the scene and the paramedic will transport the body to our cold room." He gave me a nod on his way to his patrol vehicle.

Moxmar swept past me. As she was about to enter the room, Pane stopped her. "I need you to get any witness statements. Terrance and I will handle things inside," he ordered.

Moxmar flipped toward me. Her head shook and she mumbled something like "sexist asshat" almost under her breath. By the scowl on her face, Moxmar was less than thrilled. She stood in front of me, blocking my view.

"Please Deputy Moxmar, you've got to believe me. My friend is no criminal. She went missing, and we tracked her motorcycle to the café on Main Street. It's been there since eleven-forty-five today. Ya see, her bike is her baby, and she'd never leave it," I said, without taking a breath.

"Call me, Moxy ... and hold on," she said as she held her hand to stop me. "I have to take your statement." She pulled out her pad. "First, I need some identification."

"Look, Moxy, I didn't mean to cross the line. But I am not a shitbird, tweaker criminal. No warrants or holds. I'm not known local. And I know how crazy this looks," I said again with pressured speech.

"You tracked her bike? Are you LE?" Moxy asked.

I guess using the terms "tweaker, known local and warrants or holds," gave it away that I worked law enforcement. "I am on extended leave for now. And I'd rather not go on record. In fact, disregard. Bottom line, we are not witnesses. But I assure you, our friend would never be caught dead in a motel like this." I flicked my wrist in a dismissal fashion. "Do you see an overnight bag in there? And why can't we take her home? Is she being charged with something?" I was almost nose to nose with Moxy as I stood tall.

Moxy drew her right leg back, her left hand up, the other on her weapon. "Back off!"

"Shit, I'm sorry." I put my hands up and got out of Moxy's space. "That was wrong of me."

Just then Simon, who'd been on my six the whole time, grabbed me by the elbow. "You're not helping, Rose," he mumbled in a low growl.

I spun my head and glared at him. I wore not only my game face, but I was in war mode. Simon flipped his hands and stomped back to the Sprinter. I returned my attention to Moxy.

"There is a dead body in there," Moxy spoke in a faint tone as she looked around. "It doesn't look good for her."

I widened my stance and stared at the ground for a second. "So … so she's being accused of murder?" I inquired in a calmer tone. I knew the worst thing for Lily's sake was to act like a total butt head. But my emotions ran amuck. I apologized again to the deputy marshal for my behavior.

Moxy shook her head and threw her hands out. "You all need to move along unless you have something to add or want to go on record." She leaned in and whispered. "I suggest you get your friend an attorney." She walked away to question other motel guests who were now out of their rooms, talking to one another in hushed voices. Looky loos trying to glimpse a dead body.

"Lily, it's going to be okay. Don't say a word. Wait for your lawyer," I called as loud as I could and stomped back to the van.

Kate was now in the driver's seat, while Simon stood against the vehicle. He wore a scowl.

"I apologize for 'the look'," I said with air quotes to Simon.

I've been told my face not only talks, but yells too.

"It's late and our emotions are on red alert. Apology accepted." He gave me his best *It's going to be okay* look.

I slid into the passenger side of the Sprinter and Simon closed my door. He was not only my rock, but a gentleman too. He reached in through the opened window and squeezed my hand.

I dropped my hands in my face and sucked back a stifled sob. Sue was on me within a millisecond, nuzzling in the crook of my neck. The dam almost burst. Don't be a wuss, Rose. Lily needs you to keep it together. I drew a deep breath and raised my head. "I don't suppose anyone knows of a stellar attorney … and a bail bondsman," I stated to my crew.

"No, but I'm sure your grandma does," Simon said and hopped in the backseat. "Let's get my truck and find a place to crash for the night."

Sleep was the last thing on my mind as I picked up my phone and called Grandma Lil.

CHAPTER 20

◆

"ARE YOU STILL on scene?" CK inquired as she sat in her rental in Hamilton, her feet propped on a leather recliner, sipping her tumbler of Jack Daniels.

"Affirmative. I'm across the street in the back of the van watching with night eyes," Mac said. "The cops and the meat wagon are here."

"Perfect. Now tell me *exactly* what the PI said," CK urged.

"Like I told you, the drug didn't work on him. He mentioned the flash drive and mumbled something about a chip. And before I pressed any further, he grabbed his chest, and it was lights out," Mac said. "Is that crap gonna show on a blood test? It better not come back to me."

"Leaves no trace in the system," CK said. "But wait. You said he grabbed his chest?"

"Yes."

"That is one of the potential side effects of that drug. Instant heart failure. But the autopsy should determine gunshot as his cause of death. If you did your freakin' job correctly."

Mac expelled a low, guttered growl. "What about the needle marks on their arms and behind the ear?"

"The body should absorb the mark behind their ears at a rapid rate before anyone takes notice. So, I've been told," CK said and took a swig of her drink. "And as for the ones on their arms, well, it's obvious they were using heroin. Besides, that town is still in the dark ages and not to mention they lack resources. They're gonna focus on the crime. Chances are, this was the first homicide they'd had in years."

"True. Hell, they barely have cell service out here."

"Nonetheless. Stay around to make sure there are no loose ends."

"What? It's Friday night. She won't see a judge until Monday," Mac said. "What the hell am I supposed to do?"

"You're a big boy. Figure it out," CK said. "Do I need to tell you how to do your job?"

"Fine, I have to dump the van. I'll crash at a motel on the other side of town. But I want better accommodation tomorrow," Mac said.

"I will have another vehicle. It will be parked at the vacation rental. I'll text you the location," CK said. "Are you certain you made it look like they were partying?"

"Yes," Mac said. "It's not my first rodeo, CK."

"So, you say," CK said. "What info did you get out of Lily? Does she know about this chip?"

"Don't think she knows shit. She's tough. Either that or the truth serum didn't work."

"It's *not* a truth serum. It just so happens it can act like one."

"Yeah … yeah, they designed it for something else. That part worked fairly good on her. She did everything I told her to," Mac said. "What mad scientist developed a mind control drug?"

"All I know is the agency did not sanction it. They closed those experiments years ago and destroyed the documents. It turns out there were records found in other places. Enough to reconstruct and build on the drug. Pretty disturbing."

"What do the targets have to do with any of it?"

"Not sure. My job was to terminate."

"Why the change in heart about the girl?"

"Don't know, nor do I want to," CK said. Suddenly, her phone buzzed with an incoming call. "Gotta go. Stay low. Keep me posted."

CK switched calls. "I thought we were only to communicate via e-mail."

"Just give me an update and spare me my own lecture," Alvarez said.

"On track, she's being detained as we speak. The PI has been eliminated. Unfortunately, he could not tell my guy anything. But we have the USB. The target didn't have time to look at it and she doesn't know anything." CK kept the part about a computer chip to herself.

"We need to make sure. Keep her alive for now," Alvarez said. "Rose may be a problem. Watch her closely, too."

"No kidding," CK said. "I saw her drop out of the sky with a damaged parachute and live to talk about it."

"The apple doesn't fall far from the tree," Alvarez said.

"You mean the infamous Lily Roo?"

"Yeah, although she's retired, she's got more connections than I do," Alvarez said. "Wait for the green light. Then do some house cleaning and disappear."

"Copy that." CK disconnected and downed the rest of her drink.

Did Alvarez also mean that Mac needed to disappear as well? She could kick herself for telling him about the non-sanctioned experiment.

Damn Jack.

CHAPTER 21

 ◆

SUE'S SNORING WOKE me, not to mention she was lying on my bladder. All forty-five pounds of her. I peeked at my phone and the time read 5:30 a.m. The gang was still sleeping and although the Sprinter accommodated four, it was a tight fit. We didn't have time to look for an RV park, so we opted to dry camp lakeside.

Since I'd slept in my street clothes, I was ready to go. I slipped on my running shoes and shrugged into Simon's jacket and tip-toed out the front passenger door. My teeth chattered so loud, I thought it would wake my friends, so I pulled the hood over my head. Although the temps only dropped to thirty, I was used to tropical weather and my body was cursing me.

As Sue and I trekked away from the Sprinter, I absorbed the tranquility and quietness and gazed upon the still lake before me; but an ache filled my heart. My best friend was arrested for murder. It was too much. I needed to do something, and fast. There was no way she could harm anyone.

My eyes were drawn to the mountains and a verse from the book of Psalms popped into my head: *Where does my help come from? My help comes from the Lord* ... okay, God. I trust you to guide me to my next move. Lily does not deserve this.

Just then my phone vibrated with an incoming text from Grandma: *call when you wake*. Grandma does not sleep much. She goes to bed with the party animals and rises before the roosters. I dialed Grandma and put her on speakerphone. I tried to avoid harmful radiation and used this mode when possible.

"Morning," I said.

"How was my van last night?"

"I know you don't want to discuss your van." I pursed my lips as if she could see me. "What's really up?"

"I contacted a superb attorney," Gran said. "She's a former federal prosecutor. Her name is Nala Clearwater."

"We need a good *defense* lawyer." I furrowed at the phone.

"Trust me. She is known as the pit bull. Her sheer presence makes people shiver. Nala's a trusted friend, too."

"I'm confused," I said. "How will a prosecutor help Lily?"

"That's precisely who you want defending you," Grandma replied. "She took a leave of absence to have a baby. Her husband is also a lawyer. During her maternity leave, Nala made it permanent and works for the other side. She only takes on selective cases, like Lily's, for a hefty fee."

"Gran, I can afford it and will pay … no matter the cost."

"We both can help. I'll handle her transportation. I have one of my people flying her out to my place. Nala's finishing up another murder case and will be here tomorrow," Grandma said.

"I'll ask Simon or Kate to get her."

Just then, I heard voices coming from the van.

"No, I'm going to drive Nala out there. I need to see Lily," Grandma's voice dropped to a low whisper. "She's family."

"I feel the same." I hurried back to the Sprinter.

I stepped inside and plopped on a swivel leather chair. Since everyone was awake, I kept the phone on speaker and told Grandma such. Grandma and I made a habit of advising one another when we had other ears in our conversation.

"I briefed Nala on Lily's case, to the extent of my knowledge," Grandma said.

"Can we get her bailed soon?" I asked. "I know it's Saturday, and Lily hasn't been arraigned yet. I'd hate for her to be stuck in a cell until Monday."

"I'm friends with the judge out there," Grandma Lil said. "Nala is making a phone call today to have a zoom meeting scheduled for ten tomorrow morning. And based on Lily's lack of criminal history, bail should not be an issue. It will be high, though."

"No kidding." I sighed. "I'm going to see what evidence they have on her. It's a small town. Everyone is tight-lipped. But I connected with a young female deputy marshal. She's sharp." I paused. "But they already think I'm trouble."

"Granddaughter, what did you do?" Gran's exasperation came through the phone loud and clear.

"Nothing ... well, I may have let my emotions get the best of me and I ran into the crime scene." I wrinkled my nose.

"Simon told me," Grandma said. "And you cannot let your emotions—"

"Cloud my judgment," I finished her sentence.

Simon was sitting up, grinning at me.

I gave him a crooked smile, shaking my head. "So, we have to wait another day? Can't we bail her out today?" I plead.

"Nala wants to be there. Did Lily lawyer up?"

"I advised her," I replied. "But she was out of it. And mumbling."

"Out of it? What do you mean?" Grandma asked.

"She didn't sound like herself."

"Oh boy. I will ask if Nala can break away any earlier," she said. "Speaking of attorneys, Keith called *again*. He said it was urgent."

"I promise I'll call him when this is over. I'm not in the mood to be paraded around at yet *another* fund raiser to attract more donors for the foundation." I rolled my eyes. "I feel like Bruce Wayne, without the Batman persona and outfit. Although, that would be cool."

"Granddaughter, the squirrels are loose again. Focus."

"I know, I'm sorry."

"Oh, I am looking into a larger rental for you all tonight," Grandma said. "I will text you the details later."

"Perfect. We could all use a shower and our own rooms. Besides, there are no vacancies in tow—" It hit me.

"Uh oh," Grandma laughed. "Squirrels."

"Sorry ... poor sleep. Um, well gotta go. Love you." I disconnected.

What I did not want to tell Grandma was that I needed to get inside that motel room and chat with the clerk on duty. Just as I hung up, my phone buzzed once more. It was a 406-area code. Since the whole state of Montana was 406, it was safe for me to answer.

"Hello?"

"Rose. I swear I didn't kill him!" Lily sobbed the entire

sentence.

"I know," I said. "I'm going to come see you today." My heart sank again. "Lily. I need to ask a question. Were you drugged last night?" I asked.

"I … I don't know. Maybe? But they want to transport me to the county jail until my arraignment on Monday," she whimpered. "I caan't go there. Bad people are in those places."

"I'm headed there right away," I said as I looked at my phone. The time read half-past six. I'd need to wait until at least eight. "Remember, do not say a word, or allow them to draw blood. Gran hired a lawyer."

"Too late for the blood draw," Lily groaned.

"Time's up," a male voice echoed on the line.

The call went still and then disconnected.

I texted Grandma. *Lily needs help today. They want to move her to the county detention facility.*

CHAPTER 22

I STOOD ON the steps of the Lake Simi Marshal's office. The building was constructed in the early 1900s and did not appear to be upgraded. The office was the only structure at the south end of town. I did a meditative breath as I halted. I didn't want to go in guns blazing, with a chip on my shoulder. That would be the worst. And they had a job to do.

I couldn't stand it when people told me how to do my job and that they paid my salary, yada, yada, yada. Law enforcement officers don't take to that. So, I wore my happy face. Not my *I want to throat punch you* look.

It was eight o'clock on the nose when I strolled through the front door. The inside was more modern than I expected. There were two facing desks, one empty, the other occupied by a middle-aged, slightly plump, non-custody woman. She had big bouffant, graying hair, with streaks of black running through it. Her head was down, and her long acrylic nails furiously typed away at her computer.

So, I misjudged. This was not Mayberry, and they were in the computer era. I steadily approached the clerk. Her name plate on the desk read *Peggy*.

"Good morning, ma'am." I stood with my hands behind my back and addressed her in a calm manner. I also pulled off a fake smile. All my friends knew that grin and it was BS.

"Morning, doll. What can I do ya for?" Peggy said with a cheery tone, popping her gum.

"I am here to visit Lily. Lily Cazier."

"Oh, that one," Peggy sighed and gave a raised brow. "How can

I help you?"

"May I please see her?" I asked with the politeness of a girl scout.

Peggy returned to her typing. "Nope. She's being tr—um, she is not allowed visitors."

"I know she is being transferred to the county today," I said. "She called me. I am also aware you are prohibited from telling me when." I leaned on her desk. "Peggy, please. She is family to me. She would never survive in county lockup."

"I have no control over that," Peggy said sharply. "She should've thought about that before she partied it up and committed a crime in our town." She continued tapping away at the keyboard, avoiding eye contact.

I stood with my arms crossed. "Allegedly," I growled through gritted teeth. "Wait. What do you mean, partied?"

Peggy slowly looked back at me. "You are done here," she huffed.

Crap on a biscuit. I just peed in her Cheerios. Quick Rose, be nice. "I am terribly sorry. But ya see—" I lowered my voice. "My friend, Lily, well, she's never been arrested for anything … in her life. Not a single speeding ticket. Heck, she won't even jaywalk." I put my hand on my hip and snorted and waved my other in the air. "There was this one time when we were in downtown Hamilton, and we had to—"

"Where are you going with this?" Peggy peered at me over the top of her cat eyed glasses, blinking.

"Sor—"

Just then, her desk phone rang. "Lake Simi Marshal, Peggy speaking—un hunh. Ookay. Marshal Church is out of the office. I can transfer you to the deputy on duty. Please hold." She held the phone on her shoulder. "Gary … a call for you. Line two. Some judge out of Missoula," she yelled and put the receiver down. Peggy peered back at me. "The prisoner must have friends in high places. But so ya know, Marshal Church has the final say so. And he doesn't take kindly to outsiders telling him what to do." She glared.

"Does this mean Lily won't be transferred?"

"Maybe … maybe not. I'm not at liberty." Peggy jutted her chin to a set of hard plastic chairs across from her desk. "Have a seat."

A few minutes later, Peggy's phone rang. "Yes, Gary. Un hunh—ookay," she said. "Wait. The prisoner has a visitor. Un hunh—ookay." She disconnected and looked at me. "It's Saturday. No visitors on the weekends. Short staffed and all."

I rose to my feet and furrowed my brows. I scanned the room, looking for the posted visiting hours. But didn't see any. "Look, Peggy. I apologize for coming on the way I did. I meant no disrespect," I said.

She shrugged.

I sucked my teeth, rolled my neck, and bit my tongue. It's gotta be bruised by now. I took another breath and put on my freakin' happy face again.

"May I use the bathroom?" I asked.

She looked at me and paused a spell. "Down the hall, last door on the right. But do *not* under any circumstances go through the double doors in the back," Peggy said.

I gave her a cheeky grin. As I proceeded down the corridor, I observed three offices: two on the left and one on the right. The double forbidden doors were at the far end of the hall. A sign on the door read, *Staff Only*. Out of the three offices, only one was open and occupied. The name on the doorplate boldly read DEPUTY MARSHAL G. PANE. I assumed it was Gary's office. I peered my head around the corner and the deputy sat behind a large oak desk, papers strewn across it. He held up a magnifier and was inspecting a photograph. I surmised from the only crime scene in the town.

Peggy must've been watching because she yelled, "Not that door!"

I turned back to her. "Oh, sorry. I see that now," I said, hoping to sound convincing.

Peggy's shouts startled the pudgy man behind the desk because he flinched in his seat.

He put the photo on the folder, quickly closing it. "May I help you, young lady?" he asked, stoned faced, all business.

He was the deputy from last night, Pane.

Just my rotten luck.

CHAPTER 23

"OH … I'M SORRY, *Marshal*. I was looking for the bathroom."
I smiled and blinked like a ditzy red head. My male companion,
Kevin O'Malley, said it was my azure blues that stole his heart. So,
I batted my lashes too and put my eyes to work. But I was also told
I was a terrible flirt. If I tried too hard, I resembled a serial killer.
So, I dialed down the charm … a bit.

"It's *Deputy* Marshal Pane." He inclined his head to the
nameplate on his desk.

"Oh, I just assumed you ran the place," I said with a mental eye
roll.

"How can I help you?" Gary leaned back in his chair,
interlacing his fingers.

"I'm here to see my friend, but I guess she's not allowed
visitors?" I posed it more of a question than a statement. "Um …
but I need to use the facilities."

"I remember you from last night." Gary sat tall, and he wore a
scowl. "You crossed my crime scene."

"Again, I apologize for my behavior." As I tried to convince
him, I scanned the room, looking for alternate ways to sneak back
inside. Deputy Pane's office was not as secure as one would think.
I saw a single-paned window with a twenty-year-old alarm system.
Alarms were not my forte. Yet. I pondered. "My emotions were
high, and I was worried … well am worried about my friend."

"Your *friend* has been tight-lipped. All she said was 'lawyer.'
Heck, she's been watching too many of those cop shows. Ms.
Cazier is one tough nut to crack."

I stood with my shoulders back like a proud parent. "I advised her not to. These are serious charges. I assure you Lily is innocent," I stated with a clenched jaw. So much for the ditzy routine. "Her attorney should arrive tomorrow."

"I heard." He crossed his arms. "And your friend must be well connected. They chose not to transfer her to county so she'll be here through the weekend," Gary said. "Of course, our Marshal might have something to say about that. He doesn't like anyone telling him how to run his town."

"So, I've heard," I said and started for the exit. I turned back. "Oh, and your deputy, I think Moxy, is her name. She was nice to me and my service dog. You are lucky to have her on your staff." I flashed a genuine smile.

"She is a *rising* star." He rolled his eyes. "She's hoping to take my desk as I am in line to be the next Marshal. If the city council appoints me. But being a female, this office might not happen for Moxy." Gary rose. "If you don't mind, I have work to do." He waved his hand to the hall.

Female? How condescending. I was ready to jump across his desk and throat punch him. That's why Moxy referred to him as a "sexist asshat." Instead, I let out a low, silent growl as I exited. The bathroom was next to the double forbidden doors. I looked over my shoulder to make sure I wasn't being watched and peeked through the windows.

Lily was curled in a fetal position on a wobbly metal cot with her back toward me. I wanted with every inch of my crushed heart to run in there and take her in my arms and tell her everything was going to be okay. But I would be lying. I did not know what evidence they had stacked against her. But I was aiming to find out. Even if it meant breaking a few laws.

It wouldn't be the first time.

CHAPTER 24

◆

I SHOOK MY head when I slipped behind the passenger seat of Simon's truck.

"By the look on your face, I take it things did not go well," Simon said. "Is Lily okay?"

"I didn't get to see her." I stared ahead, crossing my arms. I did not want to alarm Simon by repeating Peggy's comment about Lily's alleged partying.

Sue read my mood and jumped onto my lap, slobbering me with kisses. While she was there, I put on her service vest.

Kate parked next to us; the windows rolled down.

Rayo was standing outside between the two vehicles. "Since Sue is the only who one ate, I think we need to grab a bite," Rayo said, breaking the somber mood.

"Great idea. Let's go back to the café. Now that it's daylight, I'd like to look around." I continued hugging Sue. "Oh, Simon, is Lily's bike handled? I don't want them impounding it."

"With kid gloves. It's secure." He gave me his handsome, toothy smile.

"I should've brought you in with me." I shook my head. "Peggy would've given you the keys to the cell. She didn't take to me."

"Were you nice?" Simon asked.

I spun my head. "What kind of question is that? I'm *always* nice."

"Yeah, served with a side of snarky," Simon quipped.

I squinted at him. "Haven't you heard? Sarcasm can add a few years to your life."

"I guess you are going to live forever," Simon said, and

playfully slugged me on the arm.

Five minutes later, we pulled up to the Lake Simi Café. Since it was pouring when we arrived last night, I didn't notice the café's logo was an eye-fetching mountain lake with a canoe. We stepped inside and wood paneling lined the bottom part of the café. The top was bluish-gray lake-themed with boats, anchors, canoes in metal decals on the wall.

There were nine stools at the counter in a horseshoe shape. One in the middle had a plaque in front that read *Tony 1920-2017*. The stools faced the open kitchen where you can see the cook preparing your food. Seven booths lined the walls. All had large windows to look out at the lake and swinging double doors leading to the casino/bar in the back.

A twenty-something year old waitress greeted us and sat us at the farthest booth closest to the casino/bar. She was different than the one last night. She wore a midriff Rolling Stones t-shirt, tight jeans, and her right arm was sleeved in tattoos. She had a studded nose ring, and her pixie haircut was multicolored, bright green and pink.

"Whattya have?" she asked, stoned face and surly.

I leaned in and read her name tag. "Well ... *Zuli*. Good morning," I replied with a wide, toothy smile.

Simon murmured. "Easy with the evil clown smile."

"I'm being nice," I uttered through my teeth.

Zuli laughed. "Thanks, I needed that. I apologize. I worked at the casino bar yesterday and then the Simi last night." She yawned.

We collectively tilted our heads.

"Sorry, the Simi is the Lake Simi Motel," Zuli said. "My ass is whooped. What can I get started for you all?"

Just then, Sue perked her head up and put her paw on my lap.

"May I please have water for my girl?" I asked.

"Aww, what a cutie," Zuli cooed and knelt.

What I was lacking in the small talk department, Sue made up for it. My wing girl. "This is Sue," I said, perusing the menu.

That got another chuckle out of Zuli. "Awesome, why Sue?" She stood.

"Very long story. But I named her after my murdered friend," I answered without missing a beat.

The table went silent. I looked up and all four of them,

including the waitress, stared with opened mouths. My group knew my story, but by their looks, I could tell it was too much for someone I did not know. I would need a new tale and not the kind Sue was wagging.

I scrunched my nose. "Sorry, was that too snarky?" I asked Simon.

"Uh, noo," Simon replied. "Blunt and straight forward, yes."

I gave them a cheeky grin.

"I like you." Zuli nodded and smiled back.

We gave her our orders. "Oh, before you go, Zuli. You said you worked at the casino all day?" I inquired. "I was wondering if you recognize this lady." I pulled out my cell, scrolled and found a picture of Lily. I showed it to her.

"Yeah. She rode up on a bitchin' bike yesterday. I was surprised to see she left it."

Finally, someone saw her Genny. "Yes, my friend Lily." I sat tall. "Can you think of anything else? Was there a man with her?"

Zuli looked up and to the left. "Not that I recall. She was by herself."

I drew out a twenty and slid it on the table to her. "Please, my friend is in a lot of trouble." I did not want to tell her that someone abducted Lily. Not yet. I didn't know Zuli that well. Heck, more people could be in on her kidnapping.

Zuli slipped the money and jammed it in her jeans front pocket. "Come to think of it. A stocky man walked through the bar. He looked at her bike through the window. I could tell, because there was nothing else to look at and hers was way cool," Zuli said. "I thought nothing of it. I know the guy had a lot of money and was obviously a tourist. Only, he did not strike me as anyone interested in lake activities."

"How do you mean?" I questioned.

"Well, he had on crazy looking expensive alligator boots and a black leather bomber jacket." She walked away and turned back. "Oh, he was driving a white panel van, no windows. I thought that was odd for someone with his kind of money."

"Did you see what direction he drove?" I asked.

"He pulled his van around right next to her bike," Zuli said. "I just thought he was getting a better look."

"Do you remember what he looked like? Did you see her get in the van with him?" I urged. "Or catch a glimpse at the plate?"

She shook her head. "I was too focused on those boots, and it got busy after that. The next thing, the van was gone, but her bike was still there. I missed her leaving. She most likely walked out the front door," Zuli said.

"Thank you. Oh, does the casino have a camera system?" Simon beat me to the question.

"Yeah," Zuli said, "but it isn't working right now. The owners are getting it repaired." Zuli leaned over our table. "Please don't let that get out. We don't need anyone ripping off the casino." She left and placed our order.

Moments later, our food arrived, and we dove in mouth first. The table was still until Kate finally broke the silence. "Wow, busy girl. The café, casino, and the *motel*."

We stopped eating.

CHAPTER 25

LILLIAN SAT AT her nook and booked a lakeside rental for Rose and the crew. Just then, the front door opened.

"Griz, did you forget something?" she called out.

"Oh, hi Lillian. It's me." Charly stood at the threshold.

"Hello, Charly. Griz is not here." Lillian closed her laptop. "He went to Missoula for supplies."

"Yes, he loaned me his key," Charly said.

Lillian studied her. "Then why are you here?"

"Um … I was looking for Lily." Charly peered around the room. "Is she back?"

"I am afraid not." Lillian made her way to the kitchen and poured a cup of coffee. "Come, we need to talk." She nodded to the bar stool. "Would you like some?"

Charly tilted her head, looking like a curious puppy. "Ookay," she said hesitantly. "Thank you."

"I'm not sure if you heard, but Lily is in trouble." Lillian handed the cup to Charly.

Charly sat. "No. Is she okay?!" Her voice rose a notch.

"Physically she will be okay … at least I hope," Lillian replied. "But she has been arrested for a crime she did not commit."

"That's terrible." Charly stood and paced. "What are you going to do?"

"I have the best attorney on her case. She is arriving tomorrow."

"Oh, I'm so glad to hear that." Charly leaned on the counter and took a sip. "Is there any way I can be of assistance?" she asked.

"No, she just needs all the support and help we can give her."

"There isn't anything I would not do for her."

"Thank you," Lillian smiled.

"Where was she arrested? Is there bail set?" Charly inquired.

"The location is not important." Lillian kept some things close to the vest. "The attorney will meet with her and the judge tomorrow."

"On a Sunday?"

Lillian looked over her glasses.

"Never mind," Charly chuckled. "I forgot who I was talking to. Poor Lily. I imagined she'd be remanded to custody for a while … you know, because of her charges."

"We hope to bail her out tomorrow and bring her here, where she is safe. I fear whoever did this will not be happy if she is released."

"Absolutely." Charly shook her head. "Count me in to help." She looked at her watch. "Gotta run. Thanks for the coffee." Charly swiftly left the house.

Lillian returned to reserve the rental for Rose. And a thought occurred. How did Charly know the charges against Lily were serious? And her behavior was fickle. Could Rose be on to something? Lillian should know by now to trust her granddaughter's instincts. After all, Rose was a mirror image of Lillian when she was that age.

CHAPTER 26

"WAIT?! LAKE SIMI Motel. Why did that not register?" I said and called Zuli over again and motioned for her to sit next to me.

Zuli informed us she worked late last night *because* of the homicide. The deputies questioned everyone, including our waitress. Her honesty excluded her as one of the bad guys. Not to mention my Spidey-senses told me to trust her.

I told her the suspect was our friend, who we knew was innocent. And for a crisp Benjamin, she agreed to leave the room open for us and turn away. But it couldn't happen until late tonight.

After Zuli left the table, we finished eating our breakfast in silence. I pushed my plate back and rested my elbows on the table with steepled fingers, staring ahead.

"I see that look, Rose. What are you thinking?" Simon inquired.

"The deputy marshal was looking at photos of the crime scene and a police report. That *he* wrote, no doubt. Not that I am questioning the local LEs on their ability to investigate, but they don't have Lily's interest at heart," I said. "I've got to find out what is in that report." I shot my eyes around the table. "We need an extra body for a little B&E fun."

"B&E?" Kate asked.

"Burglary or as it's referred to as Breaking and Entering," Simon replied with a shit-eating grin.

"We can handle the motel tonight, but not the marshal's building at the same time. Not to mention the security equipment they have installed," I said. "I did some recon when I was there."

"You mean snooping," Rayo quipped.

I gave him a side look. "You *are* a smart ass. I like it. You're fitting in nicely."

Rayo sat with his shoulders back and wore a wide grin.

"I don't have the skill set yet. And I need Simon with me. But I know who does." I grabbed my phone and texted Grandma: *Need Olive's help*.

Olive Knudsen helped my grandma in the past. She was the best thief out there. Grandma Lil used her a handful of times to go in undetected and get the job done. I was a good snooper, as Rayo called it, but not B&E. Not yet.

Grandma replied: *She's in Missoula on a job. I'll send her your way, stat.*

I ordered two coffees to go. I was not a java drinker, but I was spent, and it was going to be a long day. After I paid our tab, I winked at Zuli, and we left. Since we had time to kill, so to speak, we decided to check out Main Street, but not in a touristy way. Just as I exited, I noticed a bank across the street.

"Check out the CCTV up there." I nodded.

The four of us crossed the street only to discover the bank was closed on Saturdays. Gotta love small towns. I blew out a heavy sigh.

"No doubt it's a working CCTV." I looked down at Sue, who tilted her head. "Too bad we don't have a computer hacker genius." I rolled my eyes to Rayo.

"On it," Rayo said and eagerly returned to the van.

"I'm going to join him," Kate said. "He may need an extra set of eyes."

"Can you take Sue? It's time for the princess's nap."

While the others headed back to the Sprinter, Simon and I strode the length of Main Street, scanning for the white van, other CCTVs, or even the kidnapper himself. But nothing. We continued to the south end and found ourselves in front of the Lake Simi Motel.

Imagine that.

CHAPTER 27

◆

SIMON AND I spotted a patrol cruiser parked outside room number five. Crime scene tape cordoned off the area from the stairwell to the soda machine. As we approached the vehicle, we observed Moxy in the driver's seat.

I gave Simon a wide-eyed, toothy smile again.

"Please never smile like that. You bear a resemblance to a serial killer or a rabid clown."

I titled my head and batted my lashes.

Simon laughed. "I'm going to the manager's office to see if anyone will talk to me," he said.

I continued toward Moxy's vehicle. Her windows were up with the motor running. The minute she saw me, she rolled down the window.

"Fancy meeting you here," I said, handing her a coffee.

Moxy nodded and shot me a smile. Hopefully gratitude for the coffee enough that she'd let spill some details of the investigation. "I don't find running into you a coincidence. Especially since you popped in at the marshal's office this morning." She took a sip. "I hear you met our watch dog, Peg." Moxy chuckled.

"Indeed, I did." I leaned my back against her vehicle, next to her open window. Just a concerned citizen gifting a hardworking deputy marshal with coffee and shooting the breeze. Nothing to see here. "We hired Lily an attorney," I said and blew on my hot beverage.

"That's good. She's gonna need it."

"I know you can't tell me what you found in that room. But I assure you, our friend is innocent." I stretched. Information about the van, I'd keep to myself, for now.

Simon approached, shaking his head. His look implied he struck out at the office.

Moxy beamed at him and sat high in her seat. "I remember you from last night." She looked at me. "Is this your boyfriend or husband?"

If I didn't know better, I'd say Moxy was sweet on Simon.

"Pfft. Heck no," I snorted.

Simon shoulder bumped me. "In her dreams," he said, looking at Moxy.

"This is Simon. He's more like my annoying older brother." I gave him a side bump in return. "I have a man, thank you," I said.

They shook hands, and Moxy's hazel eyes widened, and her pupils dilated.

Perfect. I could use this to my advantage.

I leaned toward her. "So, who's investigating this?" I nodded to the cordoned off room.

Moxy sat back, drinking her coffee. "We are. Well, Deputy Pane," she said with an eye roll.

"Ooh." I took a sip of java. After meeting him again this morning, I understood the eye roll. "So, you lost the coin toss?"

"Huh?" Moxy tilted her head.

"Ya know," I said, "babysitting the motel."

"Just for a while. Marshal Church has a crime scene clean-up crew coming in tomorrow," Moxy said. "His cousin's friend owns the motel and is losing money. Tourist season is in full swing. Not to mention, dead bodies tend to scare away vacationers."

"Is that why I don't see any media here? I mean, this is a big deal. Murder and all," I said.

"Pretty much," Moxy said.

"You have to sit on the room overnight?" I asked.

"We're not staffed for that. There are only two full-time deputies and one reserve, Terrance." She fidgeted in her seat. "We're done talking. There's nothing more I can tell you about the investigation." Moxy exchanged glances with Simon and me. "You and your friend need to move along."

My phone dinged with a text message. I fished it out of my back pocket. Rayo: *Got him*. I showed Simon.

"Okay. You must believe me, Moxy. Lily is innocent," I said.

"It's not me you have to convince." Moxy rolled up her window.

Just then, I received another text. This time from my attorney: *Urgent that we meet.* I ignored it again.

Keith Fenner was not on my to do list today. And what was so urgent?

I could blow off any number of calls and texts about another foundation fundraiser, but this was—what three or four urgent messages in a day and a half? Maybe it was time to call him back. In case it was really something important. At least it would get him off my back.

But not until after we met up with Rayo.

CHAPTER 28

THE INSTANT SIMON and I stepped onto the sidewalk outside the motel's parking lot, we spotted a white van, no windows. The driver inched by us, slower than the posted speed limit of twenty-five. I couldn't catch a glimpse of him. All I saw were a set of black-gloved hands and a black leather jacket. Based on the description given by both waitresses, we knew the shitbird was a male.

"You see what I see?" Simon said.

"Yep," I said as I picked up the pace. "Are you up for a drive?"

"Always." Simon remotely unlocked the truck.

We jumped in and slowly followed the van.

I called Rayo and put him on speaker. "We're driving behind a white panel van with Montana plates." I read off the numbers.

"It's the same one that was on the bank footage," Rayo said. "I ran it. The vehicle is a rental out of Missoula."

"I figured as much," I said. "Who?"

"Bee Line Industries," Rayo said.

"Rayo, did the bank's system capture Lily or her bike?" I asked.

"Only the van. But it was blocking the view of her Genny."

"Who is this guy?" I inquired. "What in the hell did he want from Lily? I mean, thank heavens he didn't shoot her. And he must have framed her for murder." I shook my head and looked over at Simon.

His jaws were clenched, and he gripped the steering wheel so hard his knuckles were white. His silence gave me pause for concern. God only knew what was going on upstairs. Because the same images were probably bouncing around in my fiery brain.

"Oh." Rayo broke the tension that filled the air. "I also got Lily's burner phone number and tracked it."

"I tried last night," I said. "Since it's off, I couldn't. She last used her cell at the café."

"Fortunately, I have your gran's computer programs," Rayo said. "It's on the move, down Main Street."

"In the van," Simon and I said simultaneously.

"Do you need a second vehicle for moving surveillance?" Kate asked. I assumed Rayo had the phone on speaker too.

"Affirmative," Simon said.

Sue must've heard my voice because she let out a whimper.

"Don't worry, baby girl," I fussed, thinking that would ease her.

"The van just turned north off the main highway, going out of town," I said.

"Copy," Kate said.

We sped up to close the gap on our suspected kidnapper. There were no other vehicles headed out of town. Most of the traffic was coming into Lake Simi.

The driver kept looking behind him and accelerated. He made a quick right. He must be doing countersurveillance because that's what I would've done.

"Kate, the van turned down a side street," Simon said. "We'll take the next turnoff."

"I just pulled over," Kate said.

"I have him on my screen. He's back on the main highway," Rayo said.

We pulled into a gas station on the right and waited. A few moments later, the white van passed.

"The driver is a white male. Dark goatee and mustache," I said.

"Copy," Kate said. "We're back on the main highway. We are one for cover."

In moving surveillance, that meant she allowed one car between her and the target. In one of my previous assignments, I was on a multi-agency task force. We trained in moving surveillance. But in this case, we didn't have a tracker on the vehicle and relied only on Lily's cell phone.

Simon waited for a car to pass after Kate. We needed at least two cars behind the lead vehicle, but traffic was too light.

I drummed my fingers on my leg, as the vehicle moved at a

turtle's pace. My heart raced, and I was crawling out of my skin. It was from either the copious amounts of caffeine or the adrenaline rush. "Can they go any slower? Ugh."

"It's okay, Rose." Simon said calmly. "We'll catch up to him." No sooner did those words pass his lips, and we were back on the road.

"We are one behind you," I said.

"Copy," Kate replied. "But the car ahead of us turned. We are right behind him. And there are no turnoffs."

The driver of the van began passing cars on a double yellow around the lake. Oncoming cars were honking at him, swerving to avoid getting hit.

"We've been made. Back off," Kate said. "Rayo is still up on the phone."

"This guy is a pro," Simon said.

Kate pulled over at the next turnout; we followed suit.

CHAPTER 29

◆

"WHAT DO YOU mean you *think* you're being followed?" the woman bellowed.

"Did I stutter, CK?" Mac said as he pressed the accelerator. "A silver Sprinter Van. But I'm pretty sure I lost them."

"How did they make you?"

"Who knows," Mac said as his wheels squealed at every turn. Out of nowhere, a deer bolted in front of him. He swerved left, then a quicker right. "Shit!"

"Easy on the rental. We don't need the highway patrol taking a report," CK said.

Just as Mac straightened the van, a phone slid to the front. He leaned over and snatched the cell from the floorboard. It was an off brand, cheap phone. It wasn't his, and he'd tossed Gil's, so that left the girl. Crap.

He flung it out the window. Mac didn't want to admit to CK his rookie move and silently cursed himself for not doing a more thorough search of the target and swiping the van clean. His focus had been questioning her and obtaining the flash drive.

"I think I lost them," Mac said as he veered down a side street. He stopped sharply at the top of a boat launch. "Are you certain I need to stick around?"

CK let out a heavy sigh. "Yes. I have eyes inside and will keep you advised of any changes."

"I am not staying another night in a crappy motel. The only decent ones have no vacancies."

"Don't you *ever* listen?" CK said. "I told you I was going to book a place. Check your damn phone. I rented an SUV, too. It'll be delivered to the rental later this evening."

He scratched his face and scrolled through the phone. Mac pulled up the address. "That's a couple of blocks from here."

"It's on the lake, but you share the beach access with the renters next to you. So, stay low."

"The last thing I want to do is play nice-nice with a bunch of freakin' tourists," Mac said.

"I'm only telling you, so you're not surprised if you see someone in your backyard."

"Fine." Mac contemplated his next move. "I hope you purchased insurance for this rental."

"What are you thinking?"

"You said to get rid of the van," Mac said.

"Are you going to set it on *fire?*" CK asked.

"That *would* get rid of the PI and the girl's DNA." Mac stared at the water. "How deep do ya think this lake is?"

"I don't care. Just do it," CK said. "Don't forget to change your appearance. You may have been spotted on a CCTV in town."

"Again, what's with the fuckin' micromanaging?" He groaned. "I'm already on it." He disconnected.

Mac climbed into the rear of the van and opened his black bag of tricks. He pulled out a mirror and perched it against the van's siding. Mac removed his gloves and black wig, exposing his bald head. After, came the goatee and mustache. Last, Mac peeled the scar off his face.

While Mac was a pro at disguises, he didn't rise to the level of Hollywood or the CIA. The agency has an entire division devoted to disguises. They could change the gender and even skin color of their spies. But Mac's work was proficient, nonetheless. The only thing Mac couldn't hide was his height, so he used lifts in his heels when needed. He wiped his face off with a moist towelette and pondered his choices. He smiled.

"Perfect."

After Mac changed, he rolled down all the windows. He snatched his bags and jumped out of the van. He scanned the parking lot for any vehicles and the lake for returning boats. As soon as the coast was clear, Mac put the van in drive and gave it a hefty push. He watched as it careened down the hill and into the water. It sank quicker than he expected.

This was not Mac's first time dumping a vehicle in this manner. After the van all but disappeared, Mac trekked the two blocks to his lakeside rental.

CHAPTER 30

◆

OUR VEHICLES SAT side by side on the turnoff. Sue couldn't wait to jump into Simon's Denali to reunite with me. She wiggled on my lap.

"We lost Lily's cell," Rayo said.

"I'm not surprised," I said. "This guy knows how to evade and must've discovered the phone."

"We need a place to land and regroup," Simon said with a yawn. "Not to mention I could use a nap."

I scrolled through my phone and found the reservation for the house Grandma had booked. "The rental is back seven miles. Five-bedroom lakeside house with a two-car attached garage. Just outside the town of Lake Simi."

"Rayo and I can get groceries in town," said Kate. "I make a mean pasta dish with lemon, chicken, and artichoke hearts."

"Thanks." I buried my face in Sue's silky coat. She looked at me and sneezed. "Okay, so I need a shower." She wagged her tail in agreement. I turned to Simon. "Whataya say we hit the motel at midnight?"

"Sounds like a plan." He pulled onto the main highway after Kate.

I stared off into the distance and sighed.

"What's wrong?" he asked.

"What if this doesn't work? I mean, what if Lily goes down for something she didn't do?" My shoulders sagged under the weight of all the possible ways Lily's frameup could send her to prison.

"Snap out of it," Simon replied. "You once told me failure was not an option." He placed his hand on my shoulder. "Do you remember when we first met?"

"Your team and I almost got blown to smithereens searching for my father."

"True," he said. "What I didn't tell you, Rose, is that I admired you. You're willing to go to any lengths for your friends and family. Heck, you not only color outside the lines, but you're on another page altogether." He chuckled.

"But this is different."

"How?"

"The odds are stacked as high as Mount Everest." I paused. "We don't have a military team to back us. We're flying solo. And I don't have a game plan or even know our enemy," I groaned. "Too many unknowns."

"And?" He threw his hand out. "From where I sit, you wouldn't let a locomotive stop you from helping the underdog. Don't start now."

"Pft, like a superhero?"

"I don't see any radioactive spider bites and from what I know, you were born in Florida, not on a distant planet. So, no, you're not a superhero."

"I've heard that before," I said, slumping with my face in my hands.

"Give yourself credit, Rose. Even Batman had years of training to reach his true potential."

"Ha, so you are comparing me to a certain caped crusader."

"No, but you do have a superhero complex." He gave me another playful slug.

"Hey, I've changed over the last year."

"Trauma does that to a person. It made you stronger."

"Yeah." I shrugged. "But what I meant is that I understand the importance of teamwork."

"Although we have a limited team, it's an excellent one. We need to train more."

"Does this mean you're going to continue working with me? Even though I've been a giant pain in the ass?"

"Yep, but more reality based."

"Jumping out of a plane with a sabotaged chute isn't reality based?"

"You know what I mean," Simon said. "I'm talking about weight training, diet, martial arts. Mental preparation is just as important to survival. It will also help with stress and an—"

I put my palm to him. "Don't say it. I'm not anxious, irritable, or angry, Simon!" I paused a spell. "Hey … ya know something. You never told me your last name?"

"Always changing the topic."

"What can I say. It's one of my superpowers." I shrugged with a snuffle.

He sighed. "Rose."

"Yeah …"

"No, I mean, it's Rose. Simon Rae Rose."

I snort laughed. "That's awesome. I guess I can't call you Rose, since that will confuse people. And why did you drop the Rae?"

"I just prefer Simon. My military buds teased me about my girlie middle name."

We shared a hearty chuckle. Moments later, we turned onto the street to our rental. And that's when I spotted an old man with a cane. He was moving fast for his age and was carrying a black bag and backpack.

"I wonder if he's okay," I said. "Can you pull over?"

Simon raised a brow. "I didn't take you for a softy."

"The elderly always hold a special place in my heart." I rolled down my window.

"Excuse me, sir."

Sue, who was still on my lap, emitted a soft growl.

"Behave, little girl," I murmured and redirected my attention to the man.

He looked at me with hard brown eyes. "Yeah?" he replied in a gruff voice, scratching his bushy gray beard.

"Are you okay? Do you need any help? A ride perhaps?" I asked.

Simon hit my leg and mumbled, "No."

I'd changed my mind about the ride and was ready to call someone for the grumpy ol' coot.

The man must've read my face because he cleared his throat and his facial features softened. "Oh, no young lady. Thank you, kindly," he said and gave us a closed-mouth smile.

Sue's hackles remained on end, and she barked at him. I held her mouth shut and considered her reaction.

"Uh, I'm just up the road here a bit. My uh … driver dropped me off at the wrong house," the man stammered and pointed with his cane.

"Okay. Have a good day," I said and rolled up the window.

Simon turned to me. "Are you kidding? A ride? He could be a serial killer." He looked at Sue. "And check out her reaction," he said.

"Yeah, yeah." I waved my hand in the air. "It's just he's old. But the second he opened his mouth, my Spidey-senses screamed 'Danger Will Robinson'," I said with a laugh.

"Good. I was ready to have your Spidey license revoked," Simon quipped.

CHAPTER 31

LILY LAID ON her cot, counting how many times this Jared person loved Emily. The 6x8 cell was for holding only and didn't even have a toilet. Deputy Moxy had to conduct an unclothed body search of Lily in the station's one and only bathroom.

Heck, the jail had no bedding. So, the gracious female deputy had brought them in from a separate storage facility. The staff told Lily their last overnight "guest" was in 2004, when a blizzard shut down the town and all roads leading in and out of Lake Simi.

Since Lily's clothes had some of Gil's blood, the deputies booked them into evidence. Moxy had to buy Lily some gray sweatpants from the local market. They hung off her slight frame. But, for her sake, her motorcycle jacket was unscathed, so she used that as a pillow. She peered at the wall clock. It was a few minutes past eleven and she was still groggy from the drugs from the prior night. Suddenly, the double doors flung wide, and Deputy Marshal Pane entered.

Lily jumped to her feet.

Pane stepped up to the bars with a clipboard in hand. "You've got friends in high places," he remarked with what sounded like an annoyed sneer in his voice.

"Huh?" Lily cocked her head.

"You're staying put, for now," Pane said. "Marshal Church agreed not to transfer you. If it were up to me, you'd be gone. Pfft. I couldn't care less what some fancy ivy league attorney requested. Not to mention the judge herself." He tugged on his utility belt and stood on tiptoes. "So, ya ready to answer some questions?"

Lily shook her head and said, "Attorney."

"Have it your way." Pane jotted something on a clipboard.

"Don't get too comfortable, princess." Peggy stepped out from behind Deputy Pane, holding a paper sack and bottled water. "Trust me, it won't be long before you're gone." She cackled. "Any hoo, here's some food." She handed them to Lily through the bars.

Wow. Were Moxy and Marshal Church the only two civil staff? She remained diplomatic and did not snap a retort.

"Thanks," Lily said as she tried to smile. "Um, I heard my friend earlier. Why didn't she come back?"

Peggy shrugged, threw her hands out to the sides, and walked away.

Deputy Pane followed Peggy without responding to Lily's question.

Lily studied them as they left. She returned to her lumpy cot and opened her bag. A bologna sandwich with American sliced cheese on white bread and plain chips. Lily lacked an appetite but couldn't remember her last meal.

She certainly did not remember meeting the likes of those two. Lily was only reintroduced to them this morning after a member of the medical staff woke her at God knew what time to draw her blood. Lily couldn't recall being arrested or booked. She looked at her arm where they drew her blood. She regretted allowing them to do that without her attorney present.

Why was her memory foggy? Must be the drugs Mac gave her. But how does she remember his name? She deliberated as she finished lunch and gulped the eight-ounce bottle of water. Lily barely remembered anything after she got to town.

Lily dropped her head in her hands and closed her eyes, trying hard to focus. It was a blur and a frightmare. That's what Lily's mom used to call her nightmares as a child. She rubbed the ligature marks on her wrists as bits and pieces floated back. Tears streamed down her face as she pondered if that man had sexually assaulted her. Her groin area did not feel any different. But she knew he took something and then it hit her. The USB flash drive. She jumped to her feet and paced.

A woman's voice echoed from the front, interrupting her private conversation. A twinge of excitement fluttered. Maybe Rose came back.

Suddenly the doors flung open, and in walked her friend.

CHAPTER 32

◆

"CHARLY." LILY SMILED for the first time in she didn't remember how long. If she couldn't have Rose, Charly was a close second. Adored by Griz and vetted by Lillian.

"Oh my gosh, Lily," Charly said, rushing to the cell. "I'm so sorry, my friend."

Peggy marched in behind Charly. "No touching," she snapped.

Charly turned and gestured her hand, "I'm aware." She spun back to Lily and rolled her eyes. "How are you holding up? And what in the world happened?" Charly's face softened.

"I … I'm not certain." Lily's smile faded. "I can't remember much."

"Your grandma hired an attorney. She'll arrive tomorrow."

"Lillian? She's not my grandma, even though she acts like it," Lily said as she leaned against the bars.

"Are you sure you don't remember … anything?" Charly urged. "Think hard because your attorney can't help if you don't have something to work with."

Lily paced the cell again with her arms crossed. A thought hit her, and she stopped. "Wait! How did you get in when Rose couldn't?" she asked with a head tilt.

"Don't know. Maybe Rose didn't try hard enough." She threw her thumb back. "Hildegard up front is a tough bird. I charmed her."

Lily furrowed her brows because she knew that was not true. Rose would come charging through like Wonder Woman to see her friend if she could. Lily shook it off. As she stood there, she felt a sharp, piercing pain in her skull. She stumbled backward, fell on her cot, and dropped her head in her hands.

"Have you eaten or been seen by a doctor?" Charly asked.

"I just finished a sack meal. And a paramedic checked me last night. I think. At least that's what they told me," Lily said, rubbing her furrowed brows.

"Did they draw your blood?"

"Mm hm. A few vials this morning."

"Did they find anything?"

"They didn't tell me," Lily's voice rose a level. "They're treating me like a drug addict who killed her dealer. I don't do drugs!" Lily shouted and grabbed her head again. "But whatever that man gave me did a number on my brain." She ran her hands through her scalp.

"I'm sorry," Charly said, as she peeked out through the double doors. "Excuse me, Peggy. Can you be a lamb and get my friend an aspirin and water, please?"

"Sure thing, doll," Peggy hollered back.

"Wow, she's certainly not that nice to me," Lily said.

"Lie back and close your eyes." Charly's voice was close to a whisper. "Tell me what you see. Smell. Hear."

Lily did what Charly told her and closed her eyes. She drew a deep breath and exhaled out. "I rode into town," Lily stated, "to meet a friend."

"A friend?" Charly asked.

"Uh … no one you know. I went to the cemetery to meet my friend. And while I waited, I visited my parents' gravesites," Lily said and opened her eyes. "I talk to them sometimes. Even though their graves are empty." Tears trickled down her cheeks. "I just miss them so much." She sat up and wiped away the dampness with the sleeve of her new oversized sweatshirt.

"But my friend never showed. So, I headed to the café on Main Street to see if he was there. I ordered lunch. I was at the café for a bit. Don't remember how long. Then I left. But … not on my bike." She stared for a spell without blinking. "And then …"

"Then?" Charly urged.

"I … I don't know, Charly. The rest of the night is a complete blur." Lily rose and rushed to the bars. She touched Charly's hands. "I swear I didn't kill him! I don't think." Lily sobbed.

"Lily, who is this man they accused you of killing?"

"I … I can't tell you." Lily stepped back and walked to the opposite side of the cell.

Charly let out a long sigh and followed along outside the cell bars. "Look, how can anyone help you if you won't tell anyone who he was? Lily, we've only known each other for a short while. But you can trust me. If you're in trouble, I want to help."

Lily looked up. "He was a PI I hired to tell me the truth about my parents."

"And?" Charly urged again.

"The PI gave me a flash drive, but that man," Lily said, "that evil man took it from me."

"Is that all he gave you? Did he say anything about your folks?" Charly sounded less her friend and more a cop interrogating her.

"I don't remember," she yelled.

Lily watched the muscles in Charly's jaw tighten. Lily stepped away and studied her friend for a sec. "Why are you so upset?"

"I … I'm upset for you. Being arrested for something you didn't do." Charly shrugged. "I'm trying to help. But if you don't want my help, I'll go."

Pane burst through the double doors. "I heard yelling. What's going on back here?" He stood, fists on his hips.

"Nothing …" Charly hesitated. "She saw a spider. Lily doesn't like spiders."

"Get used to it. Prison is loaded with them." He directed the comment to Lily, turned on his heels, and trooped away.

"Pr—prison?" Lily felt the blood rush to her head as she stumbled backwards. The room spun and her vision narrowed.

CHAPTER 33

◆

IT WAS A quarter after five when we finished the zesty pasta Kate prepared for us. I was still hungry and ready to dive into another helping when Simon seized my plate.

"What the …" I scowled at him and reached for the knife sitting on the table.

"Training, remember?" Simon said, grasping my hand. "And, seriously, you gonna stab me?" He raised a brow.

"I didn't sign up for starvation," I said and threw his hand off mine. "I'm not preparing to be on *Naked and Afraid*, ya know." I narrowed my eyes. "Besides, we can put the training on hold. Look at my face. And my ribs are killing me. Are you *really* going to deprive me?"

"Are you *really* whining right now?" Simon said. "And too many carbs are bad for you."

I snatched my plate back. "So is taking away food from a hangry person," I said, scooping a heaping spoonful of pasta from the bowl. I glanced at it and then turned my attention to Simon, who was now sitting next to me, shaking his head, laughing. I put back half the scoop. And dove in mouth first, smiling with a forkful.

Just as I swallowed, the doorbell rang.

Simon and I jerked our heads to the door, jumped to our feet, and grabbed our firearms from the kitchen counter. Kate would have joined us but was taking a shower and Rayo had yet to receive that level of training. As for Sue, she was always on my six. Kelpie ears at attention.

We darted to the front door and stood on either side, with our guns in a low ready position. I peeked through the peephole. "It's Olive," I said, lowering my pistol and shoulders.

Although I'd never met her, Gran texted her picture. Grandma spoke highly of her, as Olive was the best thief. She was so good, she never got caught, hence no criminal record to speak of. Since she was never in the CIA, I didn't completely understand how her and Gran's paths crossed. As my father and Grandma always say, "Don't ask a question you don't want the answer to."

In this case, I didn't want to know. If Olive worked for the CIA, we would call what she was going to do tonight a Black Bag Operation. A covert B&E into denied areas to obtain intel.

Olive entered and glanced at our handguns and grinned. "I like you two," she said.

I motioned for her to come inside.

Olive was in her early thirties. She stood an inch taller than me at five feet, nine inches. She was slender and wore her legs to her ears, like me. Olive's hair was long and curly brown with reddish-blonde highlights, she had hazel eyes, and smooth skin.

"It's a pleasure to *finally* meet you." Olive pulled me in for a warm embrace. "I've heard so much about you from Lillian," she said.

I stepped back.

"Sorry, I'm a hugger," Olive said, gazing at my face. "Nice shiners. I'd hate to see the other guy."

I laughed. "Not guy. My parachute attacked me. Long story." I set my gun on the coffee table. "Gran has told me about you, too. I feel like I know you."

Olive and I eased on the couch while Simon and Rayo sat across on the two matching recliners.

"Can I get you something to eat or drink?" I asked.

She shook her head, then removed a notepad from her bag and was all business. "I did a drive by. Access seems easy. I assume since Lily has been a guest at the graybar hotel, there has been someone on duty, 24/7," Olive said and showed me a detailed layout of the marshal's office. "It's an old building, but they've upgraded their systems. You know, enhanced security." Olive scanned the room. "How many do we have?"

Just then, Kate emerged from the back room and joined us.

"Here's our fourth," I said, making the introductions. I noted the three of us were around the same height, give or a take an inch. Might come in handy if we had to change posts or trade disguises like real operatives.

"What information do you need from the marshals?" Olive asked. She was a straight shooter. "Your grandma didn't go into detail."

"When I was in there, Deputy Marshal Pane had the police report on his desk. He was looking at the evidence photos." I pointed to his office on the schematics.

"No CSI?" Olive inquired.

"The marshals are it," I said. "They handle everything in-house."

"Why not wait for the attorney to get a copy of the final police report?" Olive asked.

"No time. And I don't think they have Lily's best interest in mind," Simon interjected. "I've seen how these small towns operate. They'd hang Lily if they still did that."

"Lily is guilty in their eyes." I rose and paced. "Deputy Moxy assured me of that. So, it's vital we work on clearing her as quickly as we can."

"You sound like a PI, Rose," Olive said.

"Pfft, heck no." I shrugged. "Just a concerned friend," I said. "So, Simon and I will wait until midnight to hit the motel while you and Kate tackle the marshals. Since there are few deputies on duty, I figured it's best to target them at the same time. Ya know, catch them off guard."

"Solid plan," Olive said. "Won't someone be sitting on the motel room?"

"We spoke to Moxy. There won't be anyone there overnight," I said.

"I don't think with this size town, they're worried about a burglary at the crime scene," Simon said.

"Are you getting a key?" Olive asked.

"You can say that." I grinned and told Olive about our waitress.

Sue, who'd been sitting with me the entire time, growled, fur on end.

CHAPTER 34

◆

SUE RAN TO the sliding door that led to the lake and furiously barked.

I hurried to see what caught her attention. I learned to be on alert when she acted strangely. Jumping out of a plane with a malfunctioning parachute taught me to heed her warnings.

"Hmm, it's that old man we met earlier," I murmured, turning back to Simon. Since the glass sliding door was open, I didn't want the geezer to hear us.

Simon joined me at the door. We watched the man for a spell as he plopped on a chair at the lakeside without using his cane. I glanced at Simon, and we exchanged the same curious look.

"Remember your gran mentioned we're sharing the lake access with the neighbor," Kate said.

"That's a coincidence," Rayo remarked, joining us.

"I don't believe in coincidences," Simon said.

"Me either," I retorted.

Sue continued to bark with hackles high. I eased my hand on her back to quell her. She trembled.

"What vehicle was he driving?" Kate asked.

"He was walking," Simon and I replied in unison.

"There's a vehicle in his driveway now," Olive said as she peeked out the front window.

"What kind?" I asked.

"Blue SUV," Olive replied.

"Maybe someone's visiting him," Rayo said. "Don't you guys think you're being too paranoid?"

"You have a lot to learn, Padawan." Simon smirked.

"Yeah," I said. "There was something off about him. Sue didn't like him when we first met."

"Sue has a built-in bad guy detector," Simon said.

"Or BS detector," I snorted.

We continued to study the old guy as he opened a bag from one of the fast-food restaurants in town and bit into a burger. Then he took a sip out of a tumbler.

"I agree, Rose. That dude is not right," Simon said.

"We need to keep a close eye on him," I said.

Sue must've taken that literally because she opened the screen door using her nose and charged the old guy.

I called her. She halted and retreated. "Sorry," I yelled, waving my arm at him. I looked at Sue and considered. I watched our neighbor hightail it back to his house.

Sue's hackles were not the only ones raised.

CHAPTER 35

"I ALMOST GOT eaten by a damned dog," Mac grumbled. "I swear, next time I'm gonna shoot the fuckin' thing." He walked inside his rental, closing the door. "How long do I need to stay here, CK?"

"Not long. Like you said, the girl doesn't know anything," CK said. "But I received a copy of the police report, along with the photos." She sighed. "Are you sure you didn't leave *any* evidence behind in the room?"

"Are you questioning me?" Mac set the phone on the kitchen table on speaker and poured himself another glass of Maker's Mark, since he spilled the last one outside. He tossed it back and poured a refill.

"I am. By the looks of the crime scene pictures, there was a *black* latex glove under the bed. That's *now* in evidence," CK bellowed.

"And?" Mac shrugged as if she could see his reaction. "They won't find my DNA. I don't exist, remember? I've been erased from any system." Mac walked around the living room and dining room, closing the shades. He removed his disguise and placed them on his bag to take to the SUV.

"It doesn't matter. The evidence will show a third person was in the room, not to mention it will raise more suspicion that said person is not in any system. You need to get that glove," CK barked without coming up for air. "The evidence is still sitting on the deputy marshal's desk in a marked bag."

"How do you know this?" he asked. "And why didn't you have your *inside* person ta—wait, won't that glove be on the evidence

107

log?"

"It was left off … and how I do my job is not your concern. Am I clear?"

"Yeah, yeah, whatever. It's going to cost extra," Mac said as he looked in the kitchen cabinets and freezer. "I thought this place was stocked with food. Just frozen shit."

"Didn't you eat?"

"I tried, but that damned dog scared the crap out of me, and I dropped my burger," Mac complained as he pulled out a frozen burrito and popped it into the microwave.

"And those rentals are not stocked with food. Jeezo. What's wrong with you?"

"You mean right now or in general? 'Cause I got a list, lady," Mac said with a snarl.

"I have other news." CK sighed.

"What?"

"Gil wasn't a PI. He was with the agency."

"Huh, I never would have guessed. He didn't have that spook vibe."

"He wasn't an agent. But a scientist. I thought he looked familiar."

Mac plopped on a chair at the kitchen table and stared as the microwave counted down the seconds until his beef burrito was ready.

"Mac … you there?"

"Yeah. That makes sense. But what was he doing with the girl? And does the agency know he's gone? I mean, he's been missing for two days. Doesn't he have to check in with someone?"

"Questions I don't have the answer to," CK replied. "And you know how things work."

"No, I don't! I don't know how your screwed up agency works."

"I guess you wouldn't. When someone gets close to the truth, or they've done their job … well, everyone is disposable. And don't play Eagle Scout with me. Have you looked in the mirror?" CK said.

"I'm freelance. I prefer *not* to know who employs me. And I know what kind of person I am."

"Regardless, get the glove back."

"What security system do they have?"

"Archaic. You'll be fine."

"I'll have to wait till o-dark-thirty."

"I don't care, just get it done. And don't get caught." CK disconnected.

Mac rolled his head and seethed. "Again, with the micromanaging."

CHAPTER 36

<hr/>

ELEVEN THIRTY CAME fast as I lay on my bed, listening to
Sue snoring. I couldn't nap as thoughts of Lily washed through my
mind like crashing waves. It'd been twenty-four hours since her
arrest. Who was the man they accused her of killing? Why was she
in Lake Simi?

I got up and slipped into my black 5.11 boots. I tied my hair
back in a neat braid and donned dark jeans with a long sleeved,
black shirt. The Montana spring required layering and tonight the
temps dropped to the low forties. For some Montanans that was
shorts weather, but not me. I grabbed a thick plain black hoodie
from my duffle bag.

I looked over and Sue was now running in her dreams, belly up,
chasing bad guys. At least that's what goes on in my head. I
smiled. She gave my life meaning and purpose. Not wanting to
disturb the sleepy pup, I tip-toed out of my room.

Simon was also exiting his. We slapped one another a high five,
followed by a low back five. I know, dorky, but it was our thing.
Back in the day, I had a special partner, FBI Agent James Powers.
We were assigned to a multi-agency task force together.

James and my deceased husband, Bradley, were best of friends.
James was now on the FBI SWAT team and happily married to my
sister, Saki. They have one beautiful daughter, Violet, and live in
Miami Beach. It had only been a week since I played with baby
Violet.

I sighed.

As Simon and I stepped into the main room, my nose tingled

with the aroma of java beans wafting in the air. Kate beat me to the kitchen and had made coffee for us.

"You know I didn't hire you to be a cook?" I smiled and grabbed a cup. "But thanks."

Olive was in the living room, also dressed in black and ready for her midnight op.

Kate eagerly volunteered to go with Olive to provide backup. While Simon and I hit the motel to see if there was anything left behind and to get our own impression of the crime scene. Rayo jumped at the chance to stay with Sue.

It was eleven forty-five when Simon and I edged the truck out of the garage. I looked over and noticed the neighbor's lights were on. I guess the old coot was a night owl, too.

I shook it off and pulled my iPhone out and texted Zuli we were enroute. I paid our friendly waitress to unlock the room, accidentally turn off the lights on the outside corridor, and look the other way. After inheriting money, I'd obtained a wealth of insight into human behavior. Anything or anyone can be bought, whether good or bad.

It took us ten minutes to get to the motel. The parking lot was half-full as the motel had a No Vacancy sign again. And this one was the least fancy of them. Apparently, the recent homicide didn't scare away visitors. That, or the fact the town was full of desperate, unprepared travelers who didn't care where they laid their heads.

I held my breath as I continued to scan the lot for any signs of a police cruiser.

Phew, we were in the clear. Or so I thought.

CHAPTER 37

———◆———

ZULI SAT AT the front desk; I saw her flaming pink and green hair before I saw her face. And as I'd asked, darkness filled the corridor. The Lake Simi Motel was horseshoe shaped, so Simon parked at the far end opposite the office. Room five was tucked in the corner.

I pulled my hood over my head, slipped on black leather gloves, and nodded to my partner in crime, literally. I exited the truck, gently closing it and crept down the hall with my gaze to the ground until I came upon the crime scene tape.

I paused.

For a moment, the night was still and any other evening I would have embraced the silence. But not tonight.

Then the enormity hit me. My hands trembled and my body quaked. I had walked a fine line before, but the second I crossed that yellow tape, I would be committing a crime. I'd spent my life enforcing the law, now I would be on the other side. But any of my friends would do the same for me, wouldn't they? I nodded.

As I drew in a deep breath and exhaled slowly, I scanned the corridor one more time. I ducked under the yellow tape that stated, *DO NOT CROSS*. But why wasn't it across the door itself? I snapped back to the mission.

Zuli was a woman of honor and left it unlocked. I slipped inside and texted Simon: *I'm in*. That was his cue to follow suit. I closed the privacy curtains and seconds later, Simon entered. With the low light setting on our flashlights, we scanned the room and started working. Simon took the bathroom while I stayed in the main room.

I looked under the bed where Lily had been lying and flipped up the mattress. I was careful not to disturb the crime scene and left it the way I found it. Nothing there. I peered around and found a chair on its side and a lamp shattered into pieces.

As I made my way to the other bed, my heart sank. I froze and gaped at the crimson stained bed frame; blood sprayed the walls. It brought back the nightmare of when I found my best friend from college bloodied and shot in the head in a motel room. It was a case of mistaken identity as the hit was meant for me. I shook it off.

And then something struck me. If the victim was fatally shot, there should be more blood. I contemplated as I shone my light under the bed and around the nightstand. I returned to the first bed and found a white envelope tucked in between the mattress and frame. I pulled it out. A note was inside. I started to read it when Simon stepped out of the bathroom with an empty capped syringe in his gloved hands. He slipped it into a brown paper sack. It was our version of an evidence bag.

"Where did you find it?" I whispered.

"In the trash. And given this motel, it could belong to the prior occupants," Simon responded in the same hushed tone. "Sloppy crime scene sweeping to miss it. Old or not."

He pointed to the paper in my hand.

I opened my mouth to tell him when my phone buzzed. It was a text message from Zuli: *heard on scanner cops at motel.*

I looked at Simon. "Shit," I said and showed him the text and stuffed the letter in my pocket.

We turned off our flashlights, walked over to the window and peeked out.

"It's Moxy," I muttered. "What's she doing here?"

Simon threw his hands out.

I motioned for him to join me in the bathroom. I looked up. Crap, no window. I pursed my lips. "Okay, we have a few options," I said. "One, I could walk outside and turn myself in to her, allowing you to get away. Two, I can text Zuli and have her distract Moxy. Or three, we could wait it out and pray she doesn't stay here all night."

"Door number two," Simon said.

I texted Zuli: *SOS, need distraction.*

Zuli texted back: *shit, boss sent me home after you arrived. I can go back!*

I replied: *don't! thanks.* I didn't want Zuli to get fired. She needed the money.

"Door number one," I whispered to Simon as I held up my index finger.

I slipped off my gloves and took out the envelope from my inside pocket. I pulled off my hip holster with the gun and handed him everything. If Moxy was going to arrest me, I did not want to add weapons and removing evidence from a crime scene to my list of charges.

Simon shook his head and mouthed, *no way.*

I didn't give him time to argue with me.

I threw my hood over my head and exited the room.

CHAPTER 38

◆

OLIVE AND KATE sat in Olive's black BMW X-5 behind the marshal's office. Olive grabbed her laptop from the back seat, opened it and powered it on. She scrolled through, looking for the link to the security system. She deactivated the alarm and accessed the internal CCTV.

"Okay, there's one guy. Terrance, the reserve Rose told us about. He must be on prisoner duty," she said and handed Kate her computer.

"Copy. I'll be your eyes on the outer perimeter and the inside," Kate said. "I'll text you if anyone enters."

Olive nodded as she pulled down her full-face black ski mask and exited her SUV, keeping her head on a swivel as she approached the back door. She removed her key card reader and inserted it into the slot. She waited for the electronic code to be read and the green light to illuminate. Although it was one of the easiest jobs as the marshals had not updated their systems, anything could still go wrong.

A few seconds later, the door unlocked, and she delicately opened it and glided inside with the lightness of a cat. Olive knew by studying the building's plans that she would enter near the prisoner holding area. Since the cell was only meant to be temporary, there wasn't much security. It also served as a multipurpose booking/cell room.

The second Olive entered, Lily, who'd been asleep on her cot, bolted to her feet, wide-eyed. Olive put her fingers to her lips to hush Lily.

Lily rushed to the bars. She mouthed, *who are you,* as she visibly trembled.

"Rose sent me," Olive whispered in Lily's ear.

Lily lowered her shoulders. Judging by the terror on her face, Lily undoubtedly thought the bad guys were there for her.

"Why are you here?" Lily asked in a low murmur.

"No time. Not here for you, but your report," Olive replied in kind.

Lily's brows furrowed and her bottom lip quivered. She nodded as if she understood.

Olive raised her hand to Lily to calm her. She spun on her heels and headed for the double doors and peered through them, scanning. Since the coast was clear, Olive deftly pushed through and weaved inside. She removed her lock picking kit from her rear pocket and unlocked the deputy marshal's door. There wasn't a lock Olive could not pick, and this was a piece of cake.

Just then, she heard Moxy over the radio advising Terrance she was checking on the Simi Motel. *Crap.* No time to warn Rose. Though with what Lillian had told her about Rose, she could handle it.

Olive entered the room, pulled out her flashlight, and illuminated the area. The only thing on his desk was a brown bag, sealed, marked *Evidence.* And attached was the evidence log, which was not thoroughly filled in. There were missing sections.

Olive shook her head. "They should keep this in an evidence locker. Talk about chain of custody issues," she mumbled as she took a picture of the paper sack. Not that it would stand up in court since Olive shouldn't be there.

She looked around the room for the police report but didn't see one. Rose mentioned if it wasn't on the assistant's desk, it could be on Marshal Church's.

But first she had to finish her task in this office.

CHAPTER 39

THE SECOND I exited the motel room, Moxy's police cruiser's lights blinded me. I lowered my gaze.

"Put your hands up," Moxy yelled.

I threw up my arms as I yanked off the hood.

"You?! What the hell are you doing here, Rose?" Moxy let out a low growl as she held the gun on me.

I turned my head. "Uh, can you please dim your headlights?" I stepped left with my hands still raised and continued moving. My goal was to distract her away from the room. It must've worked because Moxy re-holstered her weapon and turned off the high beams.

"Stop moving. Turn around. Put your hands on your head, interlock your fingers," Moxy commanded.

Since I knew the drill, I also walked my feet apart like an obedient felon. But I was used to standing on the other side, barking orders.

Being alone, Moxy was at a tactical disadvantage, and I assumed that's why, after she checked my waistband for weapons, she immediately handcuffed me.

Just as she slapped the bracelets on me, I took a quick peek over my shoulder and saw Simon exit the motel room. I blew out a sigh of relief.

"Don't look at me," Moxy snapped.

"Uh, sorry," I said. I knew this was the worst move to make, but I had to make sure my accomplice was in the clear.

Moxy started with the right side of my body and ran her hands down my front, up the side, into my armpit and down the back, checking my legs and ankles. Then she went to the left side, doing the same thing.

After she conducted the cursory pat-down search, Moxy spun me around and placed me against her patrol car.

"This is the *third* time I see you at my crime scene. But this time, you crossed the line, Rose. Literally! Now, before I arrest you and read your rights, do you want to tell me what the hell you are doing here?" Moxy asked with hands on hips.

"I know this looks bad, but w—, *I* needed to get eyes on the room." Sheesh. I almost let the cat out of the bag.

"Why?" she asked.

Good question. I had to tread lightly. I didn't want her thinking I believed her department was inept at handling a homicide. And then it hit me.

"Uh ... Lily said she lost a bracelet her mother gave her." I tried to bring tears to my eyes, but I couldn't.

"You broke into a crime scene ... for that? You know that yellow tape you had to *duck* under to get into the room," Moxy said. "You or Lily could've told us. And that's something the clean-up crew would find."

"It's way too sentimental to her. What if ... well, someone took it?" I asked. But the instant those words passed my lips, I regretted it.

"What are you saying, exactly? This isn't the big city, ya know."

"I ... I didn't mean any disrespect," I sighed and looked at my feet. "I'm just going to level with you." I returned my gaze to her.

"That would be a first."

I squinted. "Okay, I deserve that. I was looking to see if there was any evidence left behind that could help Lily's case." That was the partial truth.

"Now that is more believable. But still insulting. Our team is very capable of handling investigations." Moxy stood with her arms crossed and a scowl.

"I'm aware, but I wanted to see it for myself. Call it morbid curiosity." I shrugged and scrunched my nose. "Look, I'd appreciate it if you don't take me in. I'm still employed and if I get arrested, it will blow any chance of me returning to work."

"So, you really are LE?"

"I know. My behavior says otherwise." I lowered my head like a child who's being scolded. Which I was at the moment.

"I like you, Rose. So, I'm going to throw you a bone. Turn around," Moxy said, twirling her fingers in the air.

"I soo appreciate this. You won't hear another peep out of me." I relaxed my shoulders that I'd been wearing as earrings.

"Don't make me regret it." She removed the restraints. "Now move along," Moxy said as she slipped behind the wheel of her patrol car, her eyes glued to me.

Just as I made my way back to Simon's truck, I watched her key into the microphone. I hoped she wasn't radioing her boss. And then she sped off, blue and red flashing. No siren though.

"Busy town," I murmured.

The second Moxy left the parking lot, Simon popped his head up from behind the steering wheel. He glared a hole through me and shook his head.

I wore a Cheshire Cat grin as I slid into the passenger seat. And without saying a word, Simon returned my pistol, and we too sped away.

CHAPTER 40

✦

OLIVE SLOWLY OPENED the top desk drawer, pulled out the staple remover and removed the staples from the evidence bag. She peered inside and took pictures, making sure not to disturb its contents: one black latex glove and a syringe with a brown liquid substance.

That was it? While she had no clue what was at the crime scene, there should be more. Not to mention, the state crime lab should have the syringe since it held what appeared to be heroin.

After snapping photos, Olive was careful to fasten the bag using the same staple holes and made her way to the door and cracked it open. She peered left and then right and as soon as it was clear, Olive crept across the hall to Marshal Church's office and entered in the same cat-like manner.

There. On the desk. The police report, with evidence photos. After she was done taking pictures, she peeked out to see Terrance making his way down the hall, most likely checking on his prisoner. She gingerly closed the door and kept her ear plastered, listening for his return. But he didn't.

Five minutes passed, still no sound. What was he doing? Her thoughts ran amuck; male jailer, female prisoner, she'd seen the headlines. Olive would not allow that to happen to Lily. But there was no yelling coming from Lily's cell. As she put her hand to the door, the toilet flushed. Seconds later, the deputy returned to the front.

She turned the knob and her phone vibrated. A text from Kate: *man entering through north side window*. Who was this guy and what did he want? Was he here to finish Lily? Why else? Olive removed her Sig 9mm from her hip holster, slid on the silencer, and held it to her side. She waited for the intruder to open the rear entrance. But it didn't happen. After a few minutes, there was a crashing sound from Deputy Pane's office. Followed by the reserve running toward the noise.

"Who's in there?" Terrance's voice crackled and shook. He pounded on the door and tried to open it. But it was locked. Olive heard the chirping of the radio. "Moxy, it's Terrance. I think someone's in Pane's office."

"Get in there! I'm leaving the motel," Moxy responded.

As the deputy ran back to the front office, Olive heard him opening a desk drawer and returning with keys clanking. Olive slowly turned the knob and opened the door just enough to watch the young reserve fumbling through the ring, key by key. After finding the right one, he opened the door with his gun drawn. Terrance flipped on the light and entered. Moments later, he returned to the front, alone. Clearly the intruder fled.

Olive took advantage of Terrance's absence and darted through the double doors and out the back, no time to acknowledge Lily.

Kate waited behind the wheel when Olive exited. She threw the door open, jumped in, and quickly closed it as Kate drove away. Olive turned in her seat and saw red and blue descending on the marshal's office.

"That was a close call," Kate said.

"I've had closer." Olive smirked.

"Me too," Kate concurred with the same smile.

CHAPTER 41

IT WAS A quarter to one when we returned to the lake house. Simon pulled straight into the garage. I looked at my neighbor's vehicle and the headlights were on. The new vehicles' lights turn off after a brief period. So, either he just arrived, or he forgot them. And since his cabin's lights illuminated from behind his closed shades, it was safe to assume the former. Where could he have gone?

One thing was certain, something was off about him.

The second we entered the house, Sue charged me, whimpering and tapping, doing her happy dance. Sue's always eager to join me, but tonight required her to be here, safe. Rayo told me she stared at the door the whole time and did not even go out to do her business. Sue shot me a look, so I let her out back to take a wee.

Kate and Olive arrived a few minutes later and joined us inside the kitchen, where Rayo had our libations of choice waiting. Kate and I shared a love for Lake County Blend, while Simon's was whiskey.

Olive plopped on a chair and was all business at her laptop. She told me about the broken chain of custody at the marshal's office.

"I sent the police report to your e-mail, Rose," she said, eyes trained on her screen.

Simon and I removed our outer layers and set our guns on the kitchen counter and joined the gang at the table.

I imbibed some wine. It was then I remembered the note. "Simon, can you please give me the envelope I found in the motel room?"

He obliged and handed it to me.

As I silently read it, my mouth dropped. I looked around and everyone stared. I took another sip.

"Are you going to share?" Simon nodded to the paper in my hand.

"Oh, yeah." I cleared my throat. "Sorry for the secrecy, but I'm being followed. Meet me where we first met. Watch your back. Keep the drive close and don't let anyone get hold of this. If something happens to me, there's no turning back. Stay safe. Trust no one. Regards, G." I looked around the room and I could hear a pin drop. "Drive? Hmm. If I were to guess, I'd say that is what the kidnapper wanted." I gulped the rest of the wine. "And we need to know more about the vic—"

Just then, Sue let out a ferocious bark. We jumped to our feet. I snatched my gun and Simon and Olive grabbed theirs. Sue was not a vicious barker unless there was reason. I held my pistol to my side and opened the back door. Uncertain of the intruder's whereabouts, Simon exited through the garage and out the front. Olive joined him.

The instant I stepped outside, I caught an odor of a cigar and saw the cherry off the stogie. It was the neighbor, again. Twice in the same night. Go figure. I watched Sue walking in a slow, stalking motion like Kelpies do, toward her prey. He was standing this time and ready to kick Sue. I yelled for her, and she stopped and retreated.

I waved an apology at him, but what I wanted to do was beat the crap out of him. No one kicks my dog. But I cut him some slack since it was Sue that went on his turf.

He threw his hood over his head, spun on his heels, and scurried off to the house, muttering something inaudible. Awful fast for an old guy, too.

Sue trotted back with her tail wagging. If Sue were a person, she would have puffed her chest out too.

"Doggo, you can't sneak up on people like that." I scratched behind her ears. "I have to be with you first ... remember?"

The dog smiled as if she understood. In most cases, I believed she did.

CHAPTER 42

———◆———

"I ASSUME YOU'RE calling this late because you got the glove?" CK yawned.

"Affirmative," Mac said, tossing his black duffel bag on the kitchen table then removed his pistol from his hip holster.

"Any problems?"

"Negative. It was easy. The alarm wasn't on." Mac didn't tell CK he'd almost been caught. Who the hell leaves a trash basket under a window? "Now, can I get out of this town?" Mac grumbled.

"Not yet," CK said. "I'm getting a copy of the preliminary tox screen on Lily."

"How?"

"Need to know. We must make sure everything points to her. In the event it doesn't, I have a backup." CK yawned again.

"I'm sorry to wake you, princess," Mac snarled.

"I don't need your sarcasm. I've been working on this case a lot longer than you," CK said. "I'll contact you in the morning." She disconnected.

This simple job was getting more complicated. Mac made his way to the refrigerator, opened it, and sighed. He'd forgotten to stop and get food. And unlike other jobs, this town did not have a twenty-four-hour market. Mac slammed the fridge shut and turned to the Maker's Mark. He poured a double.

After his close call tonight, he deserved a stogie with his whiskey. Mac pulled his Cohiba Blue out of the cigar holder and rolled it under his nose. He closed his eyes and took in the notes of cocoa and leather and stuck it in his mouth. Although it was colder than his liking, Mac obeyed the house rules of No Smoking. Mac may have been a hired assassin and thief, but his mother also raised him to respect others' property.

So, he snatched his zipped, hooded sweatshirt that hung on the chair and shrugged into it. With his unlit cigar hanging from the side of his mouth, he grabbed his glass and headed for the lake. Mac turned and contemplated his disguise, but decided it was unnecessary. Not to mention he'd left it in his vehicle.

The partial moon illuminated his path as he made his way back to the chaise and matching table. He plopped on the longue, removed his lighter from his pocket, and lit his cigar. With the taste of caramel and cinnamon on his tongue, he puffed away, contemplating his next move. After this job, he'd go to the Bahamas ... maybe for a month. Heck, he had enough saved for a year. It was easy to do with no house note or family to consider.

Mac never married nor settled, partly because of his work, but mostly because he'd been burned with the blistering power of a dozen atom bombs by a woman years ago. Staying single was less complicated. Besides, he was knocking on forty's door and one-night stands were easier.

Just as he put his lips to his glass, he recoiled at the sound of a ferocious bark. Spilling his drink, for the second time. That damned dog from next door, *again*.

Mac jumped to his feet. "Easy girl," he said, reaching for his pistol, but it was in the house. The dog approached in a stalking motion with her hackles raised. It was obvious she did not like him, and the feelings were mutual. In fact, he couldn't stand dogs. He was attacked as a youngster and never got over his fear.

Mac pulled his leg back to kick her when someone yelled her name.

"Sue, come on girl," that neighbor lady called out.

Sue? What kind of name was that for a dog, he thought as she scampered away.

"Sorry about that, sir. Again. I hope she did not bother you." The shadow of a tall, leggy woman stood on the deck. "She means no harm," she said.

Mac threw his hood over his head, spun on his heels, and marched to the house, waving his hand in a dismissal fashion. "Forget it," he grumbled. His calm night, ruined.

Next time, he'd shoot it.

CHAPTER 43

SIMON AND OLIVE rejoined us inside, and we were back to business.

"Like I was saying, we need to learn more about the victim." I scratched my head and pondered why Lily needed to hire a PI.

"I can get a copy of the coroner's report once it's finished," Olive said.

"How long?" I asked.

"The autopsy only takes a few hours, so I could get the preliminary right away. The problem is the body is still in town," Olive replied, staring at the screen.

"How do you know?" I asked.

Olive stopped reading and looked at me.

"Never mind," I said.

Olive turned around her laptop. "Here are pictures I took at the marshal's office."

I scrolled through the police report and studied the attachments, one by one.

"The room was registered to Lily Cazier," I read to the gang. "The receptionist reported a female matching Lily's description paid in cash. No ID. My guess is someone paid off the clerk on duty. And it was not our friend, Zuli, either." I looked up from the screen. "They thought of everything." I returned to the report.

"After the deputies' forced entry, they initially found Lily unresponsive," I said in a detached tone. For a second, it was as if I was reading a work report. And then nausea kicked in. This was too close to home. I squinted to keep the tears from welling. *Stay focused, Rose.* I continued reading to myself. Her eyes were droopy and pinpoint sized, and she was nodding off. The classic signs of opioid use.

I clenched my fists under the table. The real murderer gave her heroin! That's why she sounded so out of it. Because she was.

"And?" Simon urged.

"Wait a minute," I said. "Simon, there was a hypodermic needle on the nightstand with a brown substance. Like the one you found in the trash. It was in the evidence bag. So, it was *not* from the prior occupants." I pointed to the part of the report where the deputies performed a field drug test of the syringe's contents. As I suspected, it was presumptive positive for heroin.

He studied the report and looked back at me. I saw his jaw clench.

I slowly shook my head at him with wide eyes. I did not want to admit out loud that she was given this evil drug. As I returned to the screen, something else struck me wrong.

"Wait! Simon." I looked at him again. "What hand does Lily shoot with?"

Everyone stared at me with furrowed brows. Except Simon. He knew where I was going.

"Ha. She used to shoot with both."

"Until …" I urged.

"Until she severed her left index finger roping, and they had to reattach it," Simon said.

"And why do we know this?" I asked.

He shook his head. "She showed me pictures a few days ago."

"Exactly. Lily does not have full use of her left index finger." I turned the laptop to show Simon. "What hand is her Sig Sauer in?"

Simon read it and returned his gaze to me.

"Whoever framed her, put it in her *left* hand. Lily is right-handed." I stood and paced. "That means Lily couldn't have shot Gil on her own." I leaned on the table. "And that also means this shitbird, put her left finger on the trigger and pulled," I said, as if I were pleading my case in court. "They swabbed her hands for gunshot residue."

"Her attorney needs to know this," Kate said.

I shook my head. "We're not supposed to have this report, remember? It is essential that Nala builds her own case. And when she *legally* gets the copy, we can let her in about Lily's finger," I said. "Not to mention we may have committed a few crimes obtaining the evidence."

Simon looked at me.

I lifted a finger toward him. Now was not the time to tell everyone I was in cuffs earlier and almost went to jail. Although, that would've allowed me to see Lily. Boy, Grandma was right, my squirrels were loose again. Exhaustion and all.

I returned my focus to the report.

"Let me play devil's advocate," Rayo said. "You said Lily sounded out of it. Could it be possible she was confused and didn't know what hand she was using, or maybe she shot with her right hand and put it in her left?"

"Good questions and speaking like a true prosecutor," I said. "But the report says they tested both hands for gunshot residue. None on her right."

"And to answer your first question, Rayo," Simon said. "It's an automatic reaction to use your dominant hand."

"Let me ask you something, Rayo," I said. "You're tired, and you've been drinking for the better part of the night, correct?"

"Yeah." He laughed, and his voice rose a pitch.

I threw Simon's car keys at Rayo.

He snatched them midair with his right hand.

"See, instinct." I turned to Olive. "Olive, can you please send the report to Grandma?"

"Already did," Olive replied. "Don't forget the evidence chain was broken." She smirked.

CHAPTER 44

LILLIAN SAT AT her breakfast nook overlooking her haven, sipping coffee. Her two dogs, Brian and Stevo, stationed themselves on either side of her, gargantuan towering pillars. She drummed her fingers on the table as she stared at Lily's letter and considered it for a spell. Invasion of privacy for work was one thing, but personally, it stuck like a lump in the back of her throat. Especially a letter from mother to daughter.

On the other hand, Lily was in trouble and this letter could be a clue. She pondered. As she picked up the envelope, the encrypted phone that sat in her desk drawer rang. There was only one person who had the number. Lillian put in her earbuds, placed her index finger on the biometric scanner, unlocking the phone.

"Hello, dear. You've been on my mind," Lillian said.

"That's why my ears were ringing," the woman on the other end said with a chuckle.

"So, by now you've heard about Lily," Lillian said.

"Yes. Is she okay?" the woman asked.

"I think so, physically anyway," Lillian replied.

Silence fell on the line. "It's my fault."

"Stop beating yourself up, M."

"How much does she know?"

"That's what I'm going to find out."

"I have unsettling news." M sighed. "Are you aware the victim was one of us?

"No!"

"Does the name Gil Fox ring a bell?"

"He was a scientist." Lillian blew out a gust of air. "And you're certain?"

"I may be in hiding, but, like you, I keep my finger on the pulse," M said. "I flagged anyone interested in Project X and followed the breadcrumbs. Unfortunately, they led back to Lily."

"How?"

"In reading the correspondence between the two, Gil told Lily he was a PI and would help her get to the truth about her parents."

"She stopped asking me questions about the accident months ago. I thought she let it go. Clearly, she did not," Lillian said. "That's why she's been so enigmatic lately."

"Are you aware Gil also worked on Project X?"

"I knew he was on the sensitive projects team."

"There's nothing more sensitive than X," M said. "His moral compass evidently turned. I learned he started a firestorm with his objections about X."

"I'd heard he was a whistleblower," Lillian said. "So, I guess he appropriated the agency's documents?"

"You don't think he handed them off to Lily?" M asked.

"That is a question I do not have the answer to."

"She's not with the agency. How could he involve her? Lillian, she's not safe. You've got to get her out of jail."

"I'm working on that," Lillian stated. "Nala should arrive any minute. We're driving out to Lake Simi this morning."

"Excellent, you have the pit bull on her case," M said. "Wait, isn't Nala a federal prosecutor?"

Lillian explained Nala's change in sides as she pulled up Olive's e-mail.

"No better person to handle her case … okay, I'm looking at a copy of the police report." Lillian puffed her cheeks. "It is apparent they set up Lily."

"That bad?"

"Worse, my friend."

"I don't understand. Wouldn't it have been easier to get rid of her?" M questioned. "I … I mean, I'm glad Lily is alive."

"Maybe she doesn't know much, and they needed a scapegoat, or they want to see who she talks to," Lillian said. "She is going to have a bull's eye on her once she's released."

"She needs protection."

"That's the plan," confirmed Lillian. "We'll get her bailed out today and place her in our care."

"It's Sunday, the courts aren't open," M said, hesitating before continuing. "Never mind." She chuckled. "I forget to whom I'm talking. You have more connections than the president."

"It's been difficult keeping this secret."

"Ms. Lil, you and I know some secrets are best kept."

"When the time is right," Lillian said. "I also risk getting the cold shoulder."

"A risk worth taking," M said.

"Indeed. But my Rosie has had so many secrets kept from her since she was a child."

"Teddy?" M said.

"Yes, it was only last year she and her father reunited." Lillian paused. "Rose was seven when she last saw her dad. Boy, when she found out he was an asset and the reason he disappeared, it rattled her. Rose and her sister Saki thought Teddy died in federal prison."

"I heard Rose's husband was murdered, searching for Teddy," M said.

Lillian sighed. "That was a convoluted mess. My Rose does not like surprises. I will need to brace myself when it comes out. You should've seen the look on her face when she found out what *I* did for the agency. I didn't know if she was impressed or shocked." Lillian laughed. "Too many secrets. I thought I was done keeping them."

Lillian watched as her Cessna landed in the back. "The pit just arrived. I will keep you posted."

"Take care." M disconnected.

Lillian returned the phone to the drawer, took the letter off the table, and walked it back to Lily's room.

CHAPTER 45

I TOSSED AND turned and when I popped open my eyes, it was still dark. The only noise was from the illuminated wall clock, which read three. The ticking was competing with the hamsters running on a wheel in my brain.

I shut my eyes tight and forced myself to catch more ZZs. When I finally woke, it was 6 a.m. and the smell of java mixed with pancakes tingled my nose hairs. A slight smile fell across my face for a second until I thought of Lily, who most likely hadn't had a decent meal in days.

Sue stretched and let out a loud high-pitched yawn, all fours in the air. She gave me her "I want a belly rub" look, so I obliged. As her servant, I lived to please. After five minutes of a doggo massage, we both jumped out of bed. Since I showered last night—or I should say this morning—I threw on my running leggings and navy-blue UC San Diego Tritons hooded sweatshirt. Of my alma mater clothing, this was my fav. Unfortunately, this one had a few holes from my attack in Alaska. Note to self, order a new one.

I tip-toed into the bathroom, washed my face, and brushed my teeth. My daily ritual of skin care was basic. Being a fair-skinned red head, tinted moisturizer was necessary. Not to mention I kept my face out of the sun as much as possible to avoid pre-mature wrinkles. Besides, humid Florida temps melt the makeup away the second you leave your air-conditioned home. Or in my case, yacht. So, I did something I thought I'd never do. I got permanent eyeliner. It made getting ready even quicker. I was also blessed with long eyelashes and rarely needed mascara.

By now, Sue was impatient and doing her tap dance. But this

time I was going with her. I couldn't risk her having another tangle with the neighbor. My Spidey-senses, not to mention Sue's internal BS detector, told me to watch our six. We made our way to the kitchen where everyone but Rayo was up and drinking coffee.

"Good morning," I said, peering at my watch. "Grandma and Nala should be arriving around ten. They're going straight to the jail. They're doing a Zoom meeting with the judge and the prosecutor to set bail." I poured a cup of coffee.

"On a Sunday?" Simon asked. "And a prosecutor agreed?"

I smirked. "They have a bail bondsman, too."

"Due to her charges, will they set bail?" Kate asked.

"We hope," I said. "But even with her lack of criminal history, and having the best attorney to plead her case, my guess is it'll be high." I took a sip. "And I'm ready to pay."

"One of these days, Rose, you'll have to tell me how you came into all this money," Rayo said, stretching in the entryway.

"Long story," I said, exiting the back door. I stretched the best my ribs could handle and closed my eyes, taking in the lake's serenity again. Normally, Sue and I would do a quick five miles, followed by Simon's rigorous strength training. I was an avid runner, so the jogging part was easy. It also helped clear my mind. But my recent injuries precluded me from that. So, we set out for a leisurely stroll.

As Sue and I circled around the block, we ended up at the front of the house. I noticed the neighbor's SUV was still in the driveway, so I decided to do what any reasonable person would do: a bit of recon. Since the windows of his vehicle weren't tinted, I could easily see inside.

I kept my head on a swivel to make sure our neighbor wasn't watching and tried the back door, but it was locked. I peeked in and didn't find anything to write home about, so I hustled to the front. If curiosity killed the cat, I must have murdered it a million times by now.

"What in the heck?" My jaw dropped at what I saw. I furiously snapped pictures. I hurried to the rear of the vehicle, took a photo of his plate, and bolted inside the house with Sue.

CHAPTER 46

◆

I FLUNG THE door wide and closed it as quickly as I opened it. All eyes were on me.

"Rayo, I need you to run this plate." I barked the order like a general as I handed him my cell.

Without hesitation or questioning, Rayo copied the license number and went to the couch where his laptop sat on the coffee table.

"Kate, do you have ingredients to make chocolate chip cookies?" I asked.

Simon gave me a side look.

"It's not for me," I said. "I need to get into the neighbor's house."

"Yes," Kate said. "I bought ready-made dough. Since Rayo likes cookies."

I glanced at Rayo, his face a nice shade of ladybug red.

"Okay, O'Brien, what the heck is going on?" Simon stood with arms crossed, giving me his best big brother look.

"Sue and I took the long way around and came back through the front," I said. "So, I did a bit of recon."

"It's called snooping, Rose." Rayo smirked, clicking away at the keyboard.

I squinted at him, even though his eyes were glued to his screen.

"Anyway. You won't believe what I saw in the front seat."

They collectively threw their hands in the air.

"Our old man neighbor is not *old*. I mean, not cane carrying old." I walked over and poured another cup of coffee. "I saw a gray wig and facial hair. With his cane." I scratched my head.

"And he had a pair of expensive alligator boots on the floorboard."

I looked at my crew and they stared at me like I was a few bricks short and should not be consuming more coffee.

"Remember what Paisley and Zuli told us? The guy from the café had expensive boots. These are Caiman Hornback." I showed them the pictures. "I sensed our neighbor was off. I just couldn't put my finger on it."

"I can," Rayo interjected. "Your hunch was correct." He looked up from the computer screen. "The vehicle is a rental under the name of … drum roll, please. None other than Bee Line Industries. This morning I ran the company, but it's a shell within a shell. I couldn't trace it past that."

We gathered around the kitchen table. Being the only one who hadn't eaten, I plopped on the chair. I was about to stab a pancake when Simon snatched my plate and replaced it with an egg white omelet that I assumed he made. I growled at him. But then my mother raised me to be grateful, so I thanked him. And when he wasn't looking, I snuck a pancake.

"The cookies can be ready within the hour," Kate said.

"Thanks," I said with my head in my dish.

"So, what's your plan?" Olive asked.

I set down my fork. "I'm going to put on my freakin' happy face and make amends for Sue's behavior last night."

"And what if he doesn't open the door?" Olive inquired. "What do you plan to do? Break in, kidnap him, and force him to talk?" She chuckled.

I dropped my fork. Simon, who'd just taken a sip of coffee, spit it out. We shared a look and laughed.

"What's so funny?" Rayo asked.

"Another long story," Simon and I muttered at the same time.

Simon knew about the time Lily and I drugged and kidnapped Titos. In our defense, Titos, who once worked for the FBI, went bad like sour milk. When we brought Titos to Grandma's secret squirrel lair, we used mild interrogation techniques to question him when my sisters were kidnapped. I say mild because "enhanced interrogation technique" is a euphemism for torture.

We didn't take it that far. Unless you consider cattle prod torture. But the rest of my team didn't need to be privy to that bit of information. Our little escapade turned Titos around and he ended up working with us to rescue my father. Who would've thought.

"No." I finally spoke. "I'm going to charm the crap out of him. I can be very persuasive." I gave a cheeky grin and finished stuffing my face.

"Alrighty then," Kate said. "I'll go take the cookie dough out of the fridge and get to work."

"Do we still have milk?" I asked.

"Yeeess." Kate's voice rose a note.

"Good." I turned to Rayo. "Do you have a fingerprint kit?"

He threw a thumbs up.

"Perfect." I smiled and finished my coffee.

"Luucyy!" Simon said in his best Ricky Ricardo imitation.

CHAPTER 47

"ARGH!" MAC GROUSED at his blaring cell. He pried his heavy eye lids open and blinked a few times until his vision cleared. He found himself face down in a pool of his own drool. His phone rang for the second time. And it was then he realized he fell asleep on the couch last night.

As Mac twisted to a sitting position, the call echoing magnified in his pounding head like a jackhammer. Just as he located it between the cushions, it stopped ringing. Mac closed his eyes for a moment when it started again.

"What?" Mac snapped as he answered.

"What do you mean, *what*?!" CK barked back. "It's eight o'clock."

"And?" Mac said. CK's voice pierced his brain like an ice pick, so he put the phone on speaker. Mac peered around. Oh right. The nearly empty bottle of Makers on the coffee table. Not his first time polishing off a bottle alone. Won't be the last. But the headache was new. Most likely because of a lack of nutrition.

"I need you to be running on all cylinders, Mac," CK said.

He rolled his eyes, but he couldn't get them that far back without pain.

"The target is getting bailed today," she said.

"On a Sunday? I thought with murder charges, that was unlikely." Mac shuffled to the kitchen. He pulled out a mug, grabbed a dark roast coffee pod, and put it in the state-of-the-art beverage brewing system. "Are you certain?"

"Why do you insist on questioning me?" CK said. "My source is none of your concern and very reliable. You'll need to be outside the jail when they bail her out and follow them."

He opened the refrigerator and shook his throbbing head. Damn. No milk. Just as the last drip of coffee hit his cup, someone pounded on the front door.

"What was that noise?" CK asked.

"Someone's here," Mac said. He'd heard that same banging in his younger years, but it was usually followed by some cop demanding entry with a warrant.

"Hello, sir," a female's voice softly spoke on the other side. Her tone didn't match her rap.

"Get rid of her," CK demanded.

"I … I just want to apologize for my dog's behavior. I brought you a plate of fresh cookies and milk."

"It's the irritating neighbor," Mac whispered back to CK.

Her offer piqued his interest though, as he was desperate for something to settle his stomach. He disconnected the phone—at least he thought so— and stuffed it into his sweatpants pocket. He set the coffee on the counter and lumbered to the door. He peered out the peephole and confirmed it was her. Without the dog. Perfect.

Mac opened it a crack. "Yeah, all good," he grumbled. "You can leave them on the doorstep."

"But I'd really like to apologize face to face. I feel just awful about my dog's behavior." The neighbor suddenly pressed on the door and made her way inside.

She was a pushy dame, Mac considered. "I told you, it's fine," he said, catching a glimpse of himself in the hall mirror. Shit! Where was his disguise? Shit, again, he'd left it in the SUV.

The neighbor stood there and stared at him. "I am so sorry. I thought an elderly gentleman was staying here."

"Oh … uh, that's my dad. He uh, he's in the back room sleeping," Mac whispered. "He told me about what happened with your dog. It's fine. He shouldn't be smoking, anyway." Mac grabbed the paper plate of chocolate chip cookies and the glass of milk.

"Oh, good. But can you pour the milk into another cup? You know how these rentals work. They probably count their silverware, too." She snorted and gave him a wide smile. Kinda creepy at that.

"Sure, sure. Follow me." Mac set the cookies on the counter and poured the milk into a mug. As he returned the glass to her, Mac noticed she was scanning his kitchen and living room.

"Mac ... Mac, are you still there?" CK's voice came from his sweatpants.

Mac fumbled as he removed his phone, disconnected it, and stuffed it back into his pocket. He thought he hung up on CK. He was more jacked up than he believed.

"Sorry, uh, that was my mom, you know, checking on my grandpa," Mac said. "Thanks again for the cookies. I'll make sure he gets them."

"You mean your father," she said.

"Yeah, yeah, that's what I meant," Mac said as he ushered her out the door. And just as Mac closed it, his cell rang again. He answered. "That was close."

"That woman's voice, I've heard it before," CK said. "What kind of dog does she have? What does she look like?" CK peppered him with questions.

"I don't know, some red dog. Her hair was tied back. I wasn't exactly paying attention to the color." He yawned. "She was tall and leggy. She had a good shiner under her eyes. Why?"

CK sighed. "Of all the rentals to be next to. That sounds like Rose, Lily's friend. I knew they were there. What are the odds? I need you to be certain." There was a slight pause. "Change of plans. Stay on them."

"Do you think she made me?" Mac poured the milk in his coffee and put another pod in the machine, with a larger mug under it. It was a double java morning.

"I guess you'll find out."

"I'll need a different vehicle. The gal thinks I'm here with my old man."

"Keep it. Leave for a bit so they think you're taking him home. And forget your disguise. You messed that one up," CK said.

Mac pulled the phone away and growled. "If I'm using my *actual* face, my fee just tripled." Mac disconnected.

He inspected the cookie, sniffed it, and took a bite. He followed it up with a slurp of coffee. If he was going to stay, he needed proper food. A market trip was a must-do.

CHAPTER 48

I **JETTED INTO** the house and handed Rayo the glass with the tip of my fingers.

"I got a good look at our guy next door," I said. "It appears he forgot he wasn't wearing his old man's disguise. And, if I had to bet money, I'd say he was the one who abducted Lily. How many people do you know have a protruded lower jaw with a snaggletooth? The scar was not there, though. Obviously, part of his cover up."

"It will take a bit to get his prints," Rayo said as he placed the glass in a plastic bag. He slipped on rubber gloves and went to work; his forensics degree coming in handy. He used the dark fingerprint powder, lifting the prints.

"Something struck me as odd. He was on the phone with someone when I arrived," I said. "His cell was in his pocket, and he didn't disconnect the call because the woman on the other end of the conversation called him 'Mac'."

"What's odd about that?" Olive asked.

"The woman's voice sounded familiar. But I can't place it." I peeked over Rayo's shoulder; he had a makeshift forensics lab on the kitchen counter. "How do you have the passcode to IAFIA?"

"Rayo, should I ask *how* you have access to the FBI's Integrated Automated Fingerprint Identification System?" Kate asked. "Won't they flag it?"

Rayo looked up and grinned.

"As Grandma Lil always says, 'Don't ask a question you don't want the answer to,'" Simon and I said simultaneously.

"Another thing puzzling me is why isn't the media buzzing

around," Rayo asked. "A murder in a small town. You'd think they'd be on it like flies."

"Marshal Church is keeping it hush." I grabbed a chocolate chip cookie from the plate on the counter and took a bite.

Simon glared at my choice of snack.

I jammed the rest of it in my mouth, grinning ear to ear. "Moxy said as much, not to mention it's tourist season," I mumbled with a mouthful of cookie.

"Thank God for small favors," Kate said. "Rayo, how long will the prints take?"

"I should get results within a couple of hours," Rayo replied. "Or less given the level of access."

I took a huge gulp of milk. "Speaking of Grandma," I said, looking at my watch. "It's eight twenty. They should be on their way. I need to let her know about our neighbor."

"*If* Mac is the person who abducted Lily, he'll recognize the Sprinter Van," Kate said.

"Should we put a tracker under his SUV?" Rayo asked.

"Talking like a real snooper," I said. "But it's a rental, remember?"

"I figured we could put it on there anyway," Rayo said.

"Negative. So, it's important we keep eyes on hi—" I looked out the window and noticed his vehicle was gone. "Too late. He must've caught on." I plopped on the chair. "Crap, my plan backfired." Just as I picked up my phone, my attorney called. I hit Ignore and sent it to voicemail.

I dialed Grandma and told her about the recent chain of events and advised her they may have a tail once they left the jail. Since this guy was a master of disguises, we wouldn't know his description or vehicle. I lowered my head. "I failed her," I said.

Simon walked up and put his hand on my shoulder. "You only fail if you stop trying. At least Lily's being released."

I nodded, but I didn't buy it.

CHAPTER 49

---◆---

IT WAS JUST after ten when CK drove through the charming and picturesque town of Darby. It was an old timber and mining hub, but she wasn't in tourist mode. CK continued a few more miles and turned right onto West Fort Road. She ascended for another fifteen windy minutes and took a sharp right onto a rocky dirt road. CK pulled up to a wooden handmade sign hidden from view that read *Lone Coyote Lane*. This is where CK had to ditch her Jeep to go undetected. Or so she'd assumed.

And since she did her homework, CK knew the locations of the camouflage cameras alongside the road leading up to the main gate. No one was home since Lillian left to pick up the target from jail and the rest of the staff was off for the day. So, she slipped on her ski mask, hefted her backpack onto her shoulders and set off down the mile-long road lined with pines and firs.

CK used her military training and slithered under the CCTVs. The entrance was a seven-foot black Fortress Ornamental Gate with wood pickets. The fencing around the front was the same and electrified. A recent add-on she discovered. If she jumped over onto the other side, an alarm would sound. So, the only way in was through the gate. But there was a camera pointing at the keypad.

Like a stealthy cat, she leapt up and tip-toed across the wood picket and sprayed the lens. She jumped down and punched in the security code. CK not only had special military training, but she also received multiple trophies in gymnastics in her youth.

The gate opened, and she was inside. Lily's new Ford Bronco sat front and center. CK was told it was a recent purchase. A gift from Lillian for Lily's birthday. Since the compound was secured, she knew Lily did not lock it. The complex's guard dogs, Brian and Stevo, were in their backyard but were alerted to her presence. They approached CK with their hackles raised. She knelt and removed her black ski mask to show her face, praying they would greet her like an old friend.

"Hi, boys," she whispered as they stalked toward her with their massive paws. CK trembled. It was the first time she'd been there while everyone was away. She kept her hand on her gun. Shooting them was not her first choice, but CK would if she had to. Collateral damage.

CK expected their hesitation and had two large meaty bones ready in a sealed bag in her backpack. She knew they would not take food from a stranger, but she was hardly a stranger. She remained motionless on the ground outside the Bronco. With their fur still standing high, CK tossed the bones into the back yard. Perfect landing. Those should last until her task was complete. She exhaled and went to work.

She pulled open the Bronco's door and slid behind the wheel. CK peeked under the floor mat to make sure the key fob was there and started the vehicle. She opened an app on her phone, entered the VIN number, and turned on the satellite radio. She waited for the audio and pressed the button to have a refresh signal sent. Mission accomplished.

Before she exited the vehicle, CK reached in her bag and pulled out a pre-written note and taped it to Lily's steering wheel.

She departed the premises in the same manner she came. Dodging the cameras.

CHAPTER 50

"HI, GRAN," I sighed. "I lost sight of our neighbor. Sorry."

"No worries, we picked up Lily and are driving home," Grandma said. "I just put you on speaker."

"Hi, Rose." Lily spoke in a soft tone.

"I'm so glad you are out of jail." I paced the living room with my phone on speaker, too. "Are you okay?"

"I am," Lily said. "You sound as tired as I feel."

"Don't worry about me, lil' sis." I plopped on the couch. "My concern is you."

"Thanks." Lily sighed.

"Lily. We're going to clear you. I promise."

"If anyone has the tenacity, it's you, Rose," Lily said. "I am so sorry about your skydiving accident. Lillian just told me." She sucked back a strangled sob. "It should've been me."

"Stop," I asserted, "things happen for a reason. And I have more jumps than you. My training kicked up a notch." I looked at Simon, who'd reclined in the chair, his feet elevated, eyes closed. "Not only that, but I had an amazing hero rescue me."

Simon smiled and shot a thumbs up.

"That brings me to the burning question," I said. "Who packed your chute?"

"It wasn't my parachute," Lily said. "During my jump last week, Charly was with me. After we landed, she inspected mine and noticed the lines were burned, so Charly loaned me hers." Lily paused. "I trust her, Rose."

Simon sat upright; his eyes popped open. He must've had the same thought as me. I had my suspicions about Charly. And my

144

instincts rarely failed me. Not to mention Sue's hackles rose the second she met her.

I drew a deep, meditative breath and took the phone away.

"Rose, are you there?" Lily asked. "Lillian, I think we lost the connection," she said to Grandma.

"I'm still here." I put on my fake happy face, trying to sound convincing.

I kept my suspicions about Lily's friend to myself, considering all she had gone through. And although I vowed not to keep secrets from my friends and family, in this case, truth by omission was acceptable. At least until I had facts to back my claim.

"This is not good." Grandma sounded grim.

"What?" I asked.

"I just got an alert," Grandma said. "Someone breeched my perimeter."

"What?" Simon bolted to his feet.

Grandma sighed. "I'm pulling over to the side of the road."

"Did they enter your house?" I asked.

"No. The alarm did not sound," Grandma said. "This past year I put in a tiny camera on the wood street sign."

"On Lone Coyote Lane?" I asked.

"Yes," Grandma replied.

"Who was it?" Simon inquired.

"I can't make out their descriptors, nor the vehicle," Grandma said. "But the camera captured a partial plate. Montana plate, the last four, 487H. I will text it to Rayo."

I thought I heard my grandma swear under her breath, which was way out of character.

"You can't take Lily home," I said.

"I'll be fine," Lily said. "I refuse to live in a perpetual state of fear."

"It has less to do with fear and more with getting you cleared," I said. "Until your house is clear, it's best if Lily stays here, Gran. She can bunk with me. I'd feel better with her in my custody." The second the word "custody" left my lips, I regretted it.

"I am not an inmate," Lily snapped. "I want to be far away from that town."

"I didn't mean it that way," I said. "Sorry, poor choice of words."

145

"What about your neighbor?" Gran asked.

"Don't worry about him," I said. "*If* he returns, we've got that covered." Lily didn't need to know the neighbor was her suspected kidnapper. "Gran, do you have clothes for Lily?"

"Yes," she said, "I brought them in the event Lily wanted to change at the jail."

"Perfect. Back up to the garage and open the rear door," I said. "Lily, you crawl inside through the rear of the vehicle and slip in through the garage."

"Why can't I just walk through the front door, Rose?" Lily asked.

"Uh …" I looked at Simon for help.

"Uhh … nosey neighbors," Simon said. "One of the deputy's cousins lives in the neighborhood." He raised his brows, shrugged, and threw his arms out.

"Oh, okay." Lily's voice dropped.

Simon and I stared at one another for a spell. I could almost read his mind; he too did not like lying to her.

"That's fine Rose. What about your dinner gathering?" Gran asked.

The "dinner gathering" Grandma referenced was our term for inviting our neighbor over to get a read on him. That's if he was sticking around. While she'd waited for Lily's Zoom hearing, Grandma and I talked. We knew Mac was connected to Lily and her kidnapping. And I figured I'd get him liquored up and see if he had loose lips.

"Don't worry, Gran. I'll deal with it when the time comes."

"Why are you talking in code?" Lily barked.

"It's a long story. I'll fill you in later," I said. "I promise."

"Should I know what you all have planned?" Nala chimed.

I put my hand over my mouth. I forgot she was in the vehicle.

"Negative. In fact, who is this? Gotta go. See you soon," I said and disconnected.

CHAPTER 51

◆

"STATUS," ALVAREZ SNAPPED. Her urgent tone crackled over the airwaves.

"They bailed her out," CK said as she sat in her Grand Cherokee. "Most likely headed to the old lady's house."

"Don't underestimate that 'old lady," Alvarez said. "If you only knew what she did for the agency."

"I've heard."

"And the other?"

"The tox report shows ketamine and heroin in the target's blood. As we suspected, there were zero traces of Project X. They were partying, and it got out of hand," CK said.

"And the victim's test?" Alvarez asked.

"Should be the same," CK replied. "Although his body is still in the cold room behind the Lake Simi ER."

"What about your man? Did he ask what the serum was? Or suspect anything … you know about X?"

"Um … no," CK said. She didn't dare tell Alvarez her lips grew loose when she drank. "Speak of the devil. He's on the other line." CK disconnected and switched calls. "Yes."

"I'm in town. Ya sure you don't want me to put a tail on the girl?" Mac asked.

"Unnecessary," CK said. "Get back to the rental and make nice with the neighbors."

"What if they're not who you think they are?"

"Find out," CK said. "Must I tell you how to do your job?"

"Screw you, lady. I'm not taking this." Mac disconnected.

CK glared at the cell. No one hung up on her. Blood rose to her head. She should just kill him and get a new guy.

But since time was of the essence, and she needed Mac right now, he'd get a reprieve.

Oh, crap. She had a picture of Rose.

CK let out a cleansing breath and called Mac back.

"What," Mac rumbled.

"I apologize," CK said through gritted teeth. Those two words were not the two she'd rather deliver. "I'm sending you a photo." CK massaged her chest as she tore open her second package of Tums today.

There was a pause on the line.

"Mac, are you there? Did it come through?"

"That's her. No doubt. I'm gonna ask a question, so don't bite my freakin' head off."

"Go ahead."

"If they're taking the target outta town, how are you going to tail 'em? And if they're headed back to Darby, there's going to be heightened security. You'll need my help," Mac said. "There's no way to attach a tracker. They'll sweep all the vehicles for bugs. Hell, she'll have more protection than freakin' royalty."

"Yes, and they'll be using burners," CK agreed as she sipped from her water bottle. "It's handled," CK said as she drove through Darby. "Just stick with your neighbors and we'll go from there."

She ended the call.

CHAPTER 52

$$\blacklozenge$$

THE SECOND LILY was inside, we embraced. Although my ribs pulsated to a level ten, I didn't care. She wept so hard it soaked my sweatshirt. It felt like an eternity since we last saw one another, but it had only been a few days.

"I'm sorry, Rose." Lily stepped away from our hug. "I'm such a whiny baby. My emotions are all over the map. I haven't cried this much since my parents died."

"Don't you dare apologize," I said. "Look what you've been through."

I examined my broken friend. She had bags under her red, sad eyes and the gray sweat suit hung on her wasted frame. Lily was not a sensitive person, but it was obvious the recent chain of events had taken a toll on her, both physically and emotionally. Though, I had to admit, it could also be from drugs likely still working their way through her system.

I rolled my neck, bit my tongue, and exhaled.

"Holy cow." Lily grabbed my chin, turning my head from side to side. "Your face!"

I turned to Simon and Rayo. "You guys told me it wasn't *that* bad." I squinted at them. "At least someone is honest with me."

"Gee, will ya look at the time?" Rayo pretended to peek at a watch that wasn't there. "I have to check on prints and run the other thing." Rayo grabbed his computer and went to his room.

Simon and Kate looked at the ceiling.

"Um … Simon and I are going to the market," Kate said.

"I would've told you, you look like hell, Rose," Olive said.

"But you didn't ask me." She turned to Lily and hugged her. "I'm Olive. We met at the jail. I was the one in the ski mask." She smiled.

"Yes, I remember. Thank you!" Lily said. "Thank you *all*." She looked at the floor and wiped her cheeks.

Simon stepped up to Lily and wrapped his massive arms around her. Lily's face grew still and I could tell she wasn't in the mood for that lengthy hug from him. It didn't help that Simon had a mad crush on her.

Lily, at this point in her poor relationship history, did not reciprocate. At least not yet.

"I'm going to take a long shower. You may not have any hot water after I'm done." She slung her duffel bag over her shoulder and turned to Grandma. "Lillian. I ... I don't know what to say. I owe you more than you can ever know."

I assumed Lily was referring to my grandma taking her in after her parents died in a plane crash four years ago. Grandma Lil not only gave her a home, but steady employment. In return, Lily was dedicated to her.

"I love you as if you were my flesh and blood," Grandma Lil said as she choked back tears. She handed Lily another burner phone since Mac snatched her last one. "Don't use your personal cell until we get to the bottom of who is behind your abduction."

Lily flashed a faint smile and left the room.

My heart sunk; I either wanted to have a cry fest of my own, or better yet, hit the gym and go a few rounds with a punching bag. Or Mac's face.

CHAPTER 53

◆

I TURNED TO Grandma, and the woman who I assumed was Nala Clearwater.

Nala was all business and was on her phone during our teary-eyed reunion. She approached me with a firm handshake.

"Nice to meet you, Rose," she said. "I have my work cut out if I want to clear Lily. I tried to question her on the way over here. But she is still out of it from the drugs."

"She is not a *drug* addict," I growled through gritted teeth.

Nala raised her hand to me. "Sorry, poor choice of words. But, like it or not, the tox screen will be positive for whatever drugs he gave her. I'm waiting for the report. I must prove this person gave her illicit drugs *against* her will," Nala said in a detached tone, as if she were in court.

I almost blurted out "heroin," but bit my tongue and looked at the floor.

"A prosecutor could refute the claims she was not a willing participant without evidence." Nala put her fists on her hips, scowling at me. "I am also not happy they took blood without my being there."

"Agreed," Grandma said. "Let's hit the road. I need to check on my house. And Nala, you can use any of my computer equipment."

Just as Grandma started for the door, Rayo charged in. "Wait, wait, wait!" He halted to a stop. "The neighbor's rental came back to the same shell company as both vehicles ... Bee Line Industries."

"Shell company? Who are these people?" Nala asked.

Grandma and I looked at one another and threw our hands up.

"I hope to find out tonight," I said.

"I don't want to know," Nala said, flicking her wrist. She peeked out the front window and turned. "Oh, your neighbor's returned."

"Perfect," Grandma said. She leaned in to give me a hug and whispered in my ear, "If our friend needs a little encouragement, there's some special Russian liquid in the Sprinter." She pulled away and winked.

"I saw that." I chuckled.

Grandma scared me sometimes. I could tell she missed being in the middle of the action. I think that's why she wanted me to take over for her. To live vicariously through me. Despite her retirement from the CIA two decades ago, she still had a hand in questionable affairs. Not to mention all the secret squirrel stuff she had access to.

Gran started her career during Watergate and ended just after the 9/11 attacks. She once told me she wakes up every morning looking for information that might be a precursor to something bigger.

"Remember, keep your friends close," Grandma said.

"And enemies closer," I finished. "Copy, Gran. Speaking of—" I looked around the room to make sure Lily wasn't in earshot— "We need to have a chat about Charly," I uttered in a low tone.

Grandma nodded. "It's way too coincidental that Charly gave Lily her parachute. I will ban her from the house."

"I know. Things don't add up," I said. "Who is she working for?"

"We will find out. Keep me posted," she said as she looked next door. "You better go invite your neighbor over before he packs up and leaves. And tell me how your dinner party turns out."

Just as Grandma left, my attorney called again. I declined it.

Keith sent an immediate text: *URGENT*.

I replied: *In the middle of a mess. I promise to call you.*

Keith: *Your monetary future depends on this*!

That wasn't good, I thought, furrowing my brows. I should call him. Put us both out of our misery.

Then the neighbor exited his vehicle.

I set down the phone.

CHAPTER 54

THE DINNER PARTY, as Grandma Lil referred, was anything but a welcome event. She and I had discussed what to do with Mac. If that was his real name.

I wanted to grill him and told her I could take him to her special interrogation room. She shot that down for a couple of reasons. Number one, the distance was too far, and any sedative would have worn off before we reached her house. Number two, Nala wouldn't want to know that we used "enhanced interrogation" to get the truth.

So, we devised another strategy. Turn the tables on our suspected kidnapper, play stupid, and invite the varmint over for a barbeque and alcohol. Lots of it.

At least, that was the plan. During my recon of his cabin—okay snooping— I discovered our guy liked whiskey. Simon agreed to donate his unopened bottle of Devil's Brigade, his favorite spirit from Willie's Distillery in picturesque Ennis, Montana. And a couple of his Cuban stogies.

Our simple scheme turned a bit more complicated. Mac was a professional drinker. It was only 7 p.m., the food had now settled in our stomachs, and the whiskey was gone. The only two people drinking it were Simon and Mac. Our guest appeared so sober he could probably cite the alphabet backwards while walking a straight line. On the other hand, Simon's eyes were very glossy, and he smiled … a lot. It was creepier than my pretend-I-don't-want-to-punch-you-in-the-face, smile.

"The steak and potatoes were great." Mac leaned back in the plastic lawn chair, sipping the last of his tumbler. "So, ya never told me about yourselves. Are you all related?" He scanned Kate. "And I'm curious about your shiner." He pointed to my face.

"An accident," I said. "Nothing to write home about." I rubbed my hands over the fire pit. "And family reunion." I glanced at Simon, Kate, Olive, and Rayo.

Mac rose and stood next to me; our shoulders were inches from one another. "Small family." He looked back at the crew. "I don't see a mother or father."

Sue, who'd been curled up on the deck on her dog bed, raised her head at Mac's sudden move on me, hackles high, always my protector.

I took a step left, as Mac was in my discomfort zone. I wanted with every inch of my being to put the smack down on him. Instead, I rolled my neck and sucked my teeth.

Simon must've had his eye on me and noticed my fists curled too. He stepped in between us.

"Hey. How about a cigar?" Simon said with wide eyes. He shot me his *Stand down* look and handed me my wine glass. He must've assumed I needed to keep my hands busy, or they would've been tightly wound around Mac's neck.

"Good idea ... *bro*." I stared back and took a sip. "Why don't you go get them?" Given that we were all *family*, calling Simon "bro" seemed proper. I returned to Mac. "My ... I mean, *our* parents are gone."

That was not a lie. My mother passed away from cancer a few years ago. And my father, Teddy, was in Florida playing Grandpa. Since he was absent most of his children's lives, he vowed to be a better grandpa than he was a father. It took him to get kidnapped, tortured by the cartel, and shot up for us to become a family again. I stared off into the fire pit.

"Why did you all choose Lake Simi for a reunion?" Mac said. "I mean, it's an okay place. And I don't see any paddle boards or boats out here." He inclined his head to the dock. "What else is there to do?"

"I can ask the same of you." I squinted at him and gulped the rest of my wine.

Mac met my stare.

Sue growled and started down the steps of the deck. But Rayo intercepted her on his way up.

Kate cleared her throat. "Who wants dessert?"

"I do," Olive said. "Let me help." She rose from her chair and joined Kate.

Simon returned with stogies and handed one to Mac.

Mac was too sober, and my plan was not working. I had to interrogate him. I knew with every inch of my soul he kidnapped Lily and murdered Gil. I was determined to extract that information from him.

Then it hit me. "Stop," I shouted.

Mac and Simon jumped.

"Um ... shouldn't you wait until *after* dessert to have a cigar? And you'll need something to pair with it." I shot a wide-eyed look at Simon.

"Oh ... yeah. I've got the perfect spirit that goes great with these Cubans." Simon said, glaring at me. He knew I was referring to his special reserved bottle that he had hidden in the van.

"Not for me. I've had enough," Mac raised his hands. Just as he turned, I grabbed his arm.

"I have been a shitty hostess," I said.

Mac looked at my hand, yanked his shoulder, and glared. I saw pure evil in him and knew what he was capable of. I'd stared into the eyes of deranged killers. Although Mac did not have the serial killer vibe.

Right then, Kate came out with her signature cheesecake she'd prepared earlier.

"Please," I said in a softer tone. "Kate makes the most amazing cheesecake. From scratch. You don't want to disappoint her." I turned my head to look at Kate and leaned into Mac. "I think she has taken a liking to you," I whispered in his ear.

That did it. Mac not only enjoyed his libations, but he apparently also loved the ladies. He looked past me and smiled at Kate with his snaggletooth more pronounced.

Kate and Simon gave me a head tilt.

"Oh, here. Let me help. Please." Mac took the cake from Kate's hands.

I stood behind Mac and mouthed, *sorry* to Kate.

Simon bent over and murmured, "What the hell did you say?"

"Nothing much." I shrugged and scrunched my nose. "Now follow me."

CHAPTER 55

◆

I SLIPPED INTO the garage and snuck into the Sprinter Van. I opened Grandma's black bag and removed the SP-117 and snatched Simon's bottle of Cognac from the shelf. After I returned to the kitchen, Simon had tumblers waiting for us. I set the vial on the counter.

"Olive, can you keep a lookout, so Casanova doesn't get suspicious?" I asked.

"We are going to owe Kate big time. Using her as bait," Olive said as she watched Mac make his moves. "We, meaning you Rose." She snickered.

Rayo pulled up a barstool and inspected the vial. "What is SP-117?" he asked in a low tone.

"A Russian truth serum. Works better than sodium pentothal," Lily said, emerging from the bedroom with a yawn and stretch. She'd apparently fallen into a long nap. She leaned on the bar and looked out back. "Barbeque? I'm starving. You should have woken me." She picked at the steak. "And what special guest do we have to warrant bringing out the 117?"

Simon jumped in front of her. "Um. There's someone out there you shouldn't see."

"Sorry, Lily. I anticipated you sleeping the whole night." I handed her a plate with foil over the top.

"I'll warm it up and bring it to your room," Olive said.

"What are you guys talking about?" Lily must've heard Mac's voice because her eyes widened. She tossed the paper plate on the counter and bolted for the back door. She was about to say something when I put my hand to her mouth and yanked her off her feet.

Lily wrenched my hands off her. Given that she'd recently been kidnapped, I guess grabbing her was the wrong thing to do.

"I don't have time to talk," I whispered in her ear. "Please, please keep quiet and stay inside."

Lily was smart and it must've dawned on her the SP-117 was for Mac because she nodded. "I want to hear what the worm has to say," Lily murmured through her clenched jaw.

A nap was all Lily needed, and she was back to her spunky, kick-ass self.

I returned to the kitchen.

"Why would your gran have anything like that?" Rayo inquired in a low voice.

"I told you she is unconventional," I said. "Welcome to the secret squirrel team."

"Is that why she has everyone sign an NDA?" Rayo asked.

"After she vets them," Olive quipped. "Have you ever used this stuff, Rose?"

"Yes, it works. It is the same drug we gave Titos." I looked around the kitchen. Rayo and Olive wore blank stares. "Disregard. None of you were there."

"I was," Lily said from the living room, where she plopped on the sofa.

"Won't Mac know we drugged him?" Rayo asked.

"It's odorless, colorless and has no immediate side effects," Olive said as she kept looking out for me. "I've never seen it in action."

"Yep, and after our chat, Mac will think he fell asleep," I said, stirring in the SP-117.

Simon poured a glass of wine for Kate and emptied the rest of the Cognac in his snifter.

Rayo opened the slider as Simon, and I stepped onto the deck.

"Hope you saved me some cheesecake." I tried to sound jovial as I made my way to Mac and handed him the Cognac. He was obviously attempting to be the gentleman and gave it to Kate. I snatched it back. "Oh … um, Kate doesn't do brandy."

"I don't?" she asked.

Simon handed her a glass of red wine. "I guess you've forgotten the last time you had Cognac. You made us promise to stop you next time."

I gave Mac a tight-lipped smile. "She dances on tables if she drinks too much." Another horrible lie too easily spewed from my mouth.

Kate and Simon shot me a WTF look. I shrugged again and returned my attention to Mac. Did he buy it? He swirled the Cognac around and sniffed it.

Mac shot glances between Simon and me. I didn't know Mac well enough to interpret his looks. Then he smiled. "This is good shit. Oh, sorry." He put his palm to Kate. "I meant stuff."

I lowered my shoulders and exhaled. I raised my glass. "Here's to friends."

"You mean family?" Simon said with furrowed brows.

"Ahh, of course. I … I meant to our new *friend*, Mac."

Phew. Mac nodded and took a sip.

A few moments later, Mac's glass was empty, and his eyes rolled back in his head.

Kerplunk.

CHAPTER 56

———◆———

MAC'S CHAIR TOPPLED over, feet dangling in the air. Thank God we were on sand, or we might've had to call the EMTs. When he fell back, his cell phone dropped from his pants pocket. I picked it up.

"Crap. How much did you give him, Rose?" Simon asked.

"What?" Kate snapped a look at me.

I put my fingers to my lips and mouthed *shh.*

Just then, Mac mumbled something inaudible.

Rayo and Olive, who'd stayed inside cleaning, must've seen Mac tip backward because they bolted out the back door and down the steps in a jiff. Lily on their heels.

"Sit him in the chaise," I said, sliding my arms under his armpits. I forgot about my wounded ribs and winced.

"Let me do that, Rose." Rayo tapped my shoulder and took over. He and Simon eased Mac onto the lounge chair, with his legs elevated.

Lily walked down two steps when I put my palm to halt her. She could easily trigger Mac, so she obliged and watched from the landing. The expression on Lily's face told me she wanted to hog tie the SOB and do her own interrogation. But that wouldn't help us.

I pulled a chair over and sat next to him. "Mac, can you hear me?" I inquired in a calm, even tone.

He nodded, with his eyes still closed.

"Do you know where you are?" I asked.

He opened them, staring straight ahead. "Yeah," he replied in a soft voice.

"Do you know who we are?"

"You're the ones I'm watching," Mac said. "The target's friends."

The five of us stared at each other with open mouths. We didn't anticipate the serum working so quickly, or even at all. It was a crap shoot.

"Yes. Yes, we are," I agreed, scrolling through my cell phone, hit the camera app, pressed video, and tapped the red button to record.

"Can you tell me your full name?"

"Mac Ansel Vig."

"Who do you work for?" I asked.

"Self-employed."

"What is your business?"

"Hitman."

While the answer didn't shock me, hearing it from him, out loud, was sobering. The SP-117 worked great on him. Probably the alcohol helped. I would have to remember that for the next time I use it on someone.

"Who is your target?"

"Lily Cazier."

I looked back and saw Lily's jaw drop. She put her hand to her mouth with wide eyes.

"Who else was your target?"

"Gil Fox."

"Were you hired to assassinate your targets, Lily Cazier and Gil Fox?"

"Yes," Mac replied.

The answer left a Grand Canyon-sized pit in my stomach. Okay, enough with the simple yes and no responses.

"Why did you kidnap Lily and not murder her?" I asked. I didn't look at Lily's expression this time and only imagined how cold my question sounded.

"Change in orders."

"Who's orders?"

"Lady named CK."

"Who's CK?"

"Don't know. Never met her. Only voice on the phone."

"Who does CK work for?"

"The agency."

"What agency?" I knew, but I wanted to hear him say it on the recording. It wasn't admissible in court but could assist in the defense.

"CIA."

I lowered my head and blew out the silent exhaled breath that I'd been holding. I looked at Simon and Olive and inclined my head to Mac's rental. I handed Mac's cell to Rayo. All three knew what I wanted without even asking.

While Simon and Olive tip-toed away, Rayo swiped the screen and shook his head. He showed me Mac's phone had a touch ID.

I delicately took Mac's finger and placed it on the screen, unlocking it. I returned it to Rayo, and he disappeared into our rental. I resumed probing.

"Mac, how did you kidnap Lily and Gil?"

"I knocked them out and zip tied them."

"What did you use to knock them out?"

"Ketamine."

"What other drug did you give them?"

"Heroin."

"Why did you give Lily and Gil ketamine and heroin?"

"To make it look like they were partying."

"Any other drugs?"

"A serum."

"What is the name of the serum?"

"Don't know."

I paused for a second. "Where did it come from?"

"The agency."

"How did you administer it?"

"I injected it behind their ears."

This conversation was too real, too fast.

Just then, Rayo returned with Mac's phone. Seconds later, Simon and Olive exited his cabin, shaking their heads. I shot Lily a look. Tears welled in her eyes as she ran her hand along the back side of her ear and arm. She stood and turned to walk inside, but changed her mind and sat on the step, biting her nails. Kate plopped next to her.

"Did you, Mac Vig, murder Gil Fox?"

"Yes."

"How did you kill Gil?"

"Took Lily's gun and put her finger on the trigger and pulled."

Every fiber of my being wanted to punch this jerk. I also realized it would be counterproductive and blow the interrogation. *Ohm* I silently said instead.

Mac shook his head and his eyes rolled back again. He was snoring within seconds.

CHAPTER 57

MAC FELT A sticky, liquid substance drip onto his face. When he opened his eyes, he was nose to nose with that dog. It was her drool. Her teeth were showing, but she wasn't growling. He drew his head back and furrowed his brows.

"What the hell," he grumbled. He blinked a few times to clear the double vision.

"Sue. Leave him alone." He heard Rose's voice from behind him.

Mac bolted to a sitting position. "Man, I must've passed out." He looked at his watch. "Nine-thirty?" he said, watching Simon stoke the fire.

"How about coffee?" Kate asked.

Mac thought she was hot, but based on their earlier conversation, she wasn't his type. He preferred them loose and up for a one nightstand.

"Sure, thanks." Mac grabbed the mug from her. "What happened?" Mac took a sip. "If I didn't know any better, I'd say you roofied me. But seeing how I am still dressed." Mac let out a guttered laugh.

"We would never do such an *immoral* thing," Kate said and looked at Rose.

Her expression perplexed Mac. He shook it off.

"Between the food and booze, I crashed," Mac said. "I haven't taken a nap like that since I was a kid." He patted his pockets.

"Looking for this?" Rayo asked as he handed Mac the cell phone. "It dropped out of your pocket while you slept."

"Yeah, how did I end up here?" Mac ran his hand along the

chaise.

"After you drank the Cognac, you made your way over and began snoring," Rose said with a yawn. "I passed out too." She rose from her own recliner.

"So, when do you all head home?" Mac inquired.

"Tomorrow," Rose said, scratching behind Sue's ear. The dog stared at him without blinking. It freaked him out.

"How about you, Mac?" Rose asked.

"Same." Mac stood. "Well, I appreciate the hospitality, but I'm gonna head inside." He nodded to them. Mac wasn't a touchy-feely guy and never shook hands.

The second he stepped into his cabin, his cell rang. "Yeah," he answered.

"What did you find out?" CK asked.

"Zip. They were tight-lipped." Mac poured a glass of water. "They had some lame story about being family."

"That took you *all* evening?" CK sighed. "I tried to call you multiple times."

"What?" Mac looked at his phone. No missed calls. He shrugged it off. "My job is done."

"You're done when I say so," CK said.

"No." He pounded a fist on the counter. "I'm finished when *I* say so. I'm leaving tonight."

The line went quiet.

"I'll triple your fee if you stay until morning."

Mac thought for a minute. "Okay. But I can't follow them now."

"No need. I assume they're also checking out tomorrow. Wait around. I'll give you instructions."

Mac hung up, he paced between the sliding door to the lake and the kitchen sink, brooding. Why was he still needed? They'd said nothing of importance to him. He'd been in this business long enough to know when something smelled wrong. And why was CK willing to triple his pay just to *hang* out? She was too elusive.

Did CK even know why he was staying? Judging by the uncertainty in her voice, he guessed that was a firm no.

This wasn't Mac's first job for the agency. What if she was going to send in a clean-up crew?

He knew the drill.

Mac checked his phone again. If CK called him, he would've had missed calls. But he did not. Someone must have turned it off during his *nap*. And what was with that?

Mac didn't drink enough to pass out. So … his neighbors must've drugged him. What did he say?

Mac darted his eyes around the room. Did they bug his place or phone?

The hell with this.

Mac threw his overnight bag together and smashed his cell beneath his shoe. He couldn't take his vehicle for fear CK had it tracked. He'd hitch a ride out of town or hoof it as far as he could. Better yet, hotwire something just to get out of the hell hole.

Mac hefted his duffel over his shoulder, exited the cabin, and removed his belongings from the SUV. Couldn't leave his alligator boots.

He set off down the quiet street and lo and behold, there sat a late model silver Honda Accord, just asking to be taken.

CHAPTER 58

I WOKE AROUND six in the morning to Sue doing the happy dance on my bladder. I winced. Her tippy tap did not help my bruised ribs. It was a blessing in disguise because it gave me a reason to snoop on our neighbor. I ran to the bathroom and did my thing, donning sweatshirt, yoga pants, running shoes, and snapped on my fanny pack. The others mocked me about it, but it held dog poop bags, Sue's treats, and oh, my pistol.

After I dressed and packed, I crept past Lily's room with my bags in hand. Simon, being the chivalrous man, offered his bedroom to her. And since Rayo had twin beds, Simon bunked with him. I dropped my bags in the living room and Sue and I exited out the back sliding door onto the lake access. I turned left and circled the block. The second I moved my arms to run, pain shot through my body.

I slowed to a nice leisurely stroll and my phone vibrated. I cringed. It was probably my attorney. I peeked at the cell and my heart had a party. A FaceTime call from Kevin O'Malley, my honey. I fumbled with my phone to answer before he disconnected.

"Hello, babe." I smiled into the camera.

"Hi, swee—whoa. What the hell?! Looks like you jumped out of a plane with a malfunctioning parachute."

In my excitement, I'd forgotten my black eye and cut lip. By now, my face had turned several pleasant shades of purple and black.

"Gran ratted me out again, huh?" I squinted. "Please don't tell Saki or James. They'd be fit to be tied," I said.

"My lips are sealed." He moved his index and thumb finger in a zipping motion across his lips. "I wish I was there to kiss your boo-boos."

I felt my face turn ladybug red and giggled like a schoolgirl. "Me too. I love and miss you so much."

"I love you m—" Boom! An explosion sounded.

My heart leapt. "Kevin!"

Kevin's mobile phone shook and fell to the ground. The screen showed a dark, sterile room. Metal table and chairs. No windows. Kevin picked up the phone and now I could see he wore military fatigues.

"O'Malley, are you okay? And why are you dressed like G.I. Joe?" I asked. "You're not back in D.C … are you?"

"Red, I can't talk," Kevin said. "I just wanted to see your beautiful face. I miss you and I love you."

I held back a sob. *Don't get girly, Rose.* Kevin started calling me Red when we first met in the Florida Keys. That was after I barged in on his multi-agency briefing of law enforcement officers from Key West, Miami-Dade, and his own FBI team. The nickname at first irked me. But now, hearing Red from his lips made me gushy.

"I'm fine. But, worried about yo—"

Abruptly, there was another loud explosion. My heart dropped.

"O'Malley … Kevin … babe!" I shouted, but the call ended.

He texted: *I'm ok. Talk soon. And keep your feet on the ground.*

Kevin and I had a long-distance relationship, which was fine with me. It was safe. I wasn't ready to settle and get married again and do the whole kid thing. My first marriage ended in the murder of my beloved Bradley. I wasn't ready for that level of commitment. But if I did, I knew it would be with Kevin. He was assigned to D.C., but why was he dressed for combat? Kevin's work attire was the usual khakis and Polo shirts, sometimes suits. I pondered.

Sue and I had just finished our trek around the block when something caught my attention.

Mac's front door. It looked as if someone kicked it in. Since I'm always armed, I drew my Springfield Hellcat 9mm from my fanny pack and held it to my side.

CHAPTER 59

◆

I ORDERED SUE to run to our rental as I took cover by a tree outside Mac's cabin and called Simon.

"Grab your gun. I'm by Mac's house." No sooner had I finished my sentence than Simon was standing next to me.

"What's going on?" he asked.

"Check out his front door." I jutted my chin. "I looked inside the vehicle. Most of his stuff's gone," I said. "Ready to check if there's a body?"

Simon nodded. "If there's a stiff, we call the locals."

"Agreed."

The second we stepped onto his porch, I noticed the door had been splintered. Since we weren't doing a secret squirrel entry, I called out for Mac, but there was no answer. The cabin only had a single bedroom and bath, kitchen and living room.

I took the right and Simon went left. I expected his place to be trashed, but it wasn't. There were no signs of a struggle aside from the front door. The cabin had also been cleared of Mac's items except for the vehicle rental's key fob sitting on the coffee table. As we made our way into the kitchen, I noticed his cell phone was on the floor, smashed.

"So much for us tracking him," I said, pointing to the crushed iPhone. "And by the looks of things, Mac split on his own … but how did he leave?" I pondered out loud. "His vehicle is here, and it's not like you can get a ride all this way … or can you?"

"Your guess is as good as mine. Unless he befriended someone in town." Simon shrugged.

We checked out the bedroom and bathroom again. Nothing

noteworthy, so we left and returned to our rental.

"Mac's phone is offline," Rayo called out from the kitchen table. His fingers were dancing across the laptop.

"We know," Simon and I said simultaneously.

I turned to Simon. "You don't think *they* knew about our conversation last night, do ya?" I asked.

"I doubt it," Simon said. "No exterior cameras on the units. And Rayo took Mac's phone away from the interrogation."

"Speaking of," Rayo said. "There was only one number programmed."

"CK," Simon and I spoke again at the same time.

"You two have to stop doing that," Rayo chuckled. "It's freaking me out."

Lily, Kate, and Olive emerged from their rooms, all dressed. Bags in hand. I nodded. "It looks as if you all are ready to roll, too. We can get a bite on the road," I said.

"Count me out," Olive said. "As much fun as I've had hanging out with you crazies, I have another job." She made her way to the front door.

Rayo bolted to his feet. "Wait ... um. Am I ... I mean, we, going to see you again?" He stared at the floor.

I gave Olive a closed-mouth grin. Rayo had a mad crush on her. It was easy to fall for her because Olive was gorgeous.

"Yes, I'm headed to Lillian's after," Olive replied. "Until you are cleared—" she nodded to Lily—"she asked me to stay." Olive waved goodbye and walked out the door.

The next thing we heard was, *RAT-A-TAT-TAT ... RAT-A-TAT-TAT*. An ear-piercing sound I'd heard a few months ago.

Everything was in slow motion. Windows blew out as shards of glass sailed through the air. I watched Simon, Rayo, and Kate fling their bodies to the floor. Out of instinct, I snatched Lily, threw her to the ground, and sheltered her with my body. I would've also covered Sue, but thank God, she was in the back room.

My heart beat in my throat as I waited for the attack to end. Then I realized ...

"Olive!"

CHAPTER 60

———————◆———————

I BOLTED TO the front door, pistol in hand. Simon beside me. As I flung it open, Olive tumbled back into the house. Lily and Kate dragged her inside while I took cover by a large pillar on the porch. But the attackers had fled the scene.

I re-holstered my gun, returned inside, slammed, and out of habit, locked our holey door.

Simon dropped beside Olive. "Olive ... can you hear me?" he called out.

"Yeah," Olive mumbled, shaking her head.

Rayo stood behind Simon with his hand over his mouth. Judging from his expression, this must be his first shooting.

In the distance, sirens wailed. The neighborhood we were in was mostly elderly people and rentals, so my guess is one of them, if not all, called 911.

Kate returned moments later with Simon's red medical bag.

Sue was on her heels, shaking. She undoubtedly remembered being fired upon, too. She ran to me and sniffed. I bent to show her I was okay. She gave me a reassuring kiss and then plopped next to Olive.

My little support dog on the job.

"I'm fine," Olive said. "Just a flesh wound." I think she directed her first comment to Sue, who was licking her face.

"I need to look," Simon said calmly as he removed a folding knife from his cargo pants pocket and cut away at Olive's sweatshirt.

"Not the first time I've been shot." Olive winced. "New sweatshirt too." She rolled her eyes.

"Olive, can you tell me what you saw?" I asked.

"It happened so fast," Olive replied. "I opened the door and a black SUV that was parked in front of Mac's slowly pulled away from the curb. I got suspicious and ducked behind the pillar. The next thing, they were shooting at me. I didn't have time to return fire. No clear shot either."

No sooner did Simon have Olive's wound cleaned when we heard a pounding at the door, followed by a male yelling, "Marshals. Open up."

I went to the bullet-riddled door and unlocked it.

It was Marshal Church and Deputy Pane. Seconds later, Moxy arrived with the paramedics.

Olive refused medical attention, as Simon stated her wound would only require a couple of butterfly stitches. So, we sent the paramedics away.

"I should have known it was you all," Pane said with crossed arms. "Since you and your friend—" he nodded at Lily— "came to town, it's been nothing but chaos. Heck, someone stole a vehicle last night."

I stepped up to Pane and was nose to nose. I didn't like him the second we met. My Spidey-senses agreed. "We did not cause any of this," I snarled through clenched teeth, flailing my hands in the air. "And are you accusing us of stealing a car?!"

Church snaked between us and faced Pane. "That's not how we talk to tourists. They are obvious victims," Church said. "Why don't you and Moxy have a chat with the neighbors."

Pane glared at me with a tight jaw. "Fine by me!" He turned on his heels.

"And you, young lady." The Marshal spun around. "You should know better than to talk in that manner to an officer of the law."

I lowered my head. He was right. If someone invaded my personal space like I did Pane's, I would have put them in handcuffs.

"I'm sorry, sir," I said. "You're right. We're just trying to uncover what happened to our friend. And now this."

Church put his hand on my shoulder. "I understand, dear," he said in a comforting, fatherly manner.

I liked Marshal Church. Although Moxy told me he was looking to retire in a year, he didn't seem to be winding down.

After Church looked around the rental a spell, Moxy and Pane returned.

"I checked the neighbors' cameras." Moxy said. "One of them captured a black SUV, tinted windows. No front plates. The driver wore a black ski mask. As did the shooter." She presented the photograph of the SUV she snapped from the CCTV using her cell phone. The picture was grainy.

"Email that to me," Church ordered. "I'll send it out to the highway patrol." Church turned to Pane. "I need you to stay behind and take their statements for the report. Don't forget evidence photos."

"Sir, I can do it," Moxy offered.

"That's fine," Church said. "Pane, you're with me.

Moxy waited until they were gone and flipped back to me. "We need to talk."

CHAPTER 61

———◆———

I WATCHED MOXY scan the room.

"You can speak freely," I said and nodded for her to join us at the kitchen table.

"Pane is dirty." Moxy folded her hands on the table. "I didn't want to believe it. My suspicions began at the motel. First, he lied about you—" she faced Lily— "not wanting to go to the hospital. You were so out of it and agreed to whatever Pane said. The EMT cleared you at the crime scene. That should not have happened."

"I knew she should have gone to the hospital. That SOB. I could just punch him myself," I said, my face hot.

"Second, he never volunteers to take paper and delegates to me. He calls it a learning experience." Moxy rolled her eyes. "But he did that night. And yesterday, I left the office for a shoplifting call, but forgot my cell. So, I went back. Church and Peg were at lunch and Pane was in charge. He was in his office and didn't hear me enter. But I overheard his conversation. The phone was on speaker, and he was talking to a woman he called CK. Have you heard of her?" Moxy asked.

The six of us exchanged bug-eyed glances.

"Not exactly," I replied. That wasn't a lie, just an omission. If Mac was correct and they worked for the agency, then the fewer people that knew about CK, the better, including Moxy. "But go on." I urged with a hand gesture.

"He mentioned something about being fired for evidence tampering." Moxy wrung her hands. "It's not my nature to eavesdrop. But I took exception in this case." She shook her head and paused.

"It's okay, Moxy. I would've done the same thing."

"You see, he's going through his second divorce over gambling debts. He goes to these casinos outside the area and drinks and bets his paycheck away. He owes many people. I don't have to tell you how badly that ends," Moxy said. "After he disconnected, I jetted out of there."

"That's the typical story of a dirty cop," Simon said.

"That's not all." She let out an exaggerated sigh. "When Pane and I spoke to the neighbors just now, I watched as he left the house across the street. The homeowner, Irene, approached me. She stated she did not appreciate Pane erasing her video. Irene told me he apologized for accidentally doing it, but she didn't think it was accidental."

Moxy paused again. "Why else would he erase the video if he wasn't trying to cover up something dirty? I reassured Irene it was not on purpose, and he was an upstanding guy. I had to lie through my teeth. Irene said it was a shame because the video had a clear picture of the vehicle and the rear plate number. But she couldn't recall the digits."

"Have you gone to Church with your suspicions?" I asked.

"I didn't have enough evidence until today. I will take him aside. I just don't want Pane accusing me of trying to take his job. As I've told you, Pane is in line for the Marshal's position, and I am next for his." She stood. "Please keep this under your hat. I want Church to hear it from me."

Moxy headed to the front door and turned. "Oh, I forgot to take your 'official statements'" she said with air quotes, "and evidence photos." She laughed and pulled out her notepad.

After Moxy finished, she left, as did Olive. Olive informed us she'd catch up later. I had to admire her. Shot and still up to the task.

I called Grandma and gave her an update on the recent chain of events. Although I promised Moxy not to tell Church, I made no promise about Grandma.

Evidence tampering would get Lily's case thrown out.

CHAPTER 62

◆

IT WAS NOON when CK arrived in Missoula. She pulled up to her second coffee kiosk of the day and ordered a latte and ham and cheese sandwich. After she got her order, she edged out of the drive-thru and backed into a parking spot. CK inhaled her food and opened her encrypted laptop. No return e-mail from Alvarez after she provided her daily update, nor from Mac. She blew out a heavy sigh.

CK emailed Mac last night, once she discovered his phone was off, only to get an error message. So, she tried it again. "Dammit!" She shut the screen.

Mac was smarter than she gave him credit. CK took a chance when a former asset introduced her to him. He had nothing to lose and no morals. He reminded her of, well, herself. But she also liked him; he stood up to her.

The more CK's mind raced, the more her suspicions grew of Alvarez. What was her reason for wanting Mac to stay? It made no sense. Just then, her phone buzzed. The caller ID was unknown. Most of her calls came up blocked, but her gut told her it was Cora Alvarez. CK braced herself as she answered.

"I got your e-mail. A drive by shooting in a small town, your cover is blown. *And* the targets are still alive. Did you disobey a kill order?" Alvarez seethed without coming up for air. "You need to contain this … fast."

CK removed the phone from her ear and took a deep breath. "Wait a minute. Kill order? You called red light on the targets. You told me to get her people's *attention*. That's precisely what my men did."

"Did you not read your e-mail? New orders. Green light on *all*

175

of them."

"I didn't receive any e-mail! Something that important should've been a phone call. And who's in charge of this op, anyway?" CK asked.

"That's above your pay grade," Alvarez said. "I don't answer to you."

"I'm tired of the ping-pong routine," CK growled. "Why did you select me if you didn't believe I was capable?"

"Why not? You have no family. You're a loner. No one will miss you."

"What do you mean, *miss me*?"

"Nothing. Just finish it."

"Since I'm no longer on the inside, I have another plan," CK said.

"I don't want to hear a play-by-play. Let me know when it's done. Tie up loose ends in Lake Simi. Or else." With a crisp click, Alvarez disconnected.

CK's heart palpitated, and she wiped sweat from her brow. She dialed another number.

"Yes," Deputy Pane answered.

"Did you clean up this morning?"

"Look, I hung my ass out on a line. You said nothing about a drive by in my town," Pane said. "Church is all hands-on deck. My deputy took a picture of the SUV from one of the CCTV cameras and gave it to the Marshal. I'm done."

"We own you," CK said, "or have you forgotten about your gambling debt?"

"At this point, it'd be easier if I came clean," Pane said. "I'd rather be bankrupt … unless you'd be willing to triple your fee. I want my bookie paid and a little extra in my Christmas stocking."

"Done," she said through gnashed teeth. CK disconnected and called another number. "Are you still in Lake Sim—okay. New target. I'll text the address. But wait for my call. You need to make it look like suicide—don't worry, I'll handle that." CK ended the call and pulled out another burner.

"You want to play games with me, Pane? Everyone will know your dirty secrets," CK muttered, texting him.

Panic kicked in and a paralyzing thought entered CK's mind. If she didn't take care of business, she'd become the next target.

CHAPTER 63

IT WAS ALMOST one in the afternoon when we hit the road. We tidied up the house as much as we could and didn't want to leave it in chaos. Grandma was already on the phone with the rental company to have the repairs done. Due to lost time, we grabbed burritos and coffee at Lake Simi Café on our way out of town. Zuli was on duty, so I said goodbye and thanked her again for her help. I slipped her another fifty when she wasn't looking.

Sue and I drove with Simon, while Lily hitched a ride with Rayo and Kate. She told me she needed a nap. I wasn't happy and wanted her with me. But since we were caravanning, I had eyes on her the entire time. I watched Lake Simi disappear in the rear-view mirror. As quaint as the town was, my shoulders relaxed when we passed the *Come Back Soon* sign.

We stopped for gas a half-hour into the drive home and to let Sue out. I spotted a lady resembling Charly exiting the store. She didn't see me, but the second she turned to slide behind the wheel of her Jeep, I confirmed it was her.

In the crazy chain of events, I'd forgotten my suspicions about Charly.

Until now.

I fished my cell from my jeans' pocket and snapped a picture of her license plate. I walked to the Sprinter van.

"Rayo. I need you to run another plate for me, please." I peeked in the back. Lily had just woken. Phew, she hadn't seen Charly. And before I broke the news of her traitor friend, I wanted evidence. Strong, compelling evidence. Evidence that would leave no doubt and Lily would have no choice but to believe.

"Sure thing," Rayo said. "We don't have any reception. But the second we do, I'll let you know."

"Thanks," I said and returned to the truck.

"What was that about?" Simon asked.

"I just saw Charly and snapped her plate for Rayo."

"We'd been so busy with Mac that we never discussed her," Simon said as he pulled onto the highway toward Grandma's.

We were fifteen minutes outside of Missoula when my phone rang. Rayo. I answered on speaker.

"Get ready for this," Rayo said.

Simon and I glanced at each other.

"And?" I urged.

"First, the prints came back negative on our guy. Mac is not in any government database. He's a ghost."

"Makes sense. He disappeared like one too," I said. "Unless he's sleeping with the fishes." I snorted.

Simon shook his head and laughed.

"I ran the plate," Rayo said. "None other than Bee Line Industries."

"Not surprising," Simon said.

"What am I missing?" Lily chimed into the conversation.

"I'll explain later, Lily." I disconnected.

I sat with my mouth open, staring at nothing for a spell. "C … K … Charly Kane," I said. "That's why I recognized her voice."

"What?" Simon asked.

"The woman Mac had on speaker. I've got to call Gran," I said, dialing.

"Hello Granddaughter," she answered with a pep to her voice. "I was just about to phone you."

I told her about Charly and that she was the inside mole. And she must have been the one who entered Gran's property.

But why? Could she have planted explosives? Being CIA, God only knew what she was up to.

Grandma said she was going to have her place combed for explosive materials and hidden recording devices. We also agreed not to disclose Charly's real identity to Lily just yet. She'd been through so much. After we disconnected, my mind returned to Mac's interrogation and the special needle mark on the back of their ears.

I jerked toward Simon.

"What? I know that look."

"We need to return to Lake Simi," I said.

CHAPTER 64

"WHY?" SIMON INQUIRED.

"I'll explain shortly, but stop the truck and notify Kate," I said in a single breath as I dialed Moxy's number. "Hello, Moxy. I have a huge favor."

The favor was to see Gil's body. I knew he was being picked up today and crossed my fingers I wasn't too late. I requested Moxy leave a couple of syringes, tubes to collect blood, and disposable rubber gloves in the cold room where Gil was stored. She didn't question my odd request and told me she'd call back in five. Moxy's only demand was that we leave no trace of our presence. That meant also on Gil's body.

"Do I want to know why you asked to see Gil's body? You're not planning to do something stupid, are ya?" Simon prodded.

"Not planning, doing," I said. "But it's not stupid. You remember the injection mark Mac talked about? I checked behind Lily's ear last night, but the bathroom lighting was poor. It slipped my mind … until now."

"And you want to inspect Gil's body?" Simon put the Denali in Park.

Kate pulled up behind us.

I jumped out and hurried to the passenger side of the van. I leaned into the window. "Lily, can you ride with us?"

Lily nodded without questioning me. She was likely too spent to argue.

"Grandma requests your assistance," I said to Kate and Rayo. "She needs help cleaning her house of bugs. And not the crawly kind."

"Where are you going?" Rayo asked.

"Back to Lake Simi," I replied.

Lily shook her head. "No ... no, no, no." Terror filled her eyes.

"I'll explain. You'll be safe. I promise." I grabbed Lily's hand and led her back to Simon's truck.

Just then, my phone rang. It was Moxy. "Hi, Mo—perfect. Thank you. We'll be at the hospital in forty-fi—"

"Thirty," Simon said.

"Copy." Moxy disconnected.

"Hospital?" Lily said, sliding into the back. Sue greeted her with kisses and a chin nibble.

"I have to check your arm and ear marks once more before we take off," I told Lily.

"Huh?" Lily tilted her head like Sue does when she's trying to understand what I'm saying. "Rose, what are you looking for?" she asked, sticking her arm out and turning her head.

First, I inspected the needle mark from where Mac injected the heroin and then behind her ear from the other unknown drug. I snapped pictures and zoomed in.

"The mark at the back of your ear is rapidly disappearing. The one on your arm is slower, for some reason."

"That's odd because I bruise like a peach." Lily rubbed her ear and arm.

I returned to the front passenger seat and kept quiet about the heroin injection mark. I stared straight ahead and clenched my jaw as Simon floored it. I wanted with every inch of my soul to beat the crap out of Mac and Charly.

"Did you tell your gran?" Simon inquired. "Maybe she knows something. After all, Ch—uh, this CK person works for the agency." He looked at me with wide eyes. He was about to say Charly's name.

"Not yet. It is not like any drug injection I've ever seen. It's similar to the smallpox vaccine they gave us as kids. Only in the shape of a triangle."

"What?" Lily touched behind her ear again.

"Here," I handed her my cell.

"Why are we going back to Lake Simi?" Lily asked.

"I need to examine a dead body."

"Okay ... *Scully*. You care to tell me why?" Simon quipped.

"Scully?" I furrowed my brows,

"You know the show, *X-Files*?"

"Ahh," Lily and I said in tandem.

"If I'm Scully, then you're Mulder." I gave him a half-raspberry. "No. I'm serious. I have to check Gil's body."

"You really are," Lily said. "Why not wait for the autopsy?"

"I want to compare Gil's mark with yours and draw some blood. We'll want a sample of yours as well," I said. "Besides, we don't have time to wait for the postmortem exam."

But to put it in *X-Files* terms, the mark was an anomaly of sorts. And not like anything I'd seen. And what if the mystery drug dissipates in Gil's body, as quickly as the mark behind Lily's ear? We might already be too late.

"Won't they expedite it?" Lily asked.

"Moxy thinks they will do it tomorrow, but …" I sighed. What I couldn't say is that I didn't trust Charly not to play a fast one with Gil's body. She may have tampered with Lily's blood already. Why else would we cross paths at that gas station? There was nothing in between Lake Simi and Missoula. And Lily's blood sample was most likely at the state crime lab.

"But?" Lily urged.

"Um, it takes a minimum of sixty days for the final report." Simon filled in my gap.

"I can't be in limbo that long," Lily said. "I want this behind me."

"I'm sure they will rush it," I said, attempting to sound hopeful. But a pit opened in my gut. Toxicology reports take three to eight weeks.

We were silent the rest of the way back to Lake Simi.

CHAPTER 65

IT WAS TWO-FORTY-FIVE when we passed the *Welcome to Lake Simi* sign again. It was just like *Groundhog Day*. My phone buzzed; Moxy.

"Hurry, the coroner's office is twenty out."

"Please stall them," I plead.

"How do you expect me to do that?"

"Say you can't locate the paperwork or something," I said. "We're almost at the hospital."

After I hung up with Moxy, I froze. I was clueless about how to proceed. While I was no stranger to corpses, I was out of my element in examining one or knowing what else to look for. So, I did what any reasonable person would do. I called my half-sister, Kaylee Tubberious.

Kaylee finished medical school and was in a residency program in Jacksonville, Florida. Kaylee came into my life a couple of years ago. Although she was a recent addition to the family, albeit in a very unconventional way, we connected the instant we met. Saki felt the same about her. Neither Saki nor I held the prison affair of her mother and our father against her.

I picked up the phone and dialed, hoping she would be available.

"Hey sis, what's up?" Kaylee answered. I could tell she had a smile on her face, as always.

"I need your help." I gave her the condensed version.

Silence fell on the line. Then Kaylee started laughing. That was not the reaction I'd expected.

"You never cease to amaze me at how you end up in these

situations," Kaylee said.

"Let's not revisit Florida right now."

"I guess this is not the most disgusting thing you've ever done." Kaylee chuckled.

I assumed Kaylee was referring to when I *may* have robbed my grandparents' crypt looking for a key. But not before I got into a fight at a crappy motel with Titos. Kaylee ran to my aid and sutured my gunshot wound that had re-opened during the altercation. No questions.

"So, will ya help me?" I asked.

"Of course," Kaylee said. "I'm between shifts. Oh, and send me a picture of the mark behind Lily's ear."

"Thanks. I'll call you back in a minute." I disconnected, sent the picture, then stuffed the phone in my sweatshirt, camera facing outward.

Operation *Inspect Dead Body* was underway, and we all had tasks. Mine was to examine Gil, while Simon was the photographer. Lily's task was to stand, or in her case, sit guard and call me in the event we had unwelcome guests. And of course, keep Sue company.

Simon pulled around back and hid his truck behind the dumpster.

I looked at my team and we went to work.

CHAPTER 66

THE COLD ROOM for the corpses was attached to the ER in the back. As promised, Moxy had unlocked the room. She even threw in a couple of evidence bags. Being Lake Simi was a small town, there was only one body in the cold room. Gil was front and center, bagged and tagged, lying on a sterile metal table.

We slipped on our gloves and went to work. Simon unzipped the bag while I phoned Kaylee with my Bluetooth earbuds. Since no one was supposed to be in the room, we had to keep our voices low and conversation to a minimum.

Gil had one neat hole in his forehead, but two gunshot wounds to his upper right quadrant. It is also where the blood pooled. But what I immediately observed was that Gil's hands were turned inward and arms folded. His fists clenched. Odd position if he was shot.

Simon must've noticed it too. He pointed and looked at me.

I shook it off and found the needle mark; same spot as Lily's, behind the left ear. I showed Kaylee.

"You mentioned he died of a gunshot wound," Kaylee said.

"I believe so, as Lily is being accused of his murder. But look," I said, pointing to the mark.

"I wonder what kind of needle he used?" Kaylee asked. "And his body should not be absorbing it."

I thought it odd too, since dead people don't heal. "Yeah," I spoke in a low tone like a librarian.

"Scars from, say, for instance, the smallpox vaccine, form because of the body's natural healing process. When the skin is injured, the body rapidly responds to repairing the tissue,"

Kaylee said. "But … he's dead."

"Agreed, but no time for a lecture, sis," I said.

"Of course, sorry. I just find this fascinating," Kaylee said.

I continued pointing to Gil's body, where I wanted Simon to photograph. Gil had the same ligature marks on his wrists as Lily.

Per my late-night conversation with Lily, she remembered the familiar woman's voice, that I now knew was Charly, ordering Mac not to tighten the zip ties too much. And according to Mac, the crime scene needed to look like a drug party gone bad. Hence, the needle marks on both their forearms.

"I need to draw blood," I said. "But how the heck am I supposed to do that?"

The deceased have no blood pressure or beating heart to circulate the blood inside the body, therefore their veins are not viable. So, a simple needle poke to the arm wouldn't cut it. Not to mention, getting to his inner forearm was impossible.

"The subclavian vein," Kaylee and Simon said at once.

"English."

"It's the large paired, deep vein that extends along each side of the neck."

Simon pointed.

I should've had him conduct the exam. But I felt compelled to do it.

"Copy, I jab his neck."

Simon only heard my side of the conversation and jerked back with a scrunched face. *Jab* he mouthed and shook his head.

While I drew blood, Simon gestured to a fancy black smartwatch on Gil's left wrist. I'd seen those online. Among other things, the watch measures a person's heart rate. Maybe I should give one to Simon.

He then pointed to Gil's forearm. What little we could see because of the arm's position. "Same needle mark as Lily," he said in a soft voice.

I knew beyond doubt Lily did not use drugs, but I had no knowledge of Gil. Though if I had to bet money, I'd say he didn't either. Gil was a clean-cut, handsome man. I felt gut punched. Was anyone looking for him? Did his family know he went missing? Was he a John Doe? I knew the coroner would investigate. But what if their office was so busy, they couldn't get around to it for a while? So, I put it on my to do list, after clearing Lily.

"I want his fingerprints," I said while waiting for his blood to collect in the vial.

"I have an app," Simon replied without looking up from his inspection. He scrolled through his phone, looking for the application. Within a few minutes, he was done, and so was I.

Kaylee was still on the line with me when I finished collecting the blood.

"Can you scan the rest of the body?" Kaylee asked.

I obliged her request.

"Back to the cause of death," Kaylee said.

"Go on." I knew where Kaylee was going with this because Simon and I thought the same thing.

"He's not shielding his face, no shocked expression. His body is in a decorticate posture."

"English, again, sis."

"Look at his arms. He was grabbing his chest. His fists are clenched as if he went into cardiac arrest. Without examining him, I'd say the gunshot wound was postmortem," Kaylee said. "I'm speculating without reviewing all the evidence."

If I didn't know any better, I'd say she was interested in becoming a coroner.

"Agreed," I concurred. I'd seen the shocked expression on my friend Sue's face when I found her with a bullet wound to her head. Unlike Sue, Gil most likely did not see his death coming. Not to mention there was not much blood at the crime scene.

I halted Simon from zipping the bag and touched the watch. *Grab it*, I mouthed.

He wore a horrified expression and drew his head back and slowly shook it.

I rolled my eyes and covered the mouthpiece. "I don't want to steal it. We need to analyze it."

He nodded and delicately removed the watch from Gil's wrist.

I flipped the phone toward Kaylee. "You are the bomb si—"

"O.M.G. What the heck happened to you?" Kaylee put her hand to her mouth.

I shrugged. "Eh, long story. I will tell you la—"

A text from Moxy interrupted my video call. They were coming for the body.

"Gotta go. Love you, thanks," I said and disconnected.

Before we left the cold room, I snatched a couple of extra syringes, rubber tourniquet, and vials so Simon could draw Lily's blood.

CHAPTER 67

---◆---

JUST AS SIMON and I jumped into his truck, the coroner's van arrived.

"Too close for comfort," Lily said, leaning forward. "So, what did you find?"

I gave a thumbs up as I called Moxy. "Hi, can we meet—see you there."

"Where to now, Ms. Daisy?" Simon said.

"Our favorite café," I said.

"Are you going to tell me, Rose?" Lily asked in a huff.

"I'll tell you what Moxy can't hear." I turned in my seat and sat sideways. "As I suspected, you and Gil have the same mark on the backs of your ear."

Simon handed Lily his cell.

"What is it?" Lily asked, scrolling through the pictures.

"I do not know. Kaylee was also perplexed," I said. "The unexplained mark of unknown origin on the back of both of your ears." I picked up my phone and inspected the photo of Lily I took last night. "If I were to channel my inner conspiracy theorist, I'd say, CIA alien experiment." I snorted.

"Now who sounds like a nut? I'd say you were Mulder," Simon said.

I squinted at him. "Okay, maybe not alien. But I'm serious about it being a mad scientist experiment. Mac told us the serum came from the agency," I said. "Think about it. Lily's inability to remember. A scar like the smallpox vaccine that is rapidly disappearing from her ear." I fidgeted in my seat.

"Lily, you said you bruised and scarred easily. Yet your body is

189

absorbing and healing the injection site behind your ear. However, your arm is bruised. So, it is imperative Simon draw your blood just as soon as we stop before it completely vanishes from your body."

"Is that why you took Gil's blood?" Simon inquired in a more serious tone.

"Yeah," I replied. "I smell something nefarious."

The truck went silent for a spell. The only noise was Sue snoring.

"Why are we meeting with Moxy?" Lily asked, most likely changing the topic.

"She confided in us earlier about Pane. Now it's our turn. Not to mention, Gil may have died of a heart attack," I said. "And Gil's watch measures heart rates."

"What are you thinking, Rose?" Simon inquired.

"I will ask Rayo to pull up his vitals. I want to see if his heart stopped beating before or after the witnesses heard the gunshots. My guess is before."

"I concur. Which means Gil died from a heart attack. Not the gunshot," Simon said.

"Oh my gosh." Lily turned white and put her hand to her mouth.

I snatched the phone away from her. "You shouldn't have seen that." I studied the mark again. "This is ... wrong."

"That's okay. I ... I'm all right," Lily said with a slow nod.

"And Kaylee also thinks the gunshot wound was postmortem. The coroner should discover that," I said.

"You said it could take weeks." Lily groaned. "I want to be finished with this!"

"If our assumptions are correct," I said, "then the evidence for the prosecution is not looking good."

"What if Mac poisoned *me*?" Lily said. "What if that drug will cause long-lasting effects? Or that I will die of a heart attack ... like Gil. This is a nightmare."

I looked at Simon. I hadn't thought of that.

"Lily, do you remember anything else?" I urged, watching her in my visor mirror.

"It's slowly returning to me," Lily said, sucking back a strangled sob.

Sue laid her head on Lily's lap.

"All right … I'm sorry. There are many unanswered questions. Like why you hired Gil. Or how you found him. Nala will ask the same," I said.

"She interviewed me when Lillian picked me up from jail," Lily said. "I could punch that SOB Mac in the face. You should have let me take a shot at him." Lily's neck reddened, and her fingers balled in a tight fist. "Hell, he wouldn't have known what hit him since you gave him that truth serum."

"Okay, anger works," I said, staring straight ahead. "That's it." I spun around again.

"It's too late to punch him, Rose," Lily said with a half-hearted chuckle.

"No, hypnosis," I said. "You have repressed memories. I'll meet you both in the café when you're done with Lily's blood draw."

I dialed Grandma just as Simon pulled up to the Lake Simi Café. Sue and I jumped out while Simon went to work.

CHAPTER 68

◆

GRANDMA LIL SAID we'd discuss the whole hypnosis thing when I saw her. She changed the topic and informed me we were headed for a field trip to Salmon the next day. Lily had an appointment with a hand specialist to prove she couldn't have shot Gil with her left hand.

Since Salmon was in Idaho, Nala moved to amend the bond conditions so Lily could travel out of state for her appointment. Lily had no criminal record and was a low flight risk. Grandma vouched for her. It went a long way with the judge. Nonetheless, the prosecutor was displeased.

I also told Grandma that Gil most likely died of a heart attack. I opted not to say anything about the GPS watch or my mad scientist CIA conspiracy theory. That fun fact would have to wait until I saw her in person. Phones have ears.

After my conversation, I put Sue's service vest on her, and we walked into the restaurant. The Lake Simi Café was filled with tourists and locals alike. I looked around and spotted Moxy, Simon, and Lily tucked away at a table in the back. There was a different waitress at our table. Our quirky new friend-accomplice, Zuli, was tending bar in the casino.

Moxy leaned forward, hands folded on the table. "What did you find out?" she asked in a business-like, serious tone.

I showed her the pictures of Gil's hand balled up, clutching his chest.

She stared with an open mouth as she scrolled through Simon's photos. "I didn't inspect the body before a certain someone—" she rolled her eyes "—redirected me to take witness statements,"

Moxy said. "The autopsy should prove the gunshot was postmortem. Just based on the body's response to the bullet when it entered Gil." She turned to Lily. "You'd possibly face misdemeanor abuse of a corpse as a lesser charge. Or even attempted murder, since you didn't know he was dead. I'd—"

"I did *not* shoot him," Lily yelled and pounded her fist on the table.

The café went quiet as patrons stopped conversations, all eyes fixed on our table.

"The gun was in my left hand," Lily growled through gritted teeth.

"How are you aware of this?" Moxy leaned back with arms crossed, brows furrowed.

"I uh …" Lily looked at me for help.

"Moxy, you don't want to know," I said.

"It was you all who broke into the marshal's office. You saw the report … didn't you?" she sternly asked.

I gazed at the ceiling.

"You are correct, I don't want to know." Moxy kicked her chair out from behind her and rose from the table. "As a matter of fact, you never showed me those pictures. I was never here." She spun and then flipped back to us. "When I take the stand in court, I'm going to tell the truth."

I stood too. "I'm sorry, Moxy. It was not my intention to put you in this position." I looked back at the table. "This is a major FUBAR."

"You can say that again," Simon said and sipped his coffee.

I wasn't going to reveal to Moxy that we took Gil's GPS watch, or that it may be part of a rogue CIA operation. That would send her into more of a tizzy. And then it hit me. If we found anything on the smartwatch, we couldn't use it in Lily's defense.

"I'll be in touch," Moxy said. As soon as she turned around, she received a phone call. "Yes. I see. I'll meet you at the house." Moxy disconnected, glanced over her shoulder, and nodded for us to join her.

Simon threw cash on the table for his coffee, and we exited.

Moxy was staring at the ground, hands on hips. She looked back at me. "It just gets better." She drew a deep breath with a tear in her eye. "Pane ate his gun."

"What?" I said, jerking my head toward her.

"It's all I know," Moxy said. "I don't have to ask you to keep it quiet."

"Absolutely," I said. "I'm sorry. If there's anything we can do." I placed my hand on her shoulder. While we all thought Pane was a jerk, we didn't wish him dead.

"I will," Moxy said and jetted for her vehicle that was parked curbside. She spun on her heels and returned. "Look, I'm not in favor of vigilantism or whatever you all are doing … but I understand in this case. You do what you gotta do."

"We're not vigilantes, just concerned about getting justice for Lily." I sighed. "And Moxy, it goes deep and dark. I don't have to tell you to be careful."

She nodded and silently walked to her vehicle.

We, too, were quiet as we skulked back to the truck.

As I slipped into the passenger side, I broke the silence. "Suicide or murder to look like suicide?"

"The latter," Simon responded.

"And by what Moxy told us, Pane was treading in the deep end of the pool. I didn't realize he was drowning," I said.

"Now the coroner will have her hands full," Lily said. "Is it selfish that I want her to deal with my case first?"

"Not at all," I said. "And we know they're connected."

CHAPTER 69

$\blacklozenge$

"LOOSE ENDS ARE tied up in Simi," CK said.

"And the target?" Alvarez asked.

A hush fell over the line.

"Don't make me ask twice."

"Working on it," CK snapped. "Since Mac's gone, I'll need to rely on the men who handled our problem."

"Did your men stage it as a suicide?"

"Affirmative. I was there."

"I thought you were dealing with the body."

"I can't be in two places at once! I went to the city assuming Gil's body was at the crime lab. But there was a delay." CK rubbed her face.

"Unacceptable," Alvarez barked. "You should've known about the *delay*."

"Well, I didn't, *Agent Alvarez*." CK paused. "My men called and said Pane was home early. We didn't expect him until tonight. So, I rushed over, and we made entry into the rear."

"And you're certain no one saw you enter? What about cameras?"

"I don't appreciate the accusations. It's not my first op."

"So, you say."

CK rolled her neck. *Take a deep breath. Don't piss her off.* "Of course, we took care of the CCTVs. My men scrambled the only camera that was aimed at his home. When we entered, the target was two sheets to the wind. He was growing a conscience. Pane had the cell phone in his hand. He told us he was going to turn himself in to the Marshal and was done playing games. I texted him earlier from my burner about what he did. My guys held the gun to his head, but he pulled the trigger."

"You're colder than I gave you credit. Now finish the rest and disappear for a while," Alvarez said.

CK deliberated. Was Alvarez going to facilitate CK's disappearance too after she eliminated the targets? As she ended the call, CK received a text message from a number she didn't recognize.

Hi Charly, it's Lily. This is a burner. Sorry I've been MIA. I'm out of jail, we're on the way home. We are headed out of state tomorrow.

"Can this get any easier?" CK muttered as she replied. Okay, put on your concerned friend's face. CK, a.k.a. Charly Kane, did not have real friends, so it posed a challenge. CK looked up and considered before she responded. *I was so worried about you. Glad you are free. Where are you going? I thought you were not allowed to leave the state.*

Lily: *Long story. Dr appt. When this is over, let's get together. And thanks for visiting me in jail.*

CK: *You ok?*

Lily: *I'm fine. It's for my case.*

Out of state? Doctor's appointment? Where? Washington? Idaho? Were they flying or driving? One more text shouldn't hurt, because that's what *friends* do, right?

CK: *How are you getting there?* CK held her breath, waiting for the reply. Did she go too far in her questions?

Lily: *Driving my new Bronco to Salmon (smiley face). We have a rental on the river. Who knows, I may sneak in a hike.*

The conversation bubbles appeared quicker than CK could reply.

Lily: *I shouldn't have told you.*

CK: *My lips are sealed. One more thing, don't let Rose know we texted. Don't think she likes me.*

Lily: *She will adore you when she gets to know you. Gotta go. See you soon.*

CK knew Lily loved hiking. She almost felt bad for betraying her. But it was business, and having personal feelings during an op was dangerous. She shook it off. And then it hit her. What if it was a trap?

A chance she had to take.

Now to set the final stage in her operation. In her intel of Lillian, CK knew there would be extra security detail, so she needed a chopper. She bit the bullet and called Alvarez one more time.

"Yes," Alvarez answered sternly.

"I need a chopper," Charly said. "A four-seater."

"This job is costing more than expected. Why?"

CK explained.

"She's going to Salmon. But you don't know where? How the hell do you plan on tracking them? She'll have an entourage!"

"I've got it." CK couldn't reveal that the plan relied on Lily driving her own car. "So, am I getting a chopper or not?"

"Fine, it will be waiting at the Hamilton Airport tomorrow morning."

Click. Alvarez was gone again.

CHAPTER 70

◆

WE STOPPED IN Missoula to fuel the truck. Since none of us had an appetite, except for Sue, we opted for a drive-thru. Sue knew the drill and was drooling. She would get a double burger, minus the bun and condiments. We each got a single and drove off, picking at our food.

It was a few minutes past eight when we arrived at Grandma Lil's. Simon punched in the security code, but we were denied access.

I called Grandma. "Are we on the no-fly list?"

Grandma laughed and opened the gates.

As we arrived at the house, Rayo and the dogs patrolled the perimeter. He had his tablet in his hands and a device I recalled being a bug detector.

Sue jumped out of the Denali and bolted for her buddies. All three were in dog mode. Sue loved those two; they were her big brothers. I used the term "big" loosely. Brian and Stevo had a combined weight of 180 pounds.

The second I stepped inside the house, it was as if a tornado ripped through. Grandma had furniture pulled away from the walls, pictures too. Even cardboard containers were on the counter from a restaurant in Darby. Now this was serious. Grandma Lil preferred homemade food over takeout.

"What can I do?" I asked, dropping my duffle bag in the entry.

"You mean, *we*, do," Lily said as she entered behind me.

"Lily," Grandma Lil said, "Nala has more questions for you. She's in the upstairs office. If you're up to it."

198

"Absolutely," Lily replied.

"Rosie, can you and Simon return the furniture to its proper place?"

"Of course," I responded.

"Wait, Rosebud, I forgot your ribs," Grandma said. "On second thought, Simon can do that. Let's have that chat." She inclined her head to the door leading downstairs.

"I got this, Grandma." I smiled. "It only hurts when I breathe."

I never let a fractured bone stop me. I wasn't going to now. I'd done much worse with a gunshot wound or two.

Simon stepped in front of me. "No, Rose."

I stood with my arms crossed and squinted. I wasn't a damsel in distress and didn't need him telling me what to do, unless we were training, or I was in danger. Neither of those circumstances applied at the moment.

Simon chuckled and said, "Don't use that tone with me."

I guess my face was talking again. "Okay, *brother*," I said, surrendering.

He gave me a side hug and looked down at me. "You are a stubborn little sister. Have I told you that today?" He kissed the top of my head.

I chuckled. The last person to call me stubborn was James, my old teammate, best male friend, and now brother-in-law and father to my niece.

Simon went to work, while Grandma and I headed downstairs to her war-room-James-Bond-com center. Since she was in the middle of debugging her house, the door was open. I hadn't visited in a few months, but everything was the same. The room was the size of her main floor, but on steroids, minus the kitchen. It was your average guest quarters, complete with a soft brown leather sofa sleeper, two matching recliners, coffee table, dining table, powder room. And don't get me started on her flat screens. There were four, seventy-five-inch-high-definition smart TVs.

The televisions took up the entire north side of the wall. A long L-shaped modular workstation covered the south side. She'd equipped it with one desktop computer, three laptops, a Ham radio, and a land line telephone. Grandma had five closed circuit television monitors for the surveillance cameras that surrounded her property. Since the recent security breach, everything was being updated and cleaned.

Grandma always had a secretive nature to her. Growing up, my mother told us she was a clerk for the State Department. Then I discovered she was an officer. She served thirty-two years. Most of the time overseas. She and my grandpa were what they called a CIA tandem couple.

Although she'd retired, Grandma kept her finger on the pulse and stayed well connected. She even put together the black ops team when the cartel kidnapped my father. I believe she posed a threat in certain circles. She was certainly still respected.

We plopped on the couch, and I showed her the suspicious needle marks behind Gil's and Lily's ears.

She stared straight ahead. "Delete those pictures."

CHAPTER 71

---◆---

"ARE YOU KIDDING?" I bolted to my feet.

Grandma looked up at me. "You know how I promised no more secrets after you found the truth about your father."

"Yeah. Even the truth sounds like a lie," I said. "First, I thought he died in federal prison, then I discovered he, too, was a spy." I paced.

Grandma followed me with her eyes. "Asset. Theodore was an asset."

"Same thing in my book." I stopped and stared. "This information is important to clear Lily, or have you forgotten?" I raised my voice again louder than I expected. I didn't mean to yell at my grandma, but this was not okay.

"Rose Reagan." Grandma jumped to her feet. "Don't use that tone with me."

"O'Brien, remember. We had to forget the Reagan name," I said, my eyes fixed on the floor.

"*I* am still a Reagan," Grandma snapped and threw a thumb to her chest.

"You didn't move around safe houses when you were seven, relocating every few months until the trial was over," I said with my fists on my hips, moving my head like a sassy toddler. "I have been O'Brien since I was eight when a US Marshal with WITSEC instructed us to pretend our past didn't exist!" I drew a deep breath and resumed my tirade. "Mom had to threaten to opt out of federal protection if they didn't allow us to take her maiden name."

"I thought you were over that."

"I *am*," I bellowed, and plopped back on the couch. "I'm just looking for answers and the truth, for once."

"Rosie," she said, joining me. "Sometimes the truth needs to stay hidden. At least for now." Grandma's voice shook. "But it's bigger than me ... than us."

"Mac informed us *they* worked for the agency." I enlarged the picture of the puncture marks again to show her. "If you ask me, it looks like a crazy CIA experiment."

Grandma lifted her eyes to me. "You need to leave this alone, Rose!" She stood again, staring a hole through me. "I mean it." Grandma held her hand out. "Now, where are the vials of blood?"

"In my bag," I said with pursed lips, pointing upstairs.

Heat rose to my brain cells. I was feeling betrayed by my grandmother. So, the whole exam of Gil's body was a colossal waste of time? I pondered, glaring straight ahead.

Grandma went silent too. I'd never seen this side of her, and it was scary. If my calm, cool grandma was now enraged by what we discovered, it could only mean one thing.

"Are we in danger?" I asked, my anger turned to concern.

"Yes ... we are."

I dropped my head in my hand. "So, the heightened security is more than just about—" I lowered my voice— "Charly getting in?"

She nodded.

"Gran, how big is this?"

"Grand Canyon size," Grandma replied.

"Do we have enough security to drive to Salmon tomorrow?"

"I have more people. You won't see them, but they will be there."

"How long will we be on DEFCON 1?"

Grandma shrugged.

"You can't tell me that either?"

"I'm sorry. But you must unsee those marks."

I sighed. "So do a few others."

"I know you don't like to fib, but you'll have to tell them it was nothing."

"I was hoping this would help in Lily's defense."

"Don't worry. Nala is the best. And given the evidence about Gil possibly having a heart attack, not to mention Lily's right handedness. She should be okay."

"So, I'm thinking hypnosis is a bad idea?" I asked.

"The therapist might uncover something that could put Lily in more danger," Grandma responded.

"I hate secrets." I threw my head back.

"I promise, when it's safe, I will tell you *everything*."

Just then, Simon announced to us he was done and going to the guest house for the night. With Griz still out of town, Simon stayed in his and Rayo's quarters.

I stood and looked at my watch. The time read ten o'clock, and I too was ready for bed. Mental and physical exhaustion will do that.

Grandma and I headed upstairs. She turned. "Oh, your attorney called *me*. He's firing you if you don't call him back."

"Fine." I remained downstairs and returned his call. I was relieved when it went straight to voicemail. I left a brief message apologizing for the delay and saying I'd call again in the morning.

I peered up the stairs to keep an eye out for Grandma and pulled Gil's GPS watch out of my pocket. I examined it. I had a feeling it held much more information than just his heart rate.

Like Grandma said, some secrets are okay.

CHAPTER 72

◆

THE SUNRISE HAD amazing shades of red, orange, and blue. The sky resembled a canvas where an artist's paint can was thrown to see where the colors would land. They don't call Montana "Big Sky" for nothing.

Since Sue came into my life, sleeping in was a thing of the past. But I wouldn't change it for the world. Sue owned me. I stood on Grandma's back deck and watched her romp around the fenced acre with her boys. Dogs live in the present. They don't fret about things to come or ponder the past. If only we did the same.

I considered that as I replayed last night in my brain. Grandma was terrified about the marks we found on Lily and Gil. I'd never seen her more worried. And those three words, "bigger than us" echoed through my mind. Something told me I would not get the answers this trip, but I would eventually.

At the moment, getting Lily cleared of these heinous charges was my number one priority. Not to mention protecting her. It was in my nature, as Grandma had said.

"Dare I ask what's going on upstairs?" Lily inquired as she crept up behind me. "I know that look." She chuckled and handed me my favorite morning beverage, chai latte, with a shot of espresso.

"Thanks." I took the mug, warming my hands around it. "I was just thinking of you, my friend."

She gave me a weak smile.

"I'll do everything in my power to clear you," I vowed. "If it's the last thing I do."

"I wish I had the same assurance as you." Lily sipped her

coffee. "So, do you think this … drug or whatever he injected into me was part of a CIA experiment?"

My heart sank. Ugh. I had to tell yet another lie. The CIA may have trained Grandma to lie for "the greater good." Mental eye roll. But I was not proficient at it. I felt an ulcer developing. I just shrugged.

"I don't think it will help your case to bring it up. We must prove you didn't murder Gil." I guess that wasn't fibbing. It was the truth.

"Yesterday you were convinced the marks were important," Lily said and drew her head back.

"Um … Grandma thinks it's best if we go in a different direction," I said, looking at the ground. If I made eye contact with my BFF, she'd know I was less than honest.

"Rose, whatever Mac gave me, my memory is hazy. How can it *not* be a part of my defense?" she said, plopping on an Adirondack chair. Lily motioned for me to join her.

I sat. "I … I'm not sure," I said. "We need to trust Nala to build a solid case. And having an independent evaluation aside from your doctor to prove that you couldn't fire the gun. Not to mention the whole heart attack defense."

"We can't use Mac's confession?"

"It would be considered coercion. And he's disappeared," I said. "Not to mention they will ask how we got it. The SP-117 is our dirty little secret."

"A house of cards, Rose." Lily shook her head. "So, was all that for kicks? You know, getting his confession."

"Quite the opposite. We have identified who the enemy works for." I peeked over my shoulder. "And we must keep it under wraps."

"With the family?"

"Kind of. It's for the 'greater good'." I air quoted.

"Is that some agency mumbo jumbo?" Lily asked.

"You know how I pay attention to orders," I said. "We will get to the truth. You have my word."

"I know, Rose."

"Remember, you saw nothing, and neither did I," I said with raised brows.

"Copy that." She looked away.

"Besides, I don't want to scare off Rayo. He's too new to our crazy circle. We must ease him into it." I said, giving Lily a side bump with my shoulder.

"And Olive being shot was not a proper initiation? Not to mention watching you fall from the sky, with a broken parachute," Lily said with a laugh.

"Oh yeah, I forgot about that." I snorted, stroking my bruised face.

"What are you two laughing about?" Rayo asked, joining us on the deck.

Lily and I shared a look and chuckled. "Nothing," we responded at once.

Our moment of joviality made everything bad disappear.

Too bad it was only for a millisecond.

CHAPTER 73

IT WAS CLOSE to nine when we finished consuming Grandma's famous veggie omelet, then cleaned up. It was a joint affair. Just like a genuine family. We went to our rooms and emerged with overnight bags in hand. I had limited wardrobe choices because I was only scheduled to be in Montana for two weeks.

Simon and Rayo stepped inside the main house and announced they, too, were ready to hit the road. Sue came out with her stuffed Snoopy puppy in her mouth. It was the first toy she'd probably ever had, and I bought it for her when I decided to keep her. I gave a chuckle.

Her buddies had to stay behind with their K-9 caregiver, a vetted, trusted friend of Grandma's.

We were caravanning up to Salmon. Kate, Simon, and Rayo were driving in Simon's Denali. Grandma and Nala were taking Gran's two-seater 69' Corvette. I stopped asking how Grandma could afford her fancy vehicles. She told me a few years ago she invested wisely, and I learned not to press her too hard. Olive was going to meet up with us after her assignment, wherever that was.

As for Lily, she was itching to drive her new Bronco. I think it made her feel as if all was normal and good in her world. I, being the overprotective friend, insisted on accompanying her. She started calling me her bodyguard. I was fine with that since on some level I was. Not to mention we were at DEFCON 1.

The seven of us had a meeting of the minds in Grandma's living room. By now, everyone knew we needed to keep an eye out for anything or anyone suspicious.

"Here are burner phones and the address of the rental,"

Grandma said, handing them out. "Leave your personal cells. Each vehicle will have a satellite phone when we lose cell service up the mountain." Grandma commanded the room. I felt as if I were in a briefing before hitting a house. I missed the adrenaline rush.

"The rental is on the river, with two beds per room. You all choose who to bunk with, but I get my own." Grandma flashed a cheeky smile.

"Since my appointment is tomorrow, can we go on a hike?" Lily asked. "I love that canyon in the west. It's an easy trek." She looked at me. "If your ribs could handle it."

"Is that a challenge?" I said to Lily, scanning her. She was dressed for a wilderness adventure. Her attire was straight out of an L. L. Bean catalogue. I smiled.

"That's fine. I'll make sure your security detail is aware," Grandma said.

"Wait a minute," Simon interrupted. "I'm capable of providing protection."

Grandma and I shared a look. Not everyone was privy to our conversation last night.

"Just a precaution," Grandma explained. "We don't know where Mac is or how far this goes."

"You make it sound like the whole agency is after us," Kate chimed in.

Grandma stared at me with wide eyes. By her face, she must've thought I spilled the beans.

I shrugged.

"Jeez. I'm kidding guys," Kate said.

I breathed a sigh of relief.

CHAPTER 74

SUE WAS ALREADY in the back of Lily's Bronco and wore a wide puppy grin. At least that's what I saw.

Lily was behind the wheel, smiling too as she read from a note. I jumped in and she quickly stuffed the yellow sheet of paper into the front pocket of her long sleeve hiking shirt.

"What's that?" I asked.

"Oh ... um, nothing. Just a note to me ... uh, from myself."

I knew Lily enough to know when she was telling a tall story. I chose not to push the issue and let it go. Maybe she did have a guy on the side.

The time on the dash read ten when we made it down the hill to Darby.

"According to my calculations, we should be in Salmon by eleven thirty, twelve at the latest."

"Perfect. I'm really looking forward to our hike," Lily said, pressing the control buttons on the steering wheel, trying to find a station. "We have satellite radio." She beamed.

Why was she so excited? I thought. Most vehicles come standard with it nowadays.

Lily found a classic rock channel and began head banging and shimming her shoulders to AC/DC.

I couldn't be a downer, but I needed to ask serious questions. No better time than the present. So, I ripped off the Band-Aid.

"I need to know something," I said, lowering the volume and shifting in my seat to face her. "Why did you hire Gil?"

Lily stared ahead and didn't speak for a spell. She finally reached in her back seat and pulled out a letter from her backpack and handed it to me.

"Lily, I can't read this," I said. "It's from your mom." I dared not mention Charly had possession of the envelope when Grandma and I busted her in Lily's room.

"That's okay," Lily said. "I found the envelope on my bed. I'm not sure how it got there. I was certain I put it in my drawer." She shook her head. "I'm more messed up than I realized. Anyway, it will explain things." She stroked a locket that hung from her neck.

The necklace was new. I'd have to ask her about it later. But my attention was on the letter. I knew how it got on her bed. Charly was snooping in her room, but so were we. It was for the greater good. Sheesh, I'm even thinking like Grandma. I read it and my mouth dropped.

"Your father was undergoing mandatory pilot stress testing?"

"I guess something they made pilots do, it's standard," she said with a shrug.

"Your mom said he was experiencing sudden mood changes, trance-like states, and at one point got up in the middle of the night and disappeared." I dropped the paper in my lap and stared ahead. Was this what Grandma was hiding?

I returned to the paper. "Upon his return a few hours later, he had no memory of where he went. She confronted him and they decided he was going to back out of the testing."

"Yeah, not too soon after, they flew to the Alps on a mini holiday, but their plane crashed. NTSB blamed pilot error," Lily said. "My dad was the best damn pilot!" She hit the steering wheel.

"Oh my gosh, Lily."

"My mother never mailed the letter. It was in a box of family keepsakes that arrived after I returned from Lake Tahoe last year."

"So, you hired Gil to do some digging?" I asked. "But … how did you find him?"

"Underground chat room," Lily replied. "I started searching CIA mind experiments. Boy, did a lot of bizarre things pop up, you know, alien abduction stuff. Real *X-Files* like. Most of it, I ignored. And then one day I received a private message from a man only known as G. He said he was a PI." Lily scratched her head. "But given that they murdered him, I think he was in the CIA. He knew too much, Rose."

"Agreed." I nodded. "But that stays in this car for now."

Grandma knew he worked for the CIA, hence her fear. I pondered. "Since we're sharing letters," I said and reached in the back seat, pulling out the one from Gil. I handed it to her. "I'm sorry. We had to read it. We needed clues."

"That's okay." She smiled and patted my hand. "It must've slipped out of my jacket pocket at the motel. I'm glad you found it and not the cops when they searched the room."

"Yeah, you know *who* searched it," I said with an eye roll. "Pane was only interested in finding evidence to implicate you."

"And that's why Pane killed himself?" Lily asked.

"My guess is murder," I said.

"I feel awful." Lily sucked back a sob. "Two men murdered. If I'd just let things go, none of this would've happened."

"If it's any consolation, I would've done the same thing."

"I know, Rose." Lily nodded, caressing her locket again.

"Where did you get that? It's pretty."

"It showed up in the mail. I think from your grandma."

That didn't sound like anything my gran would do. She enjoyed gifting in person.

CHAPTER 75

CK SAT ON the tarmac at the Salmon Airport when her phone buzzed. She jumped as she answered.

"Status?" Alvarez barked.

"On track," CK replied. "I'm waiting for my team."

"What's the game plan?"

That was the problem. This was the first time CK did not have a proper ops plan. But she couldn't admit that to Alvarez. It would only work if Lily and the others were out in the open. Attacking the rental house was not possible.

"I've got it handled," CK replied and put her phone on speaker. "And since when do you want a play-by-play?"

"This is a delicate situation. I don't need to tell you that my ass and yours are on the line."

"I'm aware of that. But there's more than one target." CK scrolled through her iPhone and located the satellite radio app and signed into it. CK had access that wasn't available to the public. She found Lily's location. They were still at the rental. CK rubbed her sternum and popped more antacid.

And then a paralyzing thought entered her mind. What if they changed their minds? CK looked to the heavens. Not a cloud in the sky. It was a perfect seventy-two degrees, with a light breeze out of the south. There was neither a head nor a tail wind. If it was perfect flying conditions, it would be even better hiking weather. CK was convinced Lily would not miss the opportunity.

"CK, are you there?" Alvarez snapped.

And that's when CK refreshed her app. She exhaled the breath she'd been holding when Lily's location changed.

"I'm here, but I've gotta go."

"Keep me posted." Alvarez disconnected.

With a clearer mind, CK planned her attack. She pulled up Google Earth. From a tactical standpoint, eliminating the targets should be a breeze. A couple of passes through and she and her men should have no problem taking them all out.

CK knew for certain that on the ground would be Simon, former Army Special Forces. His reputation preceded him. A gun battle was imminent, and lives would be lost. While taking out another brother did not sit well with CK, she had orders. And she refused to let her emotions cloud her judgement.

CK grew up in the foster system and aged out of it, joining the army at eighteen. She never knew a family. The closest she came were her military brothers and sisters. She began dating one soldier and envisioned marrying and having children. But he died in her arms in Afghanistan. She too sustained life-threating injuries.

From that point on, CK refused to get that close to anyone. It's a known fact that in this line of work, no one had a *real* relationship. And any interactions forged during assignments were insincere and superficial, at best. This was no exception.

Simon was not CK's only challenge. There was Lily's best friend, Rose. What little CK knew of her, one thing was certain: she would be with Lily, protecting her. Rose would take a bullet for her loved ones. She'd heard one story of how Rose, while seriously wounded, slid down an embankment in the Florida Keys, peppering a crocodile to save her partner from its jowls.

CK admired Rose's grit and brutal honesty and if they were not on opposite ends of this, she could see working with her. Perhaps in a parallel universe they could even hang out.

But not this one. No, Rose was a job. She would have to go, too.

CK's two men arrived.

She returned to the mission and went to work.

CHAPTER 76

IT WAS 1 P.M. when we pulled up to the hiking trail. Grandma and Nala did not join us. Nala had a case to prepare, and Grandma was meeting Olive in Salmon for lunch. We planned to meet at the rental around six for a cookout. And given it was on the Salmon River, Rayo brought his pole to catch a fish or two, hoping to feed his friends. But he changed his mind when we piled into our vehicles. Especially since his crush, Kate, was going. He confided in me that his brain knew he did not stand a chance, but his heart begged to disagree. He took a fancy to Olive and Kate. Young love. Or was it lust? At his age, God only knew.

We packed snacks and water in our backpacks for our seven-mile trek. The canyon was on the west side and wide open for miles. We basked in the sun's warmth, the birds chirping, and even my throbbing ribs felt better. It was the perfect spring day in the low seventies. For a moment, the terrible events of the past few days were forgotten.

Even Sue had a serious case of the zoomies.

Simon and Rayo walked ahead, chatting about the military and guns. Kate stayed back with me and Lily. Lily linked her arm in mine, and we touched heads. Although Lily and I were not blood related, she was my sister none the less. There was nothing I wouldn't do for her. She reciprocated.

"Rose." Lily addressed me. "Have I thanked you?"

"Stop," I scoffed.

Lily halted and stood in front of me. "I'm serious. I don't know what I would've done without you." She looked behind her at the guys. "And everyone else. I am blessed to have you *all* in my life."

Lily gave me and Kate a warm embrace.

"Don't be too girly," I said. "Let's not get mushy on such a pretty day."

"You're right. You suck," Lily roared. "You all suck!" she yelled through her cupped palms, her voice echoed through the canyon.

The guys, who were now two hundred feet from us, stopped. They turned and threw their hands into the air. They obviously did not share our jovial mood. Most likely they thought she was referring to them in the "you suck" comment.

Just then I heard, *chuff, chuff, chuff* in the distance. I smiled as I assumed it was Grandma's eye in the sky, our flying bodyguards. I was about to notify Gran that her men arrived, but my burner had no reception. And Simon had the satellite phone.

The chopper drew closer, and I waved my hands at them. An ease fell over me for a split second.

Sue did not agree. Her hackles were on end. She let out a low growl.

"It's okay, sweet girl, they're on our team," I said.

No sooner did those words pass my lips than the black whirly bird buzzed. I thought that was rude since the helicopter's rotor downwash pounded us. We threw up our arms to shield ourselves from the swirling sand.

"What the hell?" I bellowed and flailed my arms.

They pulled up and headed toward the guys, doing the same thing. I couldn't see the passengers or the pilot. I yanked my phone from my hiking leggings. Damn. I forgot, no cell service.

Just as Simon and Rayo turned to head back in our direction, the chopper reappeared from the south. This was too surreal and familiar.

CHAPTER 77

THE HELICOPTER, WITH two men holding AK-47s, one on each side, was headed straight towards us. The last time a whirly bird attacked me, I was in a fast-moving vehicle in the Nevada desert. Our assailants must've used suppressors because the zinging and whizzing were muffled as the bullets kicked up dirt beneath our feet. We were in a dust whirlpool again.

The chopper buzzed us as if it were a falcon hunting its prey. It was just like a slow-motion movie. I glanced to my right and saw the only place to seek shelter. A small rock alcove. My instincts thrust into overdrive.

"Take cover!" I howled as I snatched Lily by her shirt collar, yanking her off the ground. Sue grabbed hold of Lily's hiking pant leg with her teeth and pulled it. If we weren't being made into Swiss cheese, I'd have been proud of my brave service dog. But I feared our attackers would hit her. So, I yelled for Sue to go, and pointed to the cave. She obeyed my command and scampered away, a look of terror in her sweet, big brown eyes as she looked back.

I would've also seized Kate, but since she was ex-military, her training kicked in. We must've seen the cave at the same time because she tugged on the other side of Lily, and we all bolted to safety. Kate and I were in saving-Lily mode. After all, she was the target. At least, we'd always believed that. But I didn't have time to pursue that thought.

I ordered Lily to move as far away from the opening as possible. Sue joined her.

I drew my pistol from my backpack and peered out. Kate

followed suit. We watched as the guys dove to the ground with their hands over their heads. The chopper circled for another pass. Crap.

"Hurry," I yelled and waved my arms for Simon and Rayo. They took the brief absence of the helicopter and bolted toward us.

Simon had his gun out and retreated into the cave, yelling for Rayo to follow suit.

"Is everyone okay?" I hollered with my eyes to the sky, waiting for the returning irate falcon as I covered the guys. There was no response. I turned and my stomach tightened. In all the commotion, I didn't hear Lily scream.

Lily was wincing, clutching her right leg.

"Shit, Lily's shot." Simon hurried to her.

"No!" I bolted to Lily and dropped to her side.

Simon was in full-blown medic mode. He shrugged out of his backpack and flung it on the ground. He'd equipped it with a suture and burn kit, gauze, bandages, tourniquets, quick clot, antibacterial numbing spray, and scissors. With steady hands, he went to work.

"What can I do?" Rayo asked.

"Call for help," Simon and I responded at the same time.

"On it," Rayo said, grabbed the satellite phone from Simon's pack, and dialed.

"Lily, stay with me," Simon uttered.

"I'm trying … it hurts so bad!" Lily cried.

The *chuff, chuff, chuff* of the chopper in the distance returned.

CHAPTER 78

◆

I REJOINED KATE at the cave's entrance and braced for a butt whooping. Our handguns were no match for our assailants' high-powered firearms. I only had two extra fifteen round magazines, as did Kate. Simon had a 10mm, with only thirty-seven total rounds. None of us were prepared for a gun battle of this nature.

"The bullet hit the soft tissue in her upper outer thigh and went clear through," Simon said, applying pressure.

"Is that good?" Lily whimpered.

"Yes!" Simon, Kate, and I said at once.

"You're going to be okay, Lily," Simon spoke in a reassuring, low tone.

"I don't know," Lily shrieked, "it hurts so bad!"

"Repeat after me. You are going to be okay," Simon said.

"I am going to be okay," Lily responded with a shaky voice.

I would've turned around to help my friend but had to prepare for our attackers' return. I couldn't feel more helpless.

"Hello ... hello," Rayo shouted into the phone. He plugged one ear with his finger as he paced the cavern. Most likely looking for reception. "Rose, I have to get closer to the opening. The boulders are blocking my signal."

"Hurry, they're coming back," I said with my gun pointed out.

Rayo rushed to me. "Lillian ... Lillian ... can you hear me?" Rayo shouted. "We are under attack. We need help."

"Grandma," I bellowed into the receiver as Rayo held it to my mouth. "A chopper has fired upon us with AKs. Two shooters, one pilot. They're returning. Lily has been hit. We only have a little over ninety rounds."

Rayo took the phone back as he listened to what Grandma was saying. "Okay … okay." Rayo's voice crackled, and he disconnected. "Help is on its way. Her men have chopper problems. I am sending her our coordinates riight now," Rayo said.

"Good job, bud," I said. "You ever shoot a gun?"

"Uh … yeah," Rayo replied with a nervous laugh. "But only at the range."

"Take mine. It's only a nine mil. I have two extra mags in my pack," I said, removing my backpack. I bolted to Simon and pulled his gun from his chest rig. I observed as he calmly applied a four-by-four gauze in the front and back, wrapping Lily's leg.

"Ouch, that's tight." Lily grimaced.

"It has to be," I said, snatching Simon's mags from his hip holster. I flashed a reassuring look at my wounded friend. She gave a feeble smile back.

"I don't understand how they found us." I shook my head as I returned to the cave's opening. "No cell phones to track. Gran had the vehicles swept. Our sat phone is secure. No other means of tracking."

"Can satellite radio be tracked?" Lily asked with a wince.

"It can be," Simon said. "Why do you ask?"

"I'm sorry," Lily said in a weak, sad tone. "This *is* my fault."

"Huh?" I asked without looking back.

I heard the rustling of paper.

"Lily, you need to keep still," Simon said.

"I don't know how or why she would do it," Lily said.

"Who? What?" Simon asked.

"Charly," Lily said.

Simon and I shot a quick look at one another.

I returned to the incoming chopper that was ascending on our location.

"She gave me satellite radio as a birthday present," Lily said. "She left me a note on my steering wheel. I texted her we were coming to Salmon. I didn't see any harm in it."

"Shiit," I shouted as the bullets hit the outside of the cavern. I was fixed on the bad guys; no time to focus on what I was hearing. The heat rose to my face and my jaw tightened. I would've preferred to punch the witch out and go toe to toe with her, but instead we were exchanging gunfire.

The three of us aimed at the chopper returning rapid fire at its occupants. Ducking as they peppered us. From my vantage point, I could see the pilot was a female with long raven wavy hair. Charly. I remembered Grandma telling me she was a pilot.

"Ouch. It burns!" Rayo shrieked and immediately clenched his left arm.

I assumed the ejecting hot brass from our pistols hit Rayo.

It happens.

CHAPTER 79

BEING UNDER FIRE seemed like an eternity. No sooner were all our mags empty than the chopper retreated again. The cave was silent except for Rayo's moans. I glanced at him; he was teetering on his heels and his face was white as a sheet. With his arm still clutched, Rayo dropped to his knees.

Crap, I was wrong. Flying hot brass would not cause that reaction. Even in a newbie.

"Quick Kate, help me with him," I said, dragging him back.

Simon finished treating Lily and crawled over to us, bag in tow.

I ripped Rayo's shirt sleeve, exposing a small gash.

"It's okay, only grazed." Simon applied pressure.

"Yo—you mean, I've been shot?" he wailed. I could see panic in his frightened gaze.

"Welcome to the team. You get used to it," I said.

"Not helping, Rose." Simon worked his magic on Rayo.

Rayo looked me in the eyes and then at my arm. "Um, you have a little blood on your shirt, too."

No sooner did the words pass Rayo's lips when Sue crawled out from the back of the cave. She was on me, drenching me with kisses, whimpering. She was profusely licking me. And that's when I felt a searing pain. I looked at my pink, breathable shirt; it was now crimson colored.

"It's okay, girl," I said with a wince, and grabbed my left arm. I rolled up my torn sleeve and snatched a wad of gauze from Simon's bag.

"Jeezo, Rose." Simon shook his head. "James was right. You are stubborn. Can you help her, Kate?"

221

"Meh." I shrugged. "A mere flesh wound, too. We'll be okay, Rayo." I plopped next to him.

The rest of my crew let out a collective gasp. Mine was a tad more than a flesh wound. Still, nothing a few butterfly sutures wouldn't remedy.

"Don't worry," I said. "I've had worse wounds than this." It was the truth. "It's been a few months since anyone shot at me." I snorted.

Simon crawled over to me. "I thought I was crazy," he said, winking as he sprayed antibacterial numbing spray on my arm.

"Oh my gosh, Rose," Lily uttered. "I'm so sorry."

"Lily, stop beating up yourself," I said. "You didn't realize Charly wasn't on your team. I didn't want to say anything, but I had my suspicions."

"We had our suspicions," Simon declared. "You had so much going on and didn't need to know the truth … just yet."

"I wish you'd all quit treating me like a child." Lily pounded the dirt with her fist.

"Um, not to interrupt, but I'm cold." Rayo's voice shook as his lids drooped. "And it's dark in here."

"Rayo, you're cold because you're in shock." I caressed his arm. "And it's dark because your eyes are shut," I said. "Open them."

Rayo's eyes popped open. "Oh. I … I've never been shot," he said, looking at the ground.

I slunk over and showed him my wound. "See, we're all going to be fine. I promise."

Rayo turned white again, and his head lolled to the side. Lights out Rayo.

I scrunched my face. "Sorry, was my gore too much?"

The second Rayo passed out, the satellite phone dinged with an incoming call. It was Grandma. I answered on speaker. "I sure hope your men are on their way."

"They left—min—more chop—prob—"

"You're cutting out, Gran." The phone was not getting good reception. But I surmised her men had more chopper problems than they thought. I bit my lip. Did Charly have anything to do with that?

"Is ever—al—" Grandma said.

"Fine." I flinched as Simon applied Steri-Strips.

"You were hit too, huh Rosie?" Grandma's words were distinct.

"Grazed. I'm good." The moment I uttered it, the chuffing of the chopper's blades echoed in our dwelling. "They're back, Gran."

I held my breath and braced for another attack.

This time, we were sitting ducks.

CHAPTER 80

"TALK TO ME," Alvarez snapped into the phone as she paced a hole in the floor of her undisclosed location.

"Seriously? I'm busy here," CK roared over the helicopter's rotors. "I'm a man down and you want a freakin' update?"

"Casualties?" Alvarez asked.

"No, but one is bleeding like a stuck pig. I'm going to make another pass. Call you later."

The instant Alvarez disconnected with CK; her phone buzzed. Unknown number.

"Yes," Alvarez answered.

"Back down ... now," a husky voiced male growled from the other end of the line.

"Whatever are you referring?" Alvarez said.

"Do not be coy with me ... Agent Alvarez."

"You are not my superior, Agent *H*." Alvarez raised a brow.

"Correct. You do not work for me," Agent H said. "But I am still *a* superior. I've been thinking. Your eagerness to take this assignment raised suspicion."

"What are you talking about?"

"They assigned Agent Raley to Gil. But, according to what I've been told, you all but threatened him to take over," Agent H said. "And ..."

"And?" Alvarez shrugged as if he could see her.

"And then you went dark, taking Agent Charly Kane with you. We never gave you a green light on Lily Cazier, or the others. You were ordered to extract information from Ms. Cazier and, as a last resort, take her out. Gil Fox was the only one on the kill list. He was a traitor. And that got me thinking. This was personal. So, I dug even deeper. It appears you failed to disclose to the agency who your uncle was and what he did for a living. You said he was a tobacco farmer. That couldn't be further from the truth. Could it?"

"I guess it slipped my mind."

"Did it also slip your mind when you neglected to inform anyone that your uncle appeared in federal court?"

Silence fell on the line.

"One Stanley James Albrecht Cordova. A high-ranking cartel member sentenced to life in federal prison." Agent H exhaled. "You took it personal. And what is one thing they teach you at the Farm?"

"Personal feelings are a liability." Blah, blah, blah.

"Don't get me started on using agency resources for personal gain."

Alvarez sighed. "It's Teddy and Max's fault."

"But since Max was dead and Teddy, a.k.a. the Ghost, couldn't be found, you went after Teddy's daughter, Rose, and anyone close to her. Why?"

"Why? Why? I was supposed to inherit my uncle's money. Why does Rose get to sail the world and live happily ever freakin' after while my family and I suffer?" Alvarez shouted. Her Spanish accent grew thick. "It's too late."

"It's not too late. It is over," Agent H said in a calm manner.

"It's not over until I say so."

"I don't understand why now. You had her a couple of months ago."

Alvarez groaned.

"That's right. I know you got yourself assigned to her security detail in Alaska. If I were to bet, I'd say you had something to do with the bounty on her head," Agent H said. "You spread the rumor your uncle put the hit on her. But it was you. And with all the dirty money he socked away, you had the financial means to pay."

The line grew quiet for a moment. Alvarez refused to admit her criminal uncle left her cash the Feds knew nothing about. But how did Agent H?

"Correct. I had her a few months ago. That was the plan. Every safe house she was in had well-trained, heavily armed agents surrounding Rose. I knew she would grow tired of running," Alvarez said. "So, I came up with another strategy. Which worked to my advantage. What better way to get to someone than through their loved ones?"

"I am ordering you to cease at once."

"What if I don't? Are you going to make *me* disappear?"

The line went still again.

Alvarez snarled and disconnected and dialed CK.

"Stand down."

"Are you kidding me, Alvarez?"

"Do I sound like I'm joking?"

"This is just a chess game, and we are merely pawns," CK said.

"Game over … move on," Alvarez snapped.

"Copy. Send a clean-up crew for your chopper."

"Not my chopper, not my problem anymore." Alvarez disconnected.

CHAPTER 81

THE APPROACHING HELICOPTER sounded more *womp womp* and less a chuffing noise. I peeked my head out from under the rock overhang and that's when I spotted the cavalry. Charly and her band of merry men were nowhere around. Perhaps we kicked their butts, and they retreated.

"That is a sight for sore eyes." Simon waved to the advancing bird. "We need to take Lily and Rayo to the hospital." He looked at my left arm. "And you, too."

"Pfft. I'm fine," I said.

"What*ever*, Rose," Simon said. "I'm serious."

"I am too," I snapped. "No hospitals. The cops will be called for gunshot wounds."

Simon stared at me with a tight jaw. I waited for the ass chewing that didn't come. He knew I was right.

Lily moaned.

"Okay, her and Rayo." I threw a thumb back. "Make up a good story of how they were shot."

"I'm okay," Rayo interjected.

"If you're certain, Rayo," I said. "We'll leave Lily's vehicle and—" I turned to Simon— "your truck for now. We don't know when and if our friends will be returning."

Simon snapped a look at me.

"Hey, it's too far to hike down the hill ... for any of us," I said. "I promise we'll pick up your baby tonight. And we need to take Lily's Bronco to the sheriff's department and leave it there until we get the satellite radio cancelled."

Simon nodded in agreement.

227

"Hey, I appreciate your first aid skills today." I looked at my feet. "I also must apologize for being brusque with you lately."

"Apology accepted." Simon smiled. "I know I've been starving you and training you hard. But it paid off." He nodded to my wound. "No better way to test your skills than in real-life situations."

"Ha! I've had plenty of that. And did you pay Charly to shoot the bejeezus out of us?" I snorted.

"Music to my ears, Rose," Lily faintly said as Kate held her up by her waist.

Simon grabbed the other side of Lily as the helicopter landed. We welcomed the whirling dust and debris this time.

A few minutes later, we arrived at the Salmon Airport where Grandma was waiting in her Corvette and Olive in her BMW.

Since Simon double checked my and Rayo's injuries, he agreed a hospital wasn't necessary for us. Lily, on the other hand, needed a tetanus shot, antibiotics and pain meds. Maybe more. So, Simon whisked her off in Gran's vehicle to the ER. She was in excellent hands with him. I smiled at what a handsome couple they'd make.

Grandma Lil stood there, tilting her head, likely thinking the same thing.

"Should we thank you for calling off the dogs?" I asked.

She shrugged. "Wasn't me."

"If not you, then who?" I probed. "Is this related to our discussion in the war room?"

She peered around and yanked my elbow. "I told you to never *ever* talk about it," Grandma said through gritted teeth. "And you must convince Lily to drop the other thing."

I crossed my arms. "Wait a minute. She wants to know what happened to her folks." I looked away and returned a glare to Grandma. "I never dropped searching for the truth about my family."

"And look where it got you? You and your father almost died!" Tears welled in her eyes.

"At least I found him and the real story. But this is different. Lily's parents are both dead. If she wants to pursue it, I am going to help her," I sassed in my most defiant tone.

"I told you. You must stop. It's for the—"

"Greater good, I know. How about a greater cause ... the truth for once."

"Rosie." Her voice softened. I melted when she called me that. That's what Mother used to call me. "I promised you. When it is safe to do so. For now, it is not. And you must take Lily back to Florida with you."

"I was thinking the same thing. She won't be much help to you until she makes a full recovery," I said. "I know she is one of your top ranch hands."

Gran shook her head. "And with what she's been through, she needs serious R&R. No better place than safe with you and your security detail."

Grandma wrapped her arm around my waist as we made our way back to Olive's vehicle. "So, have you considered your calling?" She chuckled.

"I don't want to take over your black ops or whatever it is you do." I rolled my eyes.

"I've reconsidered," Grandma said. "I was thinking of a bodyguard." She smiled. "You'd be dynamite. You're a natural."

"Ha. They're protection agents. First, we need to get Lily's legal problems handled."

But a thought occurred. Why did Grandma change her mind about me not taking over for her?

Her secrets ran deep.

CHAPTER 82

IT WAS SEVEN when Lily and Simon arrived at Grandma Lil's river-front rental. Lily was on crutches, and Simon hovered, practically carrying her into the house.

"Will you stop!" Lily groused with a scowl and a wince.

When they entered, Grandma and I had just finished cleaning up our Chinese takeout as Gran's grand plan for a cookout had tanked. We stopped what we were doing and stared with open mouths.

"I can take care of myself. I've fallen off many horses and my motorcycle. I can deal with this!"

Simon shook his head and threw his hands up, murmuring something inaudible, and stomped into the living room, leaving Lily to fend for herself. I could've sworn "stubborn, damned woman" came out of his mouth. But that was just a hunch.

Lily was never snippy or cruel. She almost ran after Simon, hopping on one foot.

"Simon," she yelled. "Stop. I'm sorry." She eased next to him.

Grandma and I shared a wide-eyed, raised eyebrow look and leaned in, eavesdropping.

It's not every day we were witness to a lover's spat.

"I didn't mean to say those things. I appreciate everything you've done for me today. Heck, all this week." Lily's head swayed and her eyes rolled back.

"It's okay." Simon kissed her forehead. He opened a small white paper sack and pulled out a pill bottle. "Ready for your drugs?" he said in a soft tone. "You need to keep ahead of the pain. The shot the hospital gave you will wear off soon."

Grandma and I grinned at each other. They were closer than we thought.

Lily opened her palm and Simon handed her a large white tablet. "I know you've been through a lot," he said and placed a bottled water on the couch next to her.

"Exactly! I put everyone in danger because of … what?" She rolled the pill in her hand. "I wish I'd never met Gil. I mean, I am sorry he's dead. Again, because of my involvement. I'm not any closer to the truth. It died with him." Her bottom lip quivered. "I don't even have the flash drive. That shitbird took it."

I had just taken a drink of water and spit it out. Lily never swore. But I agreed with her on this one.

Lily grabbed her crutches and pulled herself to a stand. The pill dropped to the floor. She scanned the house. "This is where I would go to my room … but I'm not sure where that is," she whimpered and collapsed back on the couch.

My heart ached as I dashed over and embraced her.

Simon picked up her medication and glanced at me with a concerned expression.

I remained silent and just rocked my broken friend.

Lily pulled away and wiped her face on her sleeve. "I'm okay, Rose." She gave me a weak smile. Her big brown eyes, which were normally full of life, were droopy and red.

"I love you, sister," I said.

"I know you do. I love you too," she whispered.

"Did you kids eat?" Grandma entered the living room, leaned behind Lily, and hugged her.

"We did," Simon replied, handing Lily another pill.

"Fish and chips," Simon shared a chuckle with Lily.

"What did we miss?" I inquired.

"With the meds, Lily kept saying 'fis and chis'," Simon responded and grinned at her.

Lily turned the color of a ripe tomato, lowered her gaze, and took her medication.

So, I wasn't imagining it. Lily returned Simon's affection.

Lily struggled to stand again. "I'm gonna turn in. I know I stink and need a shower, but I go night night," she said and swayed. I grabbed her arm and Simon took her other. This time Lily allowed it. "Tanks," she garbled.

Simon and I walked Lily back to the bedroom that she and I

would share.

"So, what story did you give the hospital about the gunshot wound?" I asked.

Lily's head lolled, and she slurred with a grin. "Poacchers." She giggled.

"Oh, boy. She's out of it." I looked at Simon. "Did they buy it? You know, since it was an AK47 bullet that tore through her leg?"

Simon shrugged. "They didn't go any further with the questions. The cops never showed."

"He sharmed the pants off the nurses," Lily chuckled again.

"Alrighty then," I said.

"Lily, do you need help changing? Or washing up?" Simon asked.

Lily blushed once more when she looked at him.

Simon, being the gentleman, just smiled his Gomer Pyle grin and refrained from speaking. But I knew what he was thinking.

"I defer this to you, Rose," he finally spoke.

"Good idea," I said.

"Oh, and thanks for picking up my truck. I'll check on your and Rayo's wounds." He nodded to my arm.

"I already did. Everything is fine. Your mad first aid skills did the job on both of us." I gave him a genuine smile as we entered the room. We eased Lily onto the bed closest to the door. Her eyes shut the second her head hit the pillow.

I watched her pass out. "Those are strong meds."

Sue jumped up with the grace of a gazelle and nestled next to Lily. Although Sue was my girl and slept with me, Lily needed her more tonight. I drew the blanket over them and kissed her and Sue goodnight.

CHAPTER 83

◆

I RETURNED TO the living room, and Rayo nodded for me to join him on the couch. His computer sat on his lap.

"I pulled up the vitals that were on Gil's watch, like you requested." He smiled. "And you were right," he said, sliding the screen to me. Rayo had both the police report and Gil's vitals on the screen. "Gil's heart stopped beating at eight thirty. Witnesses heard gunshots at eight-fifty. So, Gil was dead for twenty minutes when he was shot."

"I figured as much. Thanks. You are the man," I whispered. "Let's keep this between us, for now."

Rayo nodded and closed his screen. A wide, cheeky grin fell across his face that I could only interpret as being proud.

"Let's join the others. We've earned a little R&R," I said.

Rayo and I headed to the back porch where Grandma, Simon, Kate, and Olive were sitting. As for Nala, she was at the dining room table, thumping away at her laptop. I assume working on Lily's case. They didn't call her The Pit for nothing.

The second I opened the sliding screen and stepped outside, I caught a whiff of the warming fire Grandma was stoking in the outdoor brick hearth. I zipped up my sweatshirt and pulled the hood over my head. The back porch light was off, and the stars shone brightly. Not a cloud in the sky.

A glass of red wine waited on the table, screaming my name. I plopped on the lounge chair opposite Simon. His eyes were closed, and his mouth open.

I drew a deep breath, took a long sip, and set down the glass. I joined my exhausted friend and shut my eyes, listening to the flowing river sing a gentle song. That and the popping and crackling of the firewood provided the perfect lullaby.

Just as my body drifted to Never-Never land, the screen door flung opened, slamming against the hinge. I popped my eyes wide, grabbed my pistol from my hip holster, and jumped to my feet. I had a palpitation in my throat. Simon also bolted to his feet with his gun in hand. We both were evidently still on DEFCON 1 and kept our pistols close.

"Holy cow!" Nala stood with her palms towards us like a traffic cop. "Easy. It's just me," she said. "That stupid screen door needs adjustment."

I lowered my shoulders and re-holstered my pistol. Simon mirrored me.

"Do you guys always pack ... and in sync, no less? Don't answer." She inclined her head toward the house. "Join me. I have news."

Just as my heart rate returned to normal, those five words spiked my blood pressure higher. What was she going to share? Was it good? Or did I need to pack up Lily and hide her out in another country? Preferably one without an extradition treaty. After all, I had the means.

We obliged Nala's request, and she motioned for us to sit. I stood in the event I needed a quick exit. Not to mention, my stomach was now doing jumping jacks.

Nala sat on a chair and turned her computer screen around to show us an e-mail she'd received.

I leaned over, about to combust at what I read. "Hell no," I shouted. "This is unacceptable. Lily is *not* taking a plea deal for something she did not do! They framed her." I slammed the back of the chair.

"I believe you, Rose," Nala said looking over her Gucci computer glasses. "The prosecutor knows Lily is going to the hand specialist tomorrow. Furthermore, with you all being ambushed today, it suggests third-party involvement."

"You cannot let them know we've been targeted," Grandma said. "It opens a can of worms that we need to keep closed."

"Exactly. Not to mention Gil died from a heart attack. The shot was postmortem. And we have a taped confession of the shithead who pulled the trigger!" I spoke without thinking. I gazed at Kate,

Grandma, Simon, and Olive. They looked at me with bulging eyes and wide mouths.

I can only assume they were thinking the same thing. Hell, I was too. I considered putting myself in the corner on time-out. Preferably with an entire bottle of red.

Rayo's head reared back and his jaw dropped. His face spoke loud and clear. Obviously confused at the contradiction from what I said to him moments ago.

So much for keeping the watch a secret.

CHAPTER 84

CK DUMPED HER wounded gunman off at the Steele Memorial Hospital's helipad in Salmon. She failed to get clearance or notify anyone she was dropping off a patient.

Not her problem. "It's on him to explain his gunshot," she murmured as she lifted off, returning to Montana.

Thirty-five minutes later, CK arrived at the Ravalli County Airport and ditched the chopper, retrieving her Jeep. She waited until cover of darkness to return to her downtown Hamilton rental to collect what little personal items she had. She'd been on this assignment long enough to have a safe installed in the floorboard. And since Alvarez rented it under the shell company she created, CK didn't care if the owners discovered it.

CK sat outside the house, her head on a swivel, and her nerves on high alert. Trust no one was not only a cliché, but the hard truth in her line of work.

Trust no one. Especially Agent Cora Alvarez. She was the most difficult handler CK had ever had. Alvarez's management skills needed serious improvement, as she didn't commit to a single decision during this entire operation.

Who did Alvarez answer to? Did they know CK was under her supervision or did the powers that be at Langley ask, "Agent Charly Kane, a.k.a. CK, who?" Did the agency think CK went dark and off grid or just rogue? Suddenly, her phone buzzed. She jumped.

An unknown number.

"Yes," CK answered curtly as she flipped her head in every direction. Had the person on the other end of the line been watching her? And calling to toy with her psyche? Because that's what she would do.

"The bluebird sings in the morning," a male with a husky voice said.

"Not if it's dead," CK replied.

"Agent Charly Kane?" the gentleman inquired.

"Who is this?" she asked, peering through her night vision binoculars at every vehicle parked at the curb. She looked at roof tops, heck, even a tree outside her rental.

"Agent H. I'm from the agency," the man said.

CK remained silent.

"Are you there?" Agent H questioned with a stern tone.

"Look … Agent H, I don't know who you are," CK said as she reclined in her seat, waiting for flying bullets.

"Understood. Alvarez was not a stable handler. The agency did not sanction your recent assignment," Agent H said. "Alvarez had one job. Eliminate target G. She went off book with the other hits on the O'Brien woman, her friends and family. And if you don't follow *my* orders, you will be regarded rogue, too. Am I clear?"

Agent H made sense. That's why Alvarez was so indecisive.

"Yes. Yes, sir," CK said.

"Alvarez was on a personal crusade. And you know what happens."

"Operatives get killed," CK replied. "So, was I just a throwaway?"

"The agency does not consider you expendable," Agent H said. "But Alvarez does. She is unhinged. Do you need an extraction?"

"Negative. I have this handled." CK wasn't ready to trust Agent H until she walked through the doors at Langley. Even then she learned to be mindful of who she trusted.

"Take the rest of the week to clear your head. Report Monday morning. You'll have a new assignment."

The instant CK hung up the phone, her stomach burned. She pulled out the Tums and took a handful. She couldn't shake the feeling Alvarez was going to exterminate her, too. After all, Agent Alvarez hand-picked CK for this mission because she had nothing to lose.

Those five words Alvarez told her, "No one would miss you," seared into her frontal lobe as if with a branding iron. Everyone

was disposable, like a dirty diaper.
  Another half hour went by. All still quiet.
  She was probably clear to enter her rental.

CHAPTER 85

◆

THE INSTANT CK entered the two-bedroom, one bath home, the hair on her nape stood on end like a dog's hackles. The room was dark, but she spotted a man's silhouette sitting on her living room couch. He had his feet on the coffee table.

"Damn, if I'd known you were this hot, I would've insisted on meeting you in person." A familiar male's gruff voice sounded as he turned on the lamp next to him. "It's 'bout time you got here." When his face illuminated, CK spotted the gun in Mac's hand.

"I see how it'll play out. You kill me?" CK surreptitiously eased behind her and pulled a pistol from the low of her back and leveled it at Mac. "Or better yet, I kill you."

"Something like that," Mac said with a snarl as he jumped to his feet. "Here, I thought we were friends. And then you put a hit on me."

"That was Alvarez's doing. I was ordered to have you stay another ni—wait. How did you find me?"

"Have you forgotten why you hired me?" Mac replied.

"I guess not." CK sighed. Then she spotted the red dot on Mac's chest. She snapped a look at the wall mirror behind him and saw another on her. Center mass.

Mac must've seen the dot too. The scene played out in slow motion. They dove to the floor at once. The front windows in the living room shattered as her rental became a John Wick movie. Lamps exploded, and the fillings from the cushions and pillows sailed through the air.

Mac rolled on top of CK as if he was shielding her. "Shit," he shouted with a wince.

"What the hell?" CK bellowed as she tossed Mac off her. "You came to kill me and now you're saving me?" She let out a low growl as she threw her arms over her head. Although their attackers used suppressors, CK could hear the bullets as they zinged past her.

"Maid service is here," CK shouted.

"Yeah, these cleaners don't leave mints on your pillow," Mac replied in kind.

"Damn Alvarez must've hired em'!" CK crawled quickly to her bedroom. She yanked out a black go-bag from under her bed and scurried on her hands and knees to the closet. "Who knows how many snipers." She yanked back the carpet, exposing the safe. She pressed her face to a screen, unlocking it with an iris scanner.

CK dumped the contents into her bag. US and Australian passports. A New York driver's license. Five burner phones, and enough cash to last a few months. After CK emptied the safe, she smashed the scanner with the butt of her gun. She couldn't risk leaving any identification. Fingerprints were easily altered, but not the iris.

Just as she cleaned out the safe, the gunfire ceased. It went eerily silent. Crap. It meant only one thing. They were making entry into the house to check if they'd neutralized their targets. CK rolled back over to the bed and snatched the sawed-off shotgun she'd hidden under her mattress.

"Mac, what other weapons do you have?"

"This is it." He drew a pistol from his ankle. He held a gun in each hand.

"Not enough firepower," CK said. "I have an AR in my— disregard, it's in my vehicle."

"Sorry, didn't think to bring my freakin' Uzi." Mac scoffed.

No sooner had he spoke when two men entered from the rear and two from the front.

"Been nice knowing ya," Mac said.

"You cover the front. I've got the back," she ordered.

She aimed and fired, getting hitman number one in the head. Guy two dove to the floor, but she got him in the chest. CK ranked second in her class overall at The Farm a.k.a. Camp Peary, but she excelled at firearms training and could take any weapon apart, blindfolded.

Mac emptied his magazines on the two assailants who came through the front door. The room went quiet except for CK and Mac's labored breathing. Then came the sirens wailing in the distance.

CHAPTER 86

◆

NALA REMOVED HER glasses like Clark Kent before he turned into Superman. Only there were no fancy costumes or bad guys to tackle, except for me.

"Care to enlighten me?" Nala slowly rose and leaned over, fists on the table. "How do you know this? What or who is your source?" Nala was in full-blown federal prosecutor, pit bull mode. "*I* don't even have the coroner's report yet," she said as her temples pulsed. Although Nala did not yell, I swore I heard her teeth grinding. I imagined how dynamite she would be in a courtroom.

I stood for a spell, unable to speak. Okay, the cat was not only out of the bag, but the kitty was in Florida, drinking a margarita on *my* yacht by now. As I looked around for my friends' help, I didn't find any. They all left the room, leaving me alone with The Pit and my outburst. Time to come clean with her.

I let out a heavy sigh. "Please have a seat. And I will tell you the truth," I said. "I'll understand if you recuse yourself from the case after hearing it. I just ask you to refer us to an attorney as good as you." I gave her a fake toothy smile, hoping to douse the fire I saw in her eyes.

Given Nala's blank stare, she was not amused and stood on the other side of the table, arms crossed.

I sat and nodded for Nala to do the same. Nala looked around the room, succumbing to my charm, and joined me.

I told her the partial truth from the beginning. I spouted out *my* "discussion" with Mac, leaving out the SP-117. Only that we liquored him up. I spilled the beans on my inspection of Gil's body, including Kaylee's presumptive determination that he died of a heart attack. And Gil's fancy GPS watch that showed his time of death. Which did not correspond with the time witnesses heard gunshots.

In my confession, I refused to incriminate any of my friends as accomplices and used "my," "me," and "I" statements. Per Grandma's warning, I omitted the marks on the backs of their ears. I also didn't see how that was relevant at the moment.

I figured my last revelation blew the prosecution out of the water when I told her that Deputy Marshal Pane offed himself because he was tampering with evidence. Again, I refused to throw Moxy under the bus as my source.

Nala stared at me with a tight smile. "This is all great, Rose. And quite impressive. I could use your PI skills." Her grin faded and eyes narrowed. "*However*, I need proof that I can present in a courtroom." Nala folded her hands on the table. "I must obtain the coroner's report establishing the cause and time of death. The GPS watch. The taped confession and the man you call Mac in the flesh. The prosecuting attorney can argue that anyone could've made that confession. They want a live body to cross-examine and hang for a man's murder.

"Not to mention an alcohol-induced confession will not hold up in court. The prosecutor is likely to say it was coerced. The confession is not a product of the suspect's free choice. And you said he had no memory of it? How?" Nala did not come up for air during the tirade, and her face and neck were flushed scarlet.

I mirrored Nala and stared at her. "This is precisely why I didn't tell you about any of this." I rose. "I apologize if this takes away your defense. Again, I will understand if you need to recuse yourself. I cannot stand up in court and give away my sources and how I got my intel. This is on me."

Simon, Olive, Kate, and Rayo returned to the dining room and stood on either side of me.

"It's on all of us," Simon said.

Grandma was in the living room, reclining. "Count me in too." She raised her hand.

CHAPTER 87

THE SIRENS DREW closer. While the assassins used suppressors, the sound of CK's shotgun and Mac's handguns undoubtedly sounded the alarms. Although gunshots were a common occurrence in Montana's mountains, they were not permitted within city limits.

"Let's roll," CK said as she started for the front door. "My guess is my vehicle has a tracker. Are you certain no one followed you?"

"Positive. I stole a car," Mac said. "Late model. No GPS."

"That works. Where's it parked?" She held her shotgun at her side and slung her duffle bag over her shoulder. "We gotta hurry. If they don't check in, their replacements will be here —"

Crap. Alvarez probably had her rental house bugged. CK drew Mac toward her and whispered in his ear. "I've got an insect problem," she said with an eye roll.

Mac nodded to the door, and they quickly left through the back, passing over a dead body. They escaped into the alley and dashed a block and a half in silence.

"The cops will be here in—" The first patrol vehicle flew by them, red and blues flashing, sirens blaring.

"Car's over there." Mac pointed as they turned the corner.

More police cruisers descended on the sleepy street. They swarmed like flies on a carcass.

CK yanked Mac back into the alley and ducked behind a dumpster.

"Crap," Mac yelped.

CK saw blood dripping from his arm. "How bad is it? Will you slow us?"

"Gee, thanks for your concern. And no," Mac responded. "I've got a med kit." He motioned at the Honda parked curbside a few feet away.

"When did you steal this vehicle?"

"In Simi, last night." Mac opened the driver's door, clicked a button and unlocked the passenger side.

"Need new wheels." CK looked at her watch. "It's only nine. When they find the bodies, a manhunt will be under way. And since my neighbors have seen me, they will circulate my descriptors." CK placed her bag and shotgun in the back seat and dropped into the car.

"Don't you have people at Langley to clean up or contain it, or whatever freakin' term you use?" Mac put the car in gear and pulled away from the curb.

"Negative. Nobody I trust yet." Or was there? She considered. "We need a place to lie low. There's a hotel off the highway."

She directed him to the rundown hotel a few blocks away. After he'd parked, she spoke again. "You secure us two rooms. We can rent vehicles tomorrow. Don't forget to ditch the car tonight."

"What's this *we* crap? And don't bark orders at me!" Mac said. "I'm getting far away from you, sister."

"Suit yourself." She exited the Honda. "But they won't stop until we both are toes up or the hits called off. And there's more where those guys came from. I've got a plan for getting the bounty off my head." CK spun on her heels and headed to the small office.

"Wait, wait, wait," Mac said as he caught up to CK. "What about *my* hit? You owe me. I just saved your ass."

"By jumping on me? You call that saving my ass? I'd say it was an accident you took that bullet," CK snarled as she squeezed Mac's bleeding bicep.

Mac yanked his arm away. "Fine! How do you plan on doing that?"

"I know a woman with connections," CK said with a smirk.

CHAPTER 88

———————◆———————

AFTER TOSSING AND turning all night, I woke at five-thirty the next morning. I stared at the ceiling and berated myself for last night's faux pas. As soon as I threw the pillow over my head to block out my blunder, I heard a bang against my bedroom door. Sue flew towards me and landed on the bed.

"Hey girl," I cooed. I closed my eyes as she cleaned my face. "I see you're not mad at me for having diarrhea of the mouth last night."

"I'm not either," a faint voice came from the threshold. It was Lily. She hobbled in on her crutches and eased next to me.

"Oh, you heard," I said, squeezing the pillow over my face again.

"Sue and I have been up a while talking to your gran. She told me," Lily said, pulling the pillow away from me. "Rose, I don't blame you. I'm relieved Nala knows the truth. I hate keeping secrets. Especially from my attorney."

Sue was lying with all four paws in the air, begging for morning belly rubs. I obliged.

"She's already been out and had breakfast. We wanted to let you sleep a bit more." Lily winced, rubbing her leg. "And coffee's waiting."

"I couldn't sleep if I tried. How do you feel this morning?"

"Fine," Lily said with a pained smile as she struggled to stand.

I jumped up to keep her stable. "Are you fine, fine, or the f'd up, insecure, neurotic, and emotional kinda fine?" I flashed her a cheeky smile.

"No," she laughed. "I'm good. I've got a new leash—" Lily

nodded to Sue and chuckled again— "on life. And I'm optimistic about my case. My leg … well, I'm alive. Thanks to you all."

"I'm glad your sunny disposition has returned." I hugged her. "You will be cleared and then, with your permission, I'd like to take you to Florida to bask your wounded body in the sun. You are also going to need PT and I've got a great one on speed dial. She charges a mint, but I will cover the fee … if I still have my fortune." I uttered the last part, almost under my breath.

"What?!" Lily spun so fast she almost fell off her crutches.

"Uh. It's nothing I can't handle," I said with a tight smile.

Lily frowned. "Rose, you can tell me. What's going on?"

"I don't know."

The look on Lily's face said she did not believe me.

"Honestly. Keith and I have been playing phone tag." I stood in front of the mirror, brushing my hair, pulling it up in my signature high ponytail. The routine helped me think better. "He said he needed to talk to me, and my monetary future depended on it. But I'll deal with it." I gave a shrug.

Sue jumped off the bed, sat on my foot and stared at me. She read my emotions. And Lily did too because she put her hand on my shoulder.

"Rose, I'm here for you. Like you are for me." Lily hugged me the best she could without toppling over on her crutches.

"Let's take care of your situation first," I said and pulled away. "Now go get ready for your doctor's appointment. Do you need help wrapping your leg in plastic, so the bandage doesn't get wet?"

"Simon offered." She grinned and exited the room.

My heart warmed at the thought of those two as a couple. They deserved one another. Just then Sue rubbed her face against my leg. I looked down and she was giving me her big, round, brown-eyed puppy dog, loving look. She indeed was a human lie detector. I bent and hugged her, too.

"Don't worry, girl. If Mama loses our fortune, I will still feed you the best homemade food. Even if I have to sell my blood. Speaking of, I need to check my messages." I looked around the room and spotted the landline. Grandma insisted that we leave our personal cells at her house in Darby, so I couldn't be reached. I called my phone and waited for the voicemail greeting and pressed the star key.

Nine missed calls. Five from Kevin, three from my attorney, and one unknown. I held my breath as I replayed the recordings. Kevin was worried about my lack of response. But he was also busy with work. He said he was now Stateside and would meet me anywhere I wanted. As I listened to the rest of his message, I touched my face, and it was hot. He lastly said "they" were debriefing him after his secret mission. Whoever *they* were, Kevin was not at liberty to say.

The other three were from Keith. Two were hangups, and one recording. Keith said he was in Montana and insisted on meeting with me. I quickly dialed his number. Crap, voicemail. Barring another attack from our enemies, I was going to head back to Grandma's after Lily's appointment this morning. I left him a message and *promised* to meet.

I needed to know if I was poor again. Heavy sigh. It wasn't mine to begin with. I justified in my brain.

Did I miss something in the fine print when I signed my life away? Keith was persistent and tracked me in the Florida Keys at Max's funeral to tell me I'd inherited Max's entire fortune. And could that now be gone?

While I was not money driven, having billions and not worrying about making my bills was a relief. Not to mention I enjoyed sharing my wealth.

I continued on to listening to the last message. Moxy. My jaw clenched and teeth ground.

CHAPTER 89

"TO HELL WITH that." I stewed a minute, then called Moxy. If Charly and her goon squad wanted to know where we were, come and get some. I was in no mood, and I was more than ready to have it out with her and anyone else.

"Moxmar," she answered in a professional, hard tone.

"Hey, it's Rose."

"Oh, hi," she said with a softened voice.

I told Moxy about our misadventures since we last saw one another.

"I thought my day was in the crapper. It seems like you should come with a warning label for potential friends." Moxy snickered.

"You're not the first person to tell me that." I snorted. "So, they're keeping a lid on Pane's evidence tampering? How can they and who? That's why the prosecution is offering Lily a plea deal!" I paced the room, biting my nails. "It sounds like a cover up to me. This is all bull shi … grr. I'm supposed to stop swearing to set an example for my niece."

"I'll say it for you. Yes, it's bullshit, Rose," Moxy said. "But, as far as the who, well, it's bigger than me."

"Not me. I spilled the beans to Nala, Lily's attorney last night," I said. "Heck, I did more than that. I dropped the entire case. She's looking into it. So, if it is a cover up, it won't bode well for them. Nala is tenacious. I kept you out of it, I promise." I plopped on the bed. "You don't think it's Chur—"

"Absolutely *not*. Marshal Church is a straight-up guy," Moxy insisted. "But a little anonymous birdie left a message at the District Attorney's office this morning. And not the deputy district attorney. The DA himself.'"

"I need to express my gratitude to that bird."

Lily ambled back to our room and eased down on a chair. After her shower, her hair hung wet over her shoulders and she smelled like lavender.

I gripped the phone. "Moxy. You are truly a remarkable cop and an even better friend. Thank you. If you ever want to relax on my boat, say the word."

Lily laughed. "Floating city, Rose."

"Ha, I heard her," Moxy said. "Tell Lily good luck and I'm sorry I didn't get acquainted with her. Maybe next time when she's not a murder suspect."

"Will do, and thanks again." I disconnected.

"Do I want to know why you are thanking Moxy?" Lily asked.

I held nothing back and relayed the entire conversation.

"It gets deeper, doesn't it?" Lily asked. "Who have I enraged to do this to me?"

"Or exposed."

Lily and I shared a long look.

Silence filled the room. It was so deafening; I heard the water dripping in the bathroom. If what Lily uncovered, thus far, caused so many mice to run scared, I could only imagine having the truth leaked. Whatever that was. I would eventually find out. It was in my nature. But later.

For now, getting Lily cleared was the priority.

CHAPTER 90

CK PACED HER hotel room. "Are you certain it's been called off ... on both of us?"

"Yes," a woman responded curtly on the other end of the call. "But so help you. If I hear about either of you two coming anywhere near my family, I will personally terminate you."

"You must understand, Ms. Lillian, I was following orders from Alvarez. How did I know she was on a personal crusade? I sincerely apologize."

"Accepted. But know this, there's no limit to what I would not do for my loved ones."

"How did you do it?" CK asked. "I thought you retired."

"How I do *anything* is none of your concern." Lillian's cold, detached tone didn't mask her anger. "Am I clear?"

"Yes, ma'am. Understood. This mission was too close to your family. I didn't know who Alvarez was related to ... she almost took me down with her."

"Mm hm. I've unfortunately been burned by a handler or two myself," Lillian said. "Take heed who you align yourself with."

"I'm learning that. I thought I was a better judge of character."

"It happens with the agency," Lillian said. "On to the next one, I presume."

"I don't have to tell you how it works. I go deep and shed all contacts, again." CK paused. "Soo ... Project X?"

"Project *what*?!"

CK pulled the phone away from her ear as Lillian used language she'd never heard come from a woman her age. "Uh ... nothing. Nothing at all," she said.

"That's what I thought." Click. Lillian disconnected the call.

"Phew." CK exhaled as she tossed on a black baseball cap she'd purchased from the local tourist trap. Although the hit was called off, she had to keep vigilant. She threw on an oversized gray sweatshirt that read MONTANA in big bold letters. She checked out her reflection in the mirror.

"I could pass as a tourist." She left her motel room.

CK sprinted across the street to the Cup of Java Café, where Mac sat in the corner with his sunglasses on and a black hoodie over his head.

She slid across from him. "Remove your damned glasses and throw off your hood," CK said. "You look like you're in hiding."

"Says the person who is trying too hard to blend in like a freakin' sightseer," Mac said as he slung off his glasses and set them on the table. "They're prescription if it's any business to you. And I know how to survive." He nodded for the waitress. "So, did ya make the call?"

They both went silent as the gal filled his cup. CK gestured towards her mug.

"The hits called off both our heads," CK said. "You owe me."

"I took a bullet for you. Remember." Mac sipped his coffee.

"Okay, keep telling yourself that." CK sniggered. "So, now you are free to roam the country doing whatever you do."

"Sounds good," Mac said. "What about you?"

"I'll have a new handler. They're bringing me back to Langley for a debrief. I've been dark long enough. On to the next mission."

"And your crazy boss?"

"Don't know. Don't care. My guess is Alvarez fled the country. New identity." CK drank her coffee. "And you?"

"The further I stay away from you … from all this—" Mac waved his hand in a dismissive fashion— "The safer I am." Mac threw money on the table for his beverage, along with the USB drive. "I want nothing do to with that." Mac put his glasses back on and edged out of the booth.

"I may call on you again someday," CK said.

"I'm considering retiring … somewhere tropical with a hottie or two." Mac gave a wry smile and slithered away.

CHAPTER 91

I FINISHED PACKING what little I brought with me and loaded it into Lily's Bronco. The plan was to return to Grandma's right after Lily's doctor's appointment. I had my attorney to face and the coffee I consumed when I woke wasn't cutting it. I grabbed my favorite chai latte pod and inserted it into the fancy hot beverage maker.

As I put Sue's food into her puppy cooler, I spotted Grandma Lil on the back deck, pacing as she spoke on her cell. A cell she'd told no one to bring. It must be encrypted. Grandma was giving a serious butt chewing to someone on the phone. I saw her jaw tighten.

After the last drop of tea hit my cup, I snatched it. Not that I was an eavesdropper, or snooper like I've been accused, but her conversation concerned me. The moment I opened the glass sliding door, I heard Grandma threatening someone, using colorful language.

I paused with my mug in hand. Did I go out there? It obviously had something to do with our current situation. So, I did what any irrational person would do. I stepped into the lion's den and waited for the lioness to stop devouring her prey.

"Ahem. Is everything all right, Gran?" I probed with a squint.

Grandma slipped her phone into her pocket and slowly looked up at me. "It is now, Rosie," she smiled.

Phew. Okay, the coast was clear. So, I pushed the envelope. "Soo, you wanna tell me what that conversation was about?" I asked, looking into the bottom of my empty mug. I'd guzzled my tea so fast I didn't remember tasting it.

"No," she said, pushing past me. "The threat against you all has been neutralized."

"Wait. What? You didn't do what I think."

Grandma spun. "Not that. No one has cement shoes, at least I don't think. And just leave it alone. *No* more questions, Granddaughter." She gave me a stare that could bend steel.

"Okay, fine." I leaned against the banister and watched a tree branch scream down the fast-flowing river. I wanted to know who she was talking to.

"We never had that chat," Grandma said, shifting course.

That's where I got it from. I was the queen of changing subjects to avoid uncomfortable conversations. But with Grandma Lil, it was because of a need to know. And I apparently did not.

"What are your plans when you return to Florida?" she asked.

"To stay alive," I said with a snort.

"I mean, life plan, wise acre."

"I wasn't joking about the staying alive part. That's why I hired Simon to train me to look after myself."

"About that," Grandma said. "I need to tell you something."

"Go on," I urged, hoping to hear the truth.

"Do you remember when they placed you into federal protection four months ago?"

"Kidnapped is more like it." I scoffed.

"That was on me," Grandma said. "I caught wind of the hit. I didn't know the person responsible until now."

"I assumed it was you *and* Kevin who secured me federal babysitters," I said. "Who was behind it?"

"A woman named Cora Alvarez. The niece of Stanley James."

"SJ's niece? Does she work for the agency?" I asked.

Grandma nodded. "She went rogue and tried to bring down Charly with her."

"That witch!"

"Charly was following orders. You must move forward."

"How can I?" I grumbled. "A man is dead because of what? And now Lily is fighting for her freedom."

"I understand, Granddaughter." She patted my shoulder.

"What are Lily and Gil's involvement if *I* was the target?"

She shrugged.

I rejected her pretended ignorance. But I also didn't push it. I would figure it out on my own.

"Anyway, Cora is in the wind. So, you may need to watch your back for a while."

"Why did she do it?" I asked.

"She blames you and your father for destroying her life."

"She wouldn't be the first person."

"You mean Max?" Grandma asked.

"He was a sick man."

"A sick man who left you his fortune," Grandma said with a chuckle.

"I guess that depends on what my attorney has to tell me today."

"Are you worried about it?"

"Keith has been persistent and alluded to the fact that my financial future may be in jeopardy."

"Whatever happens, you can deal with it," Grandma said. "Are you thinking of returning to your old job and your house?"

"I'm technically still employed and took a leave of absence," I said. "I have an appointment to see a shrink to give me the okay. Apparently, I've been in too many shootings. On and off duty." I rolled my eyes. "I left a year ago, so I have until the end of the month. And if I no longer have a fortune, I'll have to return to work. At least my house is paid for. But I'm considering closing that chapter and staying in Florida. I don't have the same passion for that job anymore."

"You've worn badges since you were a Girl Scout," Grandma said.

"A wise woman once told me there's life beyond the badge," I said with a cheeky grin.

She smiled back and shook her head. "I'm serious. If you don't return to your career, you're a natural at protecting people and solving crimes. You have a knack. It's in your genes."

"You mean snooping." I laughed. "That's what Rayo calls it."

"No, personal protection. Like we discussed earlier. With a twist of PI work."

"Perhaps, but I can't officially do it. I have too much net worth right now," I said. "That sounded snobbish. I didn't intend it to."

"I know, dear. But you need a purpose, unless Kevin is aiming to get you married, knocked up, and barefoot in the kitchen," Grandma said with a laugh.

"Grandma!" I giggled. "I have no immediate plans to get married. Although, O'Malley hints at it. I'm not ready. It's only been a couple of years and, well, Bradley is still in my heart." I patted my chest.

"Just as your grandfather is and always will be in mine. Embrace your memories of him but move on. You're young, and your heart is big. There's room enough in there. Kevin is a wonderful man. Bradley would've approved."

A lump developed in my throat. I cleared it. "Kevin is amazing, and I love him," I said. "I'm not ready for the whole marriage and baby carriage life. Maybe someday."

Sue ran over to me, wagging her tail.

"She is all the baby I want right now."

CHAPTER 92

IT WAS 8 A.M. and Simon, Kate, Rayo, and Lily sat in the living room with their bags at their feet, while Olive was heading out the door. We said our last goodbyes and Grandma slipped her what appeared to be a wad of hundreds. Most likely for services rendered. I gave Olive a farewell embrace. I liked her. She was also excellent at her job. And if I ever needed a professional thief again, I'd call on her.

The second Olive exited the house, Nala walked into the living room. She was talking on her Bluetooth. "You just sent it? I'll check my e-mail." She sat at the dining table, opened her laptop, and tapped away at the keys so fast I could've sworn smoke emitted from her keyboard.

We stared with open mouths and exchanged shrugs.

"Mm hm, okay then." She disconnected.

I eased into a chair across from her. "Is that a good hm or a bad one?"

"Well." Nala sat with her arms crossed and gazed at me. "Excellent," she said, pushing back from the table. "They dismissed Lily's charges."

"What?! Oh my God. That *is* excellent." I looked around the room. Grandma nodded with a grin. She seemed unsurprised by the news. Lily sat and plopped her head in her hands and wept. Sue rushed to her feet, while Simon moved over, embracing her.

"*All* the charges? And with prejudice?" Not to seem ungrateful, I wanted to make sure the prosecutor could not refile any charges, and that Lily's legal nightmare was truly over.

"Yes, to both," Nala replied. "The court reviewed the facts and made a final determination that the case should not move forward."

I lowered my shoulders. "Can we get the dismissal in writing?"

Nala laughed. "Of course, you'd ask. We'll use your grandma's printer at home."

"What caused the D.A. to change his mind?" I asked.

"Gee … I don't know." Nala looked at me over the top of her glasses and leaned on the table with her fingers interlaced. "Evidence tampering to start. But somehow, I believe you knew the answer to that question. Not to mention, they confirmed Gil died from a heart attack. And the gunshot was postmortem."

"I just wanted to hear it out loud." I nodded with a cheeky grin.

"The D.A. received a tip, and he dug deeper and found a mess. My friend, who was the prosecuting attorney and her family, were sent death threats. They're going to be placed into protective custody."

"Damn it!" Grandma said. "I've got another phone call to make." She turned back to Nala. "Tell your friend they will be just fine."

The room was silent except for Sue's panting. I've never heard Gran swear so much. I leaned my head against the chair and stared at the ceiling. For someone who was retired, Gran had a lot of pull. First, getting our hits called off, now this. Whatever "this" was. I considered as I watched her on the phone again.

I decided we were going to have a real heart-to-heart. Okay, so perhaps not this trip. Grandma was downright frightening, and I chased hardened criminals. But no one scared me more than that silver-haired woman scolding someone else today. I imagined Grandma in her prime, how ruthless she must have been. She was certainly not the bake-cookies-knit-mittens kind of grandparent. I looked out the back again and smiled. I wouldn't have it any other way.

"Does this mean we can cancel my doctor's appointment?" Lily broke the stillness.

"Absolutely," Nala said. "On it." She dialed a number.

"This day is looking brighter every minute," I said.

"Maybe your attorney has good news for you, Rose," Lily said, grunting to a stand as Simon handed her crutches.

"I'm sure he does." I faked a smile. But my stomach was in knots.

CHAPTER 93

◆

WE ARRIVED BACK in Darby at a quarter to ten. Since the hit was off, I was at ease leaving Lily at Grandma's compound. Not to mention Simon was on duty.

I was finding my niche with the whole personal protection thing, a.k.a. bodyguard. By nature, I was "smotherly and overprotective." My sister, Saki's words, not mine. I could see myself doing this. Given that I may have lost my fortune, I'd need money.

Sue and I jumped into Lily's Bronco and headed to Hamilton.

"What do you think, girl?" I cooed at Sue, scratching behind her ear. "Should we go into the personal security business? You, of course, will be my sidekick."

Sue smiled at me as she rode shotgun as if she approved. If I had a nine-to-five job, she couldn't protect me, have my back, like she'd done since we first met.

Forty-five minutes later we arrived at the hotel. The minute we exited the vehicle, my palms sweated, and my heart raced. I was fine before I became a gazillionaire and would be fine if I lost my fortune.

Sue and I made our way into the hotel and searched for Keith's room, 201. I stood at his door for a beat before knocking. I felt Sue's breath on my pant leg. I bent and caressed her. Therapy dog to the rescue.

I rapped on the door, being careful not to use my cop knock as I've been told I have. Keith opened it and smiled. He pulled me in for a warm embrace.

"I apologize. I was not ignoring you. We've had a few days of hell," I said, stepping inside.

The lodge was decorated in the typical Montana style, with a rustic log bed, matching dresser, and nightstands. But I wasn't there for a tour.

"I'm glad it worked out. I assume everyone is safe and unscathed. Except for your face," Keith said in his strong New York accent. His thin, athletic frame towered over me by a couple inches. His black hair brought out his greenish-blue eyes that were hidden behind wire-rimmed glasses. He was handsome in a Clark Kent way.

I shook off the distracting thoughts to return to business and clutched my ribs. "Mostly," I said.

Keith motioned for me to sit at the small table by the window. There was a thick, black binder with *Max Ryan Trust* in bold with Sign It tabs, waiting for me.

"Okay, just rip off the Band-Aid," I said as I eased onto the chair. Sue leaned against me the entire time. "Did I lose everything?" I asked with a wince. "I mean, it was never mine to begin with, so I am completely fine. Really, not the F'd up insecure neur—"

"Rose, breathe," Keith said as he sat across from me.

"Sorry, I … I'm rambling," I said with a nervous chuckle.

"Okay. It's just that it's time to discuss the clause." He air-quoted the last two words.

"Clause? What clause?" I took a deep breath. I'd been shot up and on pain meds when I signed the trust and will paperwork nearly a year ago and couldn't recall every detail.

"When you signed these documents at my office in New York, there was a clause in the trust."

"The trust is the size of a Florida phone book. There were a lot of clauses." I thumbed through the stack, finding the page with the yellow sticky note with the word *Clause*, in big bold print.

I read the entire page. More slowly a second time, my pulse ratcheting up and blood pounding in my ears. This couldn't be true. Could it?

"Are you fu—bloody kidding me!" I rose and kicked the chair from behind me, startling poor Sue. "That sick SOB, Max." I paced the room. "How did I miss that? I would've never agreed to such … crap." I plopped on the bed and put my head between my knees. My breath left my body.

CHAPTER 94

LILLIAN SAT ON her porch, watching Simon dote on Lily as they lounged by the pond. Lily's head rested on his shoulder. Rose was meeting with her attorney. Hopefully, she'd have good news to report. Kate was at the Ravalli County Airport preparing Rose's Gulfstream for their departure tomorrow, doing her pre-flight check. An eager Rayo accompanied her.

Since Lily was headed to Florida with Rose and the gang, Lillian was searching for a temporary ranch hand. She phoned her grand-niece, Essie Lee, but only got her voice mail. Essie was in Europe and scheduled to be in Ireland about now, visiting family. But maybe Essie would take a break from her world travels to help Lillian until Lily was back on her feet. After the Charly fiasco, Lillian had to vet her people more thoroughly. And she knew Essie could be trusted.

All was right in her inner circle for a fleeting moment.

Lillian walked back into her empty house, looked around, opened her drawer, and pulled out her encrypted phone, calling her friend.

"We dodged a bullet," M said as she answered.

"Not really," Lillian said. "Lily took one to the leg."

"What?! Is she okay?" M's voice shook.

"She will be. No surgery. The round went clean through. No vital body parts hit. Lily will have to stay off it for a while, but she'll make a full recovery."

"That's a relief. That poor girl," M said. "I hear the hit's been called off the family."

"Affirmative," Lillian said.

"If anyone could do it, it'd be you," M said.

"I first had to identify who ordered it. The rest was a simple phone call."

"Who?"

"Cora Alvarez."

"Oh, Stanley James's niece. Why?"

"Long story. She is still in the wind. Rose will need to watch her back for a while."

"I'm sorry to hear that." M paused. "But why target Lily too?"

"What better way to get to Rose than through her loved ones. Unfortunately, Lily was a potential mark. Gil was the primary."

"This *is* my fault."

"M ... it's not. Lily got too close to the truth about Project X."

"And me!" M said. "What a mess. I assume there are loose ends still out there."

"You could say that." Lillian pulled out the USB from the white envelope someone had left at her front gate. Although she had a new security system, Lillian suspected Charly. And if Charly learned anything, she would not have read the thumb drive's contents.

Lillian flipped up her laptop screen, inserted the memory stick. As she suspected it required a password. Lillian opened another program and let her computer do the work. After the document unlocked, she scrolled. She sat back and put her hand to her mouth.

"Oh my."

"What, Lillian?"

"The flash drive Gil gave to Lily." She sighed. "Let's just say it's a good thing she didn't see it."

"That bad?"

"Worse. The intelligence on this is classified. There are *unredacted* documents of the original experiment from the 50s to the 70s that were purportedly destroyed."

"Oh, that is dangerous. Anything else? I ... I mean names of those unwitting test subjects or their code names, like my husband?" M gave a heavy moan.

"That part is missing. My hunch is there's a second, maybe even third source. It's much safer to have sensitive information split. You know, professional paranoia."

"Indeed," M said. "Do you think Lily has it?"

"I'm uncertain. She was so drugged last night, she blurted out something about a flash drive that she didn't have. Nothing more. I assumed it was this one."

"She could never keep a secret." M chuckled. "You should've seen her as a child."

"She still can't. But I don't understand why Gil didn't come to me with this," Lillian said.

"My guess is he didn't know who to trust," M said. "I mean, do you blame him? They've killed anyone exposing the truth."

"Yes. And he also knew you were alive and he likely intended to tell Lily."

"Why put her in harm's way?"

"Perhaps he believed he was doing the right thing. Now we'll never know."

"I wish I could," M said.

"Not yet, too dangerous. For everyone," Lillian said. "When the time is right, we'll read in Rose and Lily and deal with the aftermath. But for now, we've got to locate the remaining data."

"If it takes my last breath to expose the rest of that wretched project!" M paused. "I'm tired of playing dead and hiding out. I'm ready to take action."

"Me too."

"How are we going to do this?" M said.

"Hunting expedition," Lillian said.

"Do you have a trusted hunter in mind?"

"I do," Lillian said. Just then, her personal cell rang with an incoming call from Rose. "Speaking of, she's on the other line. Take care, my friend. Be patient. I'll let you know when it's safe for you to rise from the dead."

"I love you and thank you again for taking care of my daughter these last four years."

"I love you too, Maisy. Lily is safe."

CHAPTER 95

———◆———

"OKAY." I STOOD once more and looked at Keith. "I'm sorry I reacted that way," I said to gain my composure. "Is this … legal for someone to do?"

"It is," Keith said.

"How long do I have to decide?" I flailed my hand in the air at the trust.

"You signed it … let's see." Keith thumbed through the document. "Last June. Eleven months ago. You had a year. The deadline is June thirtieth. You know … to begin the process."

"So let me get this straight." I drew a deep breath, although it hurt. But what I just read pained me more. "I have a *month* to decide whether I want to carry Max's sperm?!"

"Uh, you would actually raise his child," Keith said, pointing to the line that said so.

"Ho—how did I miss that? I don't remember. You know, I'd been shot to hell and was on a lot of meds. Jeezo. Can I contest it by claiming I wasn't in the right state of mind?"

He shook his head with a tight lip. "When you signed it, you noted you were of sound mind. I asked you many times about the conditions."

"Crap, I was reading about how I needed to maintain his mother's foundation with honor and respect, yada, yada, yada. Not to mention I became an instant billionaire." I wiped the sweat from my forehead. "I don't recall allowing myself to be artificially inseminated with his *sperm*. I would've totally remembered that part." I blew out a huge gust of air. "Okay. It's not your fault. But I wish you had read it to me first."

"Rose, I did. But you were in a hurry to leave my office. You didn't listen. You just nodded, signed, and left," Keith said and rose. He touched my shoulder.

I pulled away. "You should have made me listen. So, I have a month to think about it? Or I lose it all?" I asked. "What if it does not take? I mean my body. And when did he find time for this?"

"It doesn't take long ... to do this," Keith said. "And there are quite a few vials, so you need to try until you succeed."

"Oh. My. God. I knew Max was obsessed with me. He was damaged. And not in *his* right mind." I paced. "Here, I thought he redeemed himself when he took a bullet meant for me and my father. I should've known he'd find a way to get me in the end!"

I approached the door and just as I put my hand on the handle, I turned back. "I'm disappointed. I've been doing great things with the foundation and even spread the wealth, so to speak," I said. "Wait, what happens to his money if I don't do this?"

"It's distributed to various charities," Keith said.

"And who manages these charities?"

Keith gathered the papers and returned them to his briefcase. "I do," he said, without looking me in the eye.

Of course. Now it all made sense.

I stood, hands on hips, scowling at him. "You smell that?" I asked with my nose in the air.

"Huh?" he said with a head tilt.

"It's a nice bouquet of *bull shit*," I growled. "Why am I not surprised?" I stormed out. On the way to the Bronco, I phoned Grandma Lil. She advised me to call Nala for advice. So, I did. Unfortunately, I was screwed. Nala informed me there was nothing I could do because I signed a legal, notarized document. But she also said she'd contact Keith and get a copy of it.

I seethed as I sat behind the wheel. I trusted Keith, but it turned out he didn't have my best interest at heart.

In the end, if the trust proved valid, the decision to carry and raise Max's baby was up to me. It was a lot of money to throw away. But I'd also feel as if I would be selling my body and soul to the devil and raising his child.

A decision I needed to make on my own ... and fast.

THE END

Continue the adventures of Rose O'Brien in Book Two-Saving Foxy.

AUTHOR'S NOTE

I have been asked how I draw inspiration for my characters. The answer is simple: dogs, dogs, dogs. My dogs, friends' dogs, heck even ones I've just met. And like any dog lover, I wanted to pay homage to my two original fur babies, Saki and Rose. So, instead of writing about my devoted K-9 companions, I bring them to the human world by creating characters drawn from their unique furry personalities.

List of characters and their K-9 identities.

Rose O'Brien   Saki O'Brien Powers

Lily Cazier   Olive Knudson

Kate Orr   Simon Rae Rose

Rayo McQueen   Charly Kane a.k.a.-CK

Agent Cora Alvarez

Nala Clearwater

Mac Vig

Marshal Church

TJ Hooker

Kaylee Tubberious

Teddy Reagan- a.k.a The Ghost   "M." a.k.a Maisy

Tony Titianos a.k.a.- Titos   Agent H

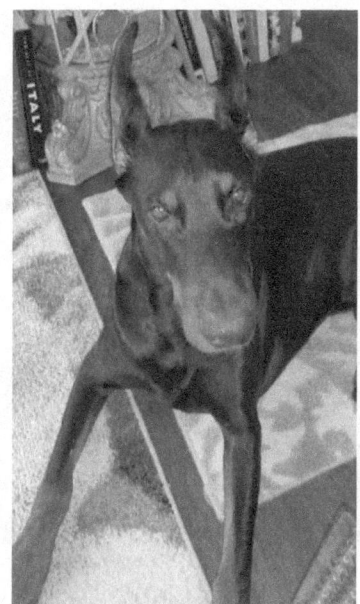

Khan Fullerton   Stanley James Albrecht Cordova
a.k.a. SJ

Deputy Moxmar, aka, Moxy   Max, a lab mix, was a childhood
pet. Pic unavailable

Last, but not least, Grandma Lil. She is the only character based on an actual person, my mother-in-law, Lillian Weinstock. Lillian was the inspiration behind Grandma Lil, and she was just as spunky as her fictional character.

RIP LILLIAN E. WEINSTOCK

ABOUT THE AUTHOR

S.S. Duskey retired from law enforcement with over 20 years of experience. She lives in the Bitterroot Mountains of Montana with her husband, Steve, and fur babies, Essie and Lilly.

When she's not plotting mischief for her characters, Sharon enjoys spending time with her family, friends, and furry children in the outdoors of the beautiful Bitterroot.

Sharon's earlier works include The Rose O'Brien Trilogy: Book One—Secrets in the Keys, Book Two—Deception in the Bitterroot, and Book Three—Redemption in the Tahoe Basin. These can be found on Amazon.

Sharon invites you to contact her at ssduskey@yahoo.com or visit her website www.ssduskeyauthor.com. She can also be found on Facebook at www.facebook.com/ssduskeyauthor and on www.instagram.com/ssduskey

NOTE TO READERS:

I hope you enjoy reading my stories as much as I have in writing them. For an indie author, reviews can have a tremendous impact on reaching more readers like you. So, if you like *A Rose O'Brien Series, Book One: Saving Lily,* please visit Amazon, Goodreads and other online retailers to leave a review.